PRAISE FOR
CASTLES OF STEEL AND THUNDER

'A brilliant tale wrapped up in local legend and the folklore of Caithness.'
Hayley @hayleyisreading

'True escapism… the Highland fae stories are enchanting.'
Susan @ahighlandblend

'I would highly recommend this for YA fantasy fans.'
Ella @booksteaandlove

'A stunning debut.'
Isla @islacwrites

PIECES OF SKY AND STONE

GAIL ANTHEA BROWN

For my boys – Christopher, Fraser, Brody and GB.

When the light comes, it lifts from the earth like a bird spreading its wings into the morning.

Yet a rising flight casts shadows, and a journey is never quite complete.

A bird sees it all from the sky – the light flickering on the sea, the shadow nestling on the mountain.

When the cold arrives, the bird accepts it, understanding this too is the nature of the world.

PART ONE

FYRISH

CHAPTER ONE

Sysa stared at her reflection in the mirror, alongside glimpses of Ida's head, which darted in and out of view like a jack-in-the box at jaunty angles. The servant was tugging at Sysa's hair in a manner uncomfortable even for fae folk.

'Ouch, Ida, you're hurting me.'

Sysa's head jerked back with the downward shift of Ida's brush.

'How you manage to get yourself into this state, and call yourself a princess,' Ida said, with a loud *tsk* of disapproval. 'You and that boy of yours, running around like a pair of wildlings.' Ida resumed her attack on Sysa's hair, making small indignant sounds as she pulled out a tiny lump of moss.

'I'm sorry, Ida, you're absolutely right, of course,' Sysa said, offering up her brightest green gaze to the mirror. After some months in the castle, she was now well used to manoeuvring her way back into Ida's favour. 'And no one does my hair as well as you.'

Ida flushed, a swell of pride blooming across her features and right to the pointed tips of her ears, which twitched under strands of hair coming loose from her topknot. The servant sniffed and smoothed down her bun, an action that seemed to dispel her irritation.

'Well, that's true,' she said, resuming her activity with a smile, and a considerably less forceful manner than before. 'There,' she concluded once Sysa's hair was gleaming like dark water a little later. 'You look beautiful.'

Sysa offered Ida a mock curtsey, followed up by a smile and a kiss on the faerie woman's cheek as she swung her way to the window to find the source of the noise that was drifting from the gardens underneath.

She looked out to see her sister and William cavorting around the fountain, and felt a sudden sense of déjà vu for a similar scene she had once witnessed between Elva and Brodie. Back then, she had been new to Fyrish, the castle – and her own family. She had also been intent on a mission to turn wayward faeries to the light. It was before they had banished Rogart, the giant who had turned out to be Brodie's father. It was before she'd turned Krystan, who was now ensconced on Selkie Island with Frode and his seal-folk tribe. It was before Luna, the mermaid who had held William captive, and then disappeared in a jealous rage after the final battle with Rogart. It was before Elva had taken off with the human William in a misguided, short-lived alliance with Rogart that had ended with William and Elva's pairing – and the source of Luna's rage. It was before Grey, Sysa's grandfather, the fae king who had bequeathed her with his powers back in Caithness. And it was before Lavellan, the shape shifter who had killed her grandfather while Grey was in the form of a unicorn – a death that had brought Brodie back to life.

Sysa shivered, thinking of Brodie and the day when the giant, revealed as Brodie's father, had tried to kill him. She thought of the magic that had come streaming from

4

Brodie's fingers after the unicorn had dripped blood on him – a revelatory kind of magic that hadn't been there until that day. She thought of herself and Brodie declaring love for each other, on that beach, on that day, after everything that had gone *before* – including a brief period of rivalry with her sister. She shivered again, thinking of those first kisses with Brodie, an image that was rudely interrupted by a vision of Lavellan and the icy blue eyes that crept so often unbidden to her dreams. She shuddered, mentally pushing Lavellan's face away, and leaned out to that familiar scene unfolding in the garden below.

So much had happened since that time *before*, and here she was, the long-lost fae princess, soon to be promoted to Queen of Steel Castle after salvaging Fyrish from the clutches of a creeping darkness. She sighed, looking out over the walled garden, the shore beyond, and the land that stretched to the Castle of Thunder, all that remained of Rogart's previous tenure.

She still had to pinch herself sometimes, thinking of everything that had happened, and the kingdom that was now hers, shared with her parents and Elva.

And Brodie, who she could not believe had not existed in her life, in her soul, before all this.

It seemed such a small word to encompass it all, that single word *before*.

'Good morning, you!' Elva's voice flew up the castle walls, breaking Sysa's concentration. Elva was waving madly with one hand, while the other rested on William, whose arms were wrapped loosely around her waist.

'At their canoodling again,' Ida tutted from somewhere behind Sysa as she clipped around, opening and shutting drawers with a swipe of her hands through air as sheets lifted in the space above Sysa's mattress. Sysa smirked at the faerie woman, who was magicking the folding of laundry with the air of someone mounting a full-scale attack on loose corners.

'They're in love,' Sysa said, a hint of reproach in her voice as she waved back at Elva, trying to stifle another laugh.

'And you and Brodie, you're no better, let me tell you.' Ida, determined to get the last word as usual, lowered her palm to drop several items into a row of drawers, before instructing them to close with a click of her fingers.

'Good morning both of you. How are you today?' Sysa called out of the window, choosing to let Ida continue with her moral outrage by herself.

'We're very well, thank you,' Elva said with a grin, speaking for William again, as was generally her custom. 'Just planning our wedding, you know,' she said, twirling around and wrapping her arms around William's neck.

'How exciting,' Sysa replied, smiling at William, who was busy looking at his fiancée with his usual puppy-dog glaze of devotion. If Sysa and her parents had had any doubts about William and his suitability for Elva, they had long since been forgotten. The man who had once cheated on his mermaid lover was a reformed character – perhaps, Sysa thought, a result of the period of reflection that had been afforded him while Luna kept him tied up in a cave. And though there wasn't much of an age difference between William and Elva – William having aged considerably slower in Fyrish than he would have done back in Caithness – the human man had developed a maturity that seemed to temper Elva's wilder instincts. Their parents had still insisted on a lengthy period of engagement, though – it wasn't that long ago that Elva had been convinced she was in love with Brodie, after all. None of this did much to hamper Elva's long-term planning, and she spent most of her time skipping around the castle dreaming of wedding gowns and harp-infused receptions. In contrast, Sysa, who was due to be married within the year after accepting Brodie's proposal, thought little of impending nuptials. She couldn't help feeling this had something to do with Lavellan, and the way he crept into both her nightmares and her dreams. She had inwardly decided that until she found out why Lavellan had killed Grey back on the cliff that day, she wouldn't be able to focus fully on her wedding, or anything else for that matter. Except Brodie, of course, who wasn't so much someone she thought about, as someone who seemed part of her, the way a finger extends from an outstretched hand.

As if to reinforce that point, Brodie's head appeared around her doorway, another echo of a time *before*, when she had first met him right here in Steel Castle. His dark hair flopped over his forehead, skimming blue eyes made brighter by the shafts of light that fell into the room. Sysa felt a familiar lurching in her chest, the same feeling she knew Brodie experienced when they came upon each other, whether after an hour, or just a moment of separation.

'Sysa.'

Her name was both a plea and an invitation. Leaving the window, she rushed across the room towards him, jumping into the arms that raised to meet her as she sprung up and wrapped her legs around his waist.

'I missed you,' he said after their kiss, which had been interrupted by a loud tutting noise from Ida.

'I missed you too,' Sysa replied, as Brodie planted her back down on the carpet, raising an eyebrow over his shoulder at the servant, who was still fussing and folding at the other side of Sysa's bed.

'Good morning, Ida.' Brodie flashed his usual bright smile towards the servant woman, who lit up briefly in the glare of it.

'Good morning, Mr Brodie,' Ida said, passing the two of them on her way out of the room.

'I'll be back to finish off in here shortly. I'll leave you to it,' she said, pushing the door open a fraction wider as she departed, while at the same time offering them a drawn-out curtsey and a disapproving sniff.

'Well, with Ida keeping guard I think it's fair to say you're safe from all manner of intruders, isn't it?' Brodie said a moment later, as Ida's footsteps retreated down the hallway. The laugh that Sysa had been holding behind her fingers escaped then, and they tumbled clumsily onto her bed.

'I thought it was Bruan I'd have to worry about, but it seems your maid is much more frightening than your father,' Brodie said with an expression of mock terror, as Sysa rolled over and pinned him to the velvet sheets beneath them.

'Oh, is Brodie scared of little Ida?' Sysa said, pouting, before dropping to kiss him, her hair falling in long strands that hung like drapes around his face. As his hands crushed around her cheeks, Sysa heard two sets of footsteps climbing the distant stairs, and not for the first time, sent

8

an imaginary note of thanks to whoever had given fae folk such keen hearing. She and Brodie sprung apart and onto their feet just as her parents were rounding into the bedroom. Behind them in the hall, Ida passed, flashing Sysa a quick, triumphant glance in the space between her parents' heads.

'Ah, good morning to you both,' Bruan said, rubbing his beard, while beside him, Elise beamed a knowing smile towards the younger couple. The king and queen of Fyrish could be mistaken for youngsters too, Sysa thought admiringly, as her parents stood in the same shaft of light Brodie had been basking in a few moments before. Her father was dressed in his usual attire of leather and soft velvet, a tunic with braided sleeves and a deep green surcoat. Next to him, Elise radiated her usual candescent glow in an emerald gown that fell like a waterfall under long lengths of straw-gold hair.

'Are you ready for the ride?' Elise enquired, reminding Sysa of the purpose of Ida's earlier fussing and preening. This morning they were leaving Steel Castle for a ride around Fyrish, an event that doubled both as a parade, and a patrol. Since Rogart had been banished from the fae lands, the family had made regular horseback rides around the kingdom, offering them an opportunity to meet with their subjects, and simultaneously survey their borders. Since Rogart's departure, there had been no sign of any disturbance from any remaining fae folk who had been turned to darkness. At the same time, it was well known that Lavellan and Luna were still at large. Although no sightings of them had been made since that day on the cliff (or at least since the day Sysa had spotted Lavellan out on the water), a strange sense of foreboding still reverberated around the castle.

Sysa knew that these were not just rides or patrols, they were hunting parties.

They were hunting for Lavellan, that icy presence who had never seemed to leave her thoughts.

★

Sysa slipped from her horse, planting her feet on the forest floor, and wondered why on earth Ida chose to dress her in such finery for riding. The horse, Sorrel, was Sysa's favourite amongst the stallions – he reminded her of Modan, the kelpie she had tamed before Selkie Island, and part of the small army who had helped her defeat Rogart on the cliff. She ran a hand over Sorrel's rump, enjoying the silky feel of his coat, a mirror to the velveteen sheen of her own cloak.

'There boy, off you go and drink,' she said, patting him, as he emitted a contended whinny, and made his way to the burn that snaked a path beside them. Nearby, Bruan, Elise and Brodie were also alighting from their steeds and offering murmurings to their respective animals.

'You look beautiful in that dress,' Brodie said, appearing beside her. She wheeled, rounding on him.

'You don't look too bad yourself.'

Brodie was dressed in black leather trousers and a brocade sleeved tunic that hugged the lines of his long, lean figure. His dark mop of hair glinted, shot through with sunlight and the pink tips of his ears, which had transformed from their human incarnation since he had first wielded his powers with Sysa on the beach. His blue eyes shone, the darkness which had once rimmed them now receded to nothing but slate-grey memory. He slipped his arm around Sysa's waist, pulling her closer.

'That seemed to go well,' he said, casting a glance around the trees.

'It did,' Sysa replied, referring to their ride through the forest lands, and their encounters with the villagers who had come out to edge paths and trails in hope of meeting the royal family. Sysa always enjoyed these excursions around Fyrish and made a point of dismounting Sorrel to wander around the smallholdings and play with the younglings, who seemed to hold her and Brodie in particular regard. Since their banishing of Rogart, the pair's status had been elevated to near-legendary proportions, and Sysa had become used to recounting details of the manner in which she and Brodie had whipped the giant into a literal ball of light and sent him flying towards a mountain.

'Like this,' Brodie could often be found saying to some wide-eyed fae child, as he demonstrated a brief flicker of light arcing from his fingers towards a nearby tree trunk. In response, the young apprentice would hold their arms up, squeeze their eyes shut, and try to emit some sort of light power from their own tiny, grasping hands. Usually, this would end with some small success, a bright spark of fire that would disappear into the air as quickly as it had left the youngling's finger. But it would be enough to let the child feel a glow of satisfaction as the couple departed.

In Fyrish, Sysa had become known as the light-bringer. She also knew that what she had offered to the people of the fae lands was something more than that. She had brought light, and with it, she had also brought them hope.

Sysa felt that hope now, as she looked around the clearing, and the place where the light forest had once scissored away into Rogart's darkness. She remembered the day when her parents had first taken her to see what had become of their kingdom, a bleak canvas scrawled with Rogart's vengeance, where light had fallen away to darkness like a cliff edge into never-ending night. Now, trees stood in the place of ragged stumps, while overhead, the sky filmed the world with an expanse of pale-blue blanket. Sysa sighed, enjoying the warmth of the sunlight that threaded the burn with streaks of ribboned gold, and pooled at their feet like searchlights. She felt it, though, that pull of another force inside her.

The Castle of Thunder.

It was still there, calling to her softly, in that place beyond the trees.

CHAPTER TWO

'They say he's back, you know, that evil one,' Sysa heard Ida whisper to one of the other maids as she rounded the corner into the kitchen.

The sound of clanging pots and crockery stilled as Sysa entered, and one or two of the servants dipped to bow and curtsey as she passed them. Sysa brushed off the servility in her usual manner.

'Please, carry on with what you were doing. Ida, what was that you were saying?' Sysa fixed her chief maid with a green stare, raised eyebrows, and one hand upon her hip.

Ida lifted her chin a fraction, as the female she had been talking to scuttled off somewhere.

'Miss Sysa, what on earth are you doing here? Haven't I told you a million times, the servants' areas are no place for the High Fae of the house?'

'Never mind about that,' Sysa replied. 'I just popped in to fetch an apple.'

Sysa stretched an arm towards the nearest counter and picked up a rosy-sheened apple that sat atop a pile of gleaming fruit.

'*Hmmpf.*'

Ida continued making disapproving noises while Sysa took a bite, eyeing the servant woman coolly. As she chewed, she tried not to betray the sense of alarm that had run up and down her spine at the mention of Lavellan. Could Ida's allusion to the *'evil one'*, she wondered, possibly apply to anyone but him?

'You said someone was back. Who's back, Ida? Is it Lavellan?'

'You'll have to ask your parents about it, Miss Sysa,' Ida replied, brushing her hands down the front of her apron and sniffing loudly. 'I've no business talking to you about such things. Now, be off with you.' Ida made a flicking gesture and scurried off in the direction of the stove.

Sysa turned, heading out of the kitchen, along the few steps to the marbled hallway, and then up the sweeping staircase that rounded to the first floor, and the room she had entered with her family on the first day she had arrived in Fyrish. At one side, the fire roared deeply, warming the dog Telon, who was languishing in his usual spot beside it, while at the table, her parents and Brodie sat, greeting her with matching expressions as she burst into the room.

'He's back, isn't he? Why didn't you tell me?' Sysa cried, flying towards the table, which she leaned over, her fingers splayed across the wooden surface.

Bruan stood first, and rubbed at his forehead, exhaling loudly.

'I'm sorry, Sysa. We were waiting for the right moment. We knew how upset you'd be. We were just discussing it now, in fact, with Brodie.' Bruan gestured in Brodie's direction.

Brodie stood up and walked around the table, his expression one of wary appeasement as he reached out a hand and dropped it lightly on Sysa's arm.

'Don't touch me!' Sysa seethed, flicking her arm up so

that Brodie staggered back, raising his palms in a hurried gesture of surrender. 'You knew about this?' she spat out, her eyes narrowed in fury.

'I only just found out, Sysa. Your parents were telling me when you arrived there. We were trying to work out how to break the news to you. No one was trying to keep anything from you, I promise.'

Brodie took a step closer, while Sysa turned her attention to her parents, who by now had gathered at her other side.

'And how long have you both known, dare I ask?' Sysa said, the anger she had felt bubbling up inside her dispelling as she looked into Elise's concerned expression.

'Not long. Just since yesterday,' Elise answered. 'We heard about it from Arno, just after we returned from the ride.'

Sysa thought back to the previous day's outing, and how little she had noticed of her parents' manner during – or after – the activities. Had they seemed subdued at dinner, she wondered? With her own thoughts consuming her, she had to admit she hadn't noticed anything amiss. She knew that Arno, the eagle sky seer, would have wasted no time in alerting Bruan and Elise at the first sign of Lavellan's return to the kingdom of Fyrish, though. She also knew that everyone in Steel Castle was aware of her hatred for Lavellan, and she could hardly blame them for their caution in advising her.

'I see,' she said finally, rubbing at her forehead in a mirror of Bruan's earlier gesture. 'So where is he? At the Castle of Thunder?' she asked, although in her heart she already knew the answer.

The way the distant castle had called out to her, grabbing at a place deep inside her as she'd stood in that clearing.

He had been calling to her, and she'd known it all along.

'Yes, we believe he's back at the castle. With Luna,' Elise replied, apparently oblivious to the awful sense of recognition that was churning inside Sysa's stomach.

'Well, we need to go there. Now,' Sysa said, her eyes sweeping around the room as she mentally gathered up the others, before swivelling on her heel towards the door.

'Wait. We need to think this through, work out a strategy.' Bruan's voice reached Sysa as she approached the doorway.

Sysa stopped, sighing loudly into the doorframe, then she pivoted, turning on them.

'A strategy? There's only one strategy, Father. Get to the castle, and finish this thing off for good.'

'Sysa, come, sit down please.' Her mother gestured to the seat beside her. 'Your father's right, we can't just go storming off to the Castle of Thunder without a plan. Besides, we need to involve Elva in this.'

Sysa shook her head, remembering how Elva had reacted after being sidelined in their quest against Rogart. She made her way to the table and sat down, the wood of the chair screeching against stone and rousing Telon from his rest beside the fire.

'I propose we call a family meeting, first thing in the morning,' Bruan said, eyeing Sysa warily. Her father was well aware of her headstrong spirit, and Sysa knew he was trying to bridge the gap between the group and her own urgent need to act.

She reached down to where Telon's soft muzzle rested

on her thigh, and stroked his head as he looked up at her adoringly. A flurry of silver-coloured motes surrounded him, the result of a displaced crackle that had released from Sysa's hands as she had made her way back from the door. She was getting better at controlling it, the release of the power that emanated from her fingers whenever she felt angry. Right now, though, she felt that control slipping away from her. Thankfully, it didn't seem to bother Telon, who wriggled under the cloud of dispersed magic, evidently enjoying the fizzing crackle of the motes along his back.

'All right,' Sysa said eventually, looking at her father steadily across the table. 'Will you talk to Elva?' Bruan nodded back at her, and then looked down at his folded hands.

'I will. Come, it's late now.' He rose from his chair, turning towards the doorway.

'First thing tomorrow then.' Sysa stood too, and swept across the room.

'Sysa.' Her mother's voice called out from behind her. 'We all love you so much, you know that, don't you, my dear?'

Sysa stopped and turned. 'Of course I know that, Mother. I love you too. I just want to find out why he did it – why he killed Grey – I want this to be over.'

'We all do,' Brodie said, staring back at her, Sysa's arm resting on the doorway in the same way his own had during his first appearance in her life all those months ago.

★

'Sysa.' Sysa felt Brodie's breath on the back of her neck, as he caught up with her in the hallway. 'I'm sorry.' His hand reached out for hers, and she took it, turning towards him in the dark.

'I know. I was just angry, that's all. You know how I feel about Lavellan.' She looked down at the floor, until Brodie placed his hand under her chin and lifted it up towards him.

'I do. And I also know how I feel about *you*, and what we can do, what we can *be* together. We'll fix this.'

She nodded back at him and stepped up on tiptoe, wrapping her arms around his neck. As they kissed, Sysa felt that familiar heat light up her body, the same warmth she felt every time they touched; a feeling that flooded every inch of her being, like a counter to her anger.

'Come on.' She pulled away, leading him down the hall.

In the distance, the sounds of the castle stilled, settling into slumber.

Brodie traced Sysa's footsteps through the hallway, content to follow her, just as he'd promised he always would.

★

In Sysa's room, they stood facing each other in the half-light. Brodie lifted her hand to his chest, placing her fingers so they lay in the space above his heart. 'Yours,' he said, as he covered her hand with his own, so that she felt the thrum of his heart beating under the skin there.

'Mine,' she replied, holding his eyes for a moment, before taking his hand and guiding it towards the same place on her skin. 'Yours,' she said, as his fingertips rested on her, following the rise and fall of her breath, which came faster as he traced the softness of the flesh there.

'Forever,' he said, as he lowered his head towards her and drew her in, the warm bite of his breath tugging softly against her lips. As they dissolved into one another, the moon cast shadows on their skin, painting their love in time with the rhythm of their breathing. And all at once, the world around them stopped, ended, and began again, the only sound left in the darkness the beating of two single, tethered hearts.

★

Sysa opened her eyes, feeling the cool river of her silk bedsheets wrapped around her. Brodie was lying on his back with one arm under her, while Sysa was tucked into his side, her mouth pressed against his hair. She stretched one arm lazily across his chest, and breathed in the scent of him, damp and salty against her nostrils. Earlier, she had felt the waves of his breath soften, and had known that he was sleeping. She closed her own eyes again, willing the same rest to find her.

She knew it wouldn't, though, not with Lavellan out there in that space beyond the trees.

She rose and padded over to the window, where the moon had lit up the glass with its milky, snowy softness. Out in the garden, the silvered light sheened the surface of the grass and lit up the sea behind the walls with a trickle of zig-zagged white that pointed to somewhere beyond the dark. Sysa opened the window, hearing a sound like the echoing chime of a finger rubbed around the rim of a goblet, a sound that seemed to be coming from the sea, or the sky, or perhaps from somewhere deep inside her.

She leaned her body further out of the window, tracing the path of the light along the garden, where it pooled on a figure that seemed to rise up out of the night-drenched air.

It was Grey's statue, the stone form of the unicorn, built in honour of her grandfather.

Was the noise coming from within it?

Sysa turned, fumbling into her gown and her cloak, and raced out of her room and out into the hall.

She rounded the stairs, descending onto the tiled marble of the entranceway. Tiptoeing across the floor, she pushed her way out of the large oak doors and felt the icy air of night sting sharply at her face. She pulled up the hood of her cloak and turned towards the garden, hurrying over to where the statue rose from the earth, frozen on its hind legs in eternal gesture. She placed her fingers on the stone, willing it to guide her.

The chiming sound, no longer just a sound, but a feeling, reverberated through her hand and echoed inside her chest.

'Tell me, tell me what to do,' Sysa said, resting her head against the stone, the cold dampness of it searing across her skin like a weapon.

The chiming feeling rose, swirling around and inside her, pulling at the fabric of her cloak and whipping her hair across her face. Beyond the wall, the sea sang out to her, and beyond that, the sky churned like a restless veil above the world. In the trees, the leaves rustled, passing a song with words Sysa couldn't decipher.

Yet, she had felt this feeling before once, back in Caithness.

Whatever called out to her pulled at her like a magnet.

There was no way to refuse it.

Lavellan was calling to her, and she hated him for it.

'I'll go to him. I'll find out why he killed you.' Sysa spoke to the statue, her fingers sparking tiny fires to life around the stone.

She dropped her hand and stepped back, staring up at the stony form of the unicorn above her. She remembered that day back at the cliff face, her face turned up towards the creature, the way she had cried out to him as he sent his blood towards Brodie on the sand. How he had passed her all that knowledge, all that wisdom, everything she had needed to defeat Rogart, to turn that dark and awful forest back to the light place it was now. And yet here, on this journey towards Lavellan, he couldn't help her.

'I miss you,' she said into the darkness. 'Grandad, how will I do this without you?'

The stone unicorn stared back at her, its only answer the silence and the dark.

CHAPTER THREE

Sysa padded through the forest, no longer dark with the threat of a creeping evil, but of nighttime.

Still, something about the silence that hung around the air felt ominous, as if the flowers and insects had retreated, curling away into themselves as if they too felt wary of Lavellan's return amongst the trees. A twig snapped under Sysa's foot, and she felt herself jolt sharply.

'Pull yourself together. This is ridiculous,' she said into the darkness. In response, a small bird flew out from its resting place, almost crashing into the hand Sysa had brought up towards her face.

She continued on through the dark tunnel of the forest, the air damp with the shroud of midnight. She didn't look back towards Steel Castle; she knew this was something she had to do alone. She kept her head up, feeling the curtain of her hood fall softly around her cheeks and over her forehead. Where was it, she wondered, the place where the light had once fallen away into darkness? She looked around, as if she could somehow decipher the point where Rogart's dark kingdom had once begun.

For now, though, all she could see were the trees merging into one, their crowns rushing and rustling against each other in a state of living, breathing quiet. She heard their hushed voices whisper and knew the Castle of Thunder could not be far away. She turned, twisting on the track until she found herself in a small clearing. And then she saw it, screened by the wall of trees that had grown since Rogart's departure: a turret rising from green darkness. Atop the square of grey stone, a flag flew, emblazoned in blue and white cresting patterns. She shuddered. Lavellan wanted her to know a new master was at home.

Sysa carried on, winding her way through the track that rose up towards the castle. With each step, the trees closed in on her, as if the world was shrinking to this track, this place, this time. The night felt heavy, laden with whispering leaves and a growing sense of claustrophobia. The air smelled of pine and a cloying sort of sweetness. It was intoxicating. She strode on, feeling the small winds that gathered behind her, propelling her closer to the castle. From ahead, the whispers called out to her, a blanket of need surrounding her in the dark.

Finally, she reached the end of the track and a gate framed by two large stone pillars, around which ivy climbed like curling serpents. Beyond the gate, the castle loomed, its square and rectangular towers peering out like angry grey faces against the night. A row of trees hugged the walls surrounding the castle lands, which were not really gardens, Sysa noted, but an expanse of bare earth that appeared to have been kept deliberately barren despite the new growth made possible by Rogart's departure. She looked up, half-expecting the boom of thunder and lightning that had emanated from the castle during Rogart's rule there. Those forces from the fae lines that lay around the castle boundaries were now strangely quiet, only the stars left suspended in the sky they had once shook.

Sysa rattled at the steel bars of the gate, shaking them defiantly. It was an unusual touch, she thought to herself with a grimace, the link to her surname, a ruse to make her feel vulnerable perhaps. She felt anything but vulnerable, though, in fact sensing a rising power surge up within her as she stepped back from the gated entrance. She lifted her arms, pointing her hands towards the castle. With an outward flick of her palms, the gate opened, like the call to heel of an obedient dog.

From somewhere above, Sysa heard a flapping noise, and peered around, wondering if the sky seer Arno had followed her on her passage. There was no sign of him amongst the trees, though, and only the thrumming flag atop the turret answered her searching look. Below the flag, a window was lit with the glow of a hanging candelabra, just visible in the uppermost corner. Sysa inhaled deeply, starting down the gravelled track that led to a huge, arched entrance, and a pair of heavy black doors shuttered with several rows of gleaming steel.

She waited in front of the entrance and planted her feet wide, ready to unleash her growing sense of anger. She raised her hands in preparation, but before she could release her stream of light against the doorway, the bars slid sideways and the doors opened, like two large arms beckoning her in.

He's expecting me, Sysa thought, stepping into the entrance and making her way along a stone-walled corridor lit with the glow of candles that lined the hallway. The corridor soon opened onto a large oval-shaped area, from which a staircase rose abruptly. The place had nothing of the curved lines and sweeping arcs of Steel Castle, Sysa thought, as her eyes swept around warily. Everything here was straight and square, boxy-looking and dark. She looked left, to where a portrait of the giant Rogart stared in amber-coloured fury back at her. She tilted her head, momentarily entranced by the giant's beauty, undeniable even in two dimensions, and his currently exiled state. She stared into his almond-shaped eyes, so similar to the ones that had bored into her just a few hours previously, and felt a pang of longing for Brodie, her son of a giant. She brushed the thought off, turning towards the staircase and the sound of a tinkling laughter that was drifting towards her, as if descending down the steps.

She climbed, feeling the hum of the laughter press down like an assault against her senses. There was another sound too, the murmured whispers of a female. And a smell – something animal, Sysa thought, as the tang of it wafted down and curled its way around her nose. She reached the first floor, remembering the lit window near the highest peak of the castle. She climbed to the second floor, hearing the sounds of the laughter not far above her head. At the third landing, she stopped and turned into a passageway that bloomed with the voices that were still calling to her. She stepped along a corridor, lined with painted scenes of the castle's history – a spotter here, another portrait of Rogart further along the wall. As she passed each gilded frame, they breathed to life, emboldening whatever memory the scene evoked, as a black-winged spotter stretched its wings to flight inside the painting closest. She stepped past it, turning her head sharply as she heard a familiar cry inside the frame. There she saw Brodie, held suspended by the spotter above the cliff, back on the day they had first kissed, a living memory of their horror. Sysa squeezed her eyes shut, willing the scene away as quickly as it had come. When she opened her eyes again, the memory had breathed itself gone, leaving only the dark spotter, staring out at her through watercoloured eyes that held a hint of triumph. Further along, another portrait of Rogart smirked to life as she moved past it. She pivoted, daring it, until Rogart's smile settled once again into a frozen, painted line.

Sysa lifted her chin and stared ahead, determined to avoid the goings-on of the castle's artwork. She rounded a corner, closer to the source of the laughter that now ballooned around her head. The passageway, which was lit by candles, suddenly felt cold, as if an icy chill had descended on the place. She knew that feeling – she had felt it before, every time Lavellan had been near. She nudged open a door, through which a sliver of light peeked out, as if goading her.

As the door swung open, a dark shape loomed towards her, emanating a sudden warmth Sysa hadn't expected from the room. Before she could step back, the dark, warm thing was in front of her face, its hot breath clawing against her features.

Next, a large mouth opened, fangs shining white against the darkness.

The mouth growled at her.

Sysa had come face to face with Lavellan's wolf.

★

'Now, now, Sirius, is that really any way to welcome visitors?' A familiar voice clipped the air from somewhere behind the creature.

Sysa staggered back as the wolf sat, then stretched its front legs across the marble, suddenly radiating obedience and calm. Now able to see past the bulky form of the grey wolf, Sysa peered towards the back of the room, where Lavellan sat on a velvet-backed throne, one leg draped lazily over an armrest. At his feet sat Luna, coiling a strand of golden hair around her hand and alternating smug looks between the pair. On the other arm of the chair was a raven who peered at Sysa through buttoned ebony eyes that seemed to bore into the depths of her.

Sysa anchored her gaze on Lavellan, who leaned forward in his seat, resting his elbows on his knees.

They stayed like that for some time, just staring at each other, as a strange silence hung around the room like a waiting, willing dagger. Lavellan fixed Sysa with his usual icy eyes, his eyebrows slightly arched, as if inviting her to speak. His white-blond hair hung around his head in its usual arrangement, a sheen mirrored by tight leather trousers and a jerkin that clung to him like dark water. Finally, he rolled his eyes up and down Sysa's body before exhaling loudly.

'Well, well, well. If it isn't the light-bringer. How nice of you to come.'

Sysa took a deep breath, feeling the crackle of her powers awaken inside her fingers. The surge was met with something else, though, a feeling that came from somewhere deep inside her chest. It was that pulling, jarring feeling she had felt before, as if a rope had been attached to her ribs, reeling her in no matter how much she tried to resist it.

Something flickered across Lavellan's face then, an expression Sysa didn't have time to place before he quickly rearranged his features.

'I think you knew I was coming, Lavellan. And I see you have company.' Sysa's eyes drifted towards the mermaid Luna, who sat simpering at Lavellan's feet, her currently human form clad in a few silken shreds that swam over her sun-kissed torso. Sysa exhaled loudly, returning her attention to Lavellan.

'I want to know why you killed Grey.'

'Such accusations! And we've only just reunited.' Lavellan stood up, placing a hand over his heart and sticking his bottom lip out in a façade of being wounded. He took a step closer, Luna's arms falling from his thighs as he brushed her off like an over-zealous pet.

'Oh no, no,' he said, tilting his face in Sysa's direction. 'We'll come back to questions later. For now, my dear, we have so much catching up to do. For a start, you haven't been properly introduced to my new friends.'

Lavellan swept his arms about to indicate the wolf and then the raven, who remained on the armrest, still peering at Sysa with interest.

'That's Sirius,' he said pointing at the wolf again. 'He's been *such* a good friend to me since all those silly spotters dispersed when Rogart, well – you know.' Lavellan made a face.

Sysa thought back to the painting in the hall, and recalled Rogart's companions with a shudder. If they had scattered after the giant's departure, she certainly didn't feel any regret about their loss.

'And that's Three-Wings,' Lavellan continued when

Sysa didn't answer. 'My raven.' Lavellan looked over proudly at the bird, who responded by ruffling his feathers, revealing the likely source of his naming – on one side were two stacked wings instead of one.

'Imaginative name,' Sysa said as Lavellan whipped his head back round to face her.

'Ah! I see you haven't lost any of that spark I enjoy so much about you. This is going to be fun, I just know it.' Lavellan cooed at the bird, stroking him in an exaggerated manner. 'What did the bad female say about you, *mmm*, Three-Wings? Such a good boy. You're such a special boy.'

Sysa sighed, rolling her eyes as Lavellan proceeded with his drawn-out performance. Eventually, he dismissed the raven with a wave of his hand, and the bird flew to an open window, where he alighted, apparently deciding between the stone walls of the castle and the sky.

'Off you go, my lovely. Off you go, boy. Fly. Enjoy yourself.' Lavellan flicked his hand in the direction of the window. The bird flew off, beating his way across the darkness. 'My own sky seer.' Lavellan folded his arms across his chest, watching his charge depart.

Sysa made a small snorting noise. The bird was being sent to check if she had been followed, and she and Lavellan both knew it.

Lavellan was still watching the open window, with the look of a wistful parent.

'They must have their fun, mustn't they? Our children.' Lavellan sighed again, swivelling on his heel and casting a glance between Sysa and Luna. 'So, what's next? Mermaid versus faerie?' He clasped his hands together. Luna made a hissing noise and stood up, before Lavellan wagged a finger at her. 'Not yet, my dear. We're only just getting started.' Luna sat down, a cloaked fury spreading across her face.

Sysa shot a look at the mermaid, who was clawing at Lavellan's legs again. 'Enough with the dramatics, Lavellan. You know exactly why I'm here.'

'Oh, do I?' Lavellan cast his eyes to the ceiling and rubbed his chin with a curled finger.

'I came here to find out two things,' Sysa said. 'Why you killed Grey, and what you're doing back here now. I'm glad you've made some new friends—' Sysa's voice dripped with the same mocking edge Lavellan's had a few moments earlier— 'but, in truth, I don't really care about that.'

'*Mmm*,' Lavellan replied, tapping his finger against his lower lip in a slow rhythm. 'You see, the thing is – if I tell you the answers to those questions, you're either going to kill me, or you're going to leave, and neither of those options really feel good for me right now.'

'I know! Why don't we start with why Luna's here?' Lavellan trilled, his eyes widening as he swivelled, inclining his head towards the mermaid.

'That's an interesting story.' Lavellan nodded once at Luna, encouraging her to speak.

'I've come for William, of course.' Luna's voice was as tight as the narrowed look she levelled at Sysa. 'I heard he and your sister are engaged to be married? We'll see about that. First, I take William back, then I punish your sister for what she did.'

'What *she* did?' Sysa felt a crackle of light spark up inside her fingertips. 'Falling in love with a man and then choosing *not* to tie him up in a cave surrounded by riches? Since when was that a crime?'

'Stealing is still a crime in the fae lands, Sysa, if I'm not mistaken,' Luna answered, rising up from her seated position. 'And your sister stole from me.' The mermaid walked slowly around Sysa, circling her. 'I punish those who steal from me. Severely.' Her hot breath wafted against Sysa's cheek.

In the background, Lavellan stood, arms folded across his chest, apparently amused by the scene in front of him.

'You go near my sister, or William, and I swear I'll...' Sysa bunched her fists, feeling her nails dig into her palms.

'You'll do what?' Luna raised her eyebrows. 'Kill me? I thought you were the light-bringer, the *good* one, the perfect Seelie faerie.'

'Oh, she's far too much of a goody-two-shoes for violence.' Lavellan's words tugged at Sysa's fingers, infuriating her.

'She is, isn't she? I'll do exactly what I want to her sister, and William, and she won't be able to stop me.' Luna's face flashed with a grin that lit up the room with an ugly brightness.

In response, another light moved into the darkness, flying from Sysa's fingers and exploding across the mermaid's face.

CHAPTER FOUR

For a moment, everything went completely black, as if the light from Sysa's hands had extinguished everything that existed in the castle. Sysa blinked into the darkness. She could feel a vague sense of her arms, hanging limp at her sides beside her, but they felt empty, as if she had pushed all the power that lived there out of her flesh and deep into the room. The air around her felt thick, weighed down with a sense of foreboding that pressed against her senses. She smelled burning, a scent that collided with the tang of something else that wafted under her nostrils. *Was it blood?* she wondered, looking around into the darkness.

The silence was broken by a shifting noise and the sound of the wolf, Sirius, growling.

Sysa felt an awful desire to vomit rise up inside her throat.

'Well, that was a little unfortunate.' Lavellan's words cut the air and were followed by a clicking noise and the bursting to life of the candles that had snuffed out during the explosion.

In the light, Lavellan stood over the crumpled heap of Luna's form, curled up like a sleeping apostrophe on the floor. A streak of red scissored its way along her cheekbone, mirroring the jagged threads of her garment that streaked silken welts across her skin.

Sysa put her hand to her mouth, her mind filled with a vision of what she had once done to the faerie Krystan in a similar fit of anger. Yet, then, the fight had at least been equal. This time she hadn't given her opponent even the semblance of a chance.

'Did I do that?' she asked, her voice trembling into the darkness.

'Well, it certainly looks that way.' Lavellan looked around, as if checking for some invisible assailant in the room.

'Is she... dead?' Sysa whispered, for once not succumbing to anger at Lavellan's mockery.

Lavellan bent down, swiping the blood on Luna's cheek with an outstretched finger. He inhaled deeply, holding the bloodied finger level with his eyeline, turning it this way and that.

'Not dead. Very close to it, though,' he said as he rose up to his full height and made a face while wiping his finger on a cloth draped over a nearby table.

Sysa allowed herself a second's relief before she flew at him.

'Don't you care? Isn't she meant to be your friend?'

'Well, I don't know if I'd go that far,' Lavellan said. 'She's become something of a nuisance these last months, actually. Did you see the way she was hanging off me earlier?' He made a sort of tutting sound. 'You might have done me a favour. And yourself, too. Saved your family a lot of trouble, by the looks of it. Let's just leave her.' He swaggered over to his throne and flopped down on it, before casting an eye at his wolf friend who was on the other side of the room, sniffing at the blood-tinged air.

'Sirius. Are you hungry?' He motioned in the direction of the mermaid.

The wolf, head hung low, made a few steps towards Luna's prone form, droplets of saliva hanging from his jaws.

In an instant, Sysa was in front of the wolf again, this time matching his growl with the web of light she pushed out from her fingers. The wolf pressed his face against the web, and it sealed over into a hardened arc of air, preventing his passage any further. He sat down, making a small whining sound.

'All right, Sirius, no dinner for you tonight. She's in one of her moods again.' From his throne, Lavellan made a sympathetic face towards the wolf.

Still holding on to the arc of light, Sysa turned her head towards Lavellan. 'You can't be serious?'

'It was just an idea.' He sniffed at the air, wounded. 'You can let it go now.' He gestured towards the light-arc. 'Sirius will be a good boy, I promise.' He nodded at the wolf, who slunk back to his earlier position and lay down, resting his muzzle on the floor with a discontented noise.

Keeping her eyes on Lavellan, Sysa lowered her arms until the wall of light receded away into nothing. She walked around in small circles, pressing her fingers against her forehead. 'Think,' she said to herself in rings of repeated agony. From his throne, Lavellan watched, flinging his leg over the armrest and making lazy circles with his foot. 'I know. I'll go back to Steel Castle, speak to my family, Brodie too, he might be able to do something to bring her back.' Sysa stood still at last, her only movement a hurried glance towards the mermaid.

'Your family? Brodie? You really want them to know you did this?' Lavellan pointed at Luna's heaped body for emphasis. 'What will they think, once they know what you're capable of? I'm not sure they'll be as eager to help you as you assume.'

'Of course they will. They love me.' Sysa bit at her lip, feeling a surge of uncertainty rise up inside her body. What if Lavellan was right? What if her family were as horrified as her by what she'd done here? 'Not that you would know anything about love, of course.' She shot a cool look towards him. 'Unless you count your wolf there, and that raven.' Sysa raised her chin, wanting to hurt him, punish him. An odd look passed over Lavellan's face for a moment before it was swallowed by another expression.

'Oh, love again. That old chestnut.' Lavellan waved his hand around in the air beside his head. 'Well, perhaps you ought to think about the one you love so dearly, before you go scurrying back to Steel Castle.'

'What do you mean? Are you talking about Brodie? Brodie will help me. He's my fiancé.' Sysa realised her final words had sprung out with a desperate tone, and instinctively splayed her fingers at her sides.

Lavellan's eyes dropped to her hands and then shifted back up again.

'There it is. That anger. Don't you see it? What you're going to do to him with all that burning rage? Don't you remember it, that darkness in him? The darkness that was only extinguished when you came to him with your heart of shining light? Don't you see that this—' Lavellan was suddenly beside her, his breath goading against her cheek the same way Luna's had— 'this rage of yours, what you've done here, it's only going to send him to the dark. Your light fuels his light, your darkness fuels his hate, don't you see it, Sysa?' Lavellan was walking around her, his breath warm on her neck now. Sysa had never heard him say her name like that before, and she winced, something inside her springing to the surface. 'You take him here, to this, and you'll destroy him. Is that what you want, Sysa?'

That feeling again.

'No, it's not what I want. So, what do I do?' Sysa's voice cracked, the thought of doing anything that might hurt Brodie utterly unbearable. And there was something else too – that sense of the deep-seated connection between them, their souls, forever entwined either in darkness or in light.

She knew that Lavellan was right, that she held the force of Brodie's power within her fingers. She had felt it on the beach that day with Rogart, the sense that she somehow *owned* it, that it was hers to direct as either a force for good or bad. Brodie was Rogart's son – the capacity for darkness still lived inside him. Sysa cast another glance towards the mermaid, her face flushing with shame and horror.

That capacity for darkness obviously existed somewhere inside her too.

'Well, there is something we might consider, if you're really intent on saving her,' Lavellan said, apparently oblivious to Sysa's inner torment.

'Of course I want to save her,' Sysa snapped back, eyes burning. 'So how do we do it?'

Something lurched in the region of Sysa's stomach. All of a sudden, she and Lavellan were a 'we'.

She felt a sudden longing for Grey and his stories, which in that time *before*, had given her all the answers she needed. She squeezed her eyes shut, but there were no stories, no visions. Just the dark curtain of her eyelids, and Lavellan's voice ringing out across the room.

'*We*,' he said with a smile, as Sysa snapped her eyes back open, 'go back to Never Night.'

'Never Night? You mean Caithness?' Sysa repeated, her voice lifting at the mention of the place she'd lived in with Grey before arriving in Fyrish. 'Why there?' She took a step towards him, remembering their last encounter in Caithness, and the awful day when he had attacked Grey at the river beside their cottage. 'What could possibly be in Caithness that might solve this? Is this some kind of trap, Lavellan?' She fixed him with an icy stare and placed her hands on her hips.

'A trap? Don't be ridiculous. I'm trying to help you. But no, no, if you don't believe me, then hurry home to that family of yours and let them tidy up your mess.' He turned away.

Sysa inhaled, letting her breath back out in a furious stream through her nostrils.

'Just tell me. Please,' she added, after a pause of several seconds. 'What is there in Caithness that will help bring Luna back?'

'A healing stone,' Lavellan said, swivelling on his heel and turning back towards her.

'A healing stone?' Sysa answered, inwardly chastising herself. Was she just going to stand here repeating everything Lavellan said?

'Yes, a healing stone. A stone that has the power to heal,

salve, make better.' Lavellan smirked, obviously enjoying his new role as teacher.

'I know about healing stones. Grey told me about them.' Sysa thought back to Grey's stories of objects imbued with magical properties, and their use in treating illness. Hugh, the boy who had lived on the croft nearest them in Caithness had once alluded to his father's possession of such an object, which he ministered to his livestock when they were affected by a sickness of some or other sort. Hugh's father had also been a staunch advocate of faerie darts, and other protections against the fae folk, Sysa remembered, wondering what the man would now think if he saw her. Like many Caithness people, Hugh's father had feared and revered the fae in equal measure. Sysa snapped back from her memories, realising with a jolt that Grey's stories had found a way back to her through Lavellan's mention of the stone.

'There are lots of supposed healing objects in Caithness, though, Lavellan,' Sysa said, feeling his name roll off her tongue with the same odd feeling she'd experienced earlier when he'd said her own name. 'What is it about this healing stone that would help save Luna? Is it special in some way?' She stepped towards him, suddenly enlivened by the prospect of an antidote to Luna's near-death.

'Yes, this one is special. It has the power to return someone back from the brink of dying.'

Sysa swallowed, thinking of Grey again, and the unicorn blood that had saved Brodie from death at the hands of his father. But Grey wasn't here now, and the power of the unicorn was gone. She sank down into herself – for now she had no option but this, and Lavellan.

She raised her head again.

'So, do you know exactly where in Caithness this magical stone is?'

'Not so much where, but *who*,' Lavellan said, wandering around the room, a fist bunched at his chin, his crossed arm cradling his elbow. 'I know who has it, so we find them, and then we find the stone.'

'And who has this stone then?' Sysa snapped, feeling furious again. She knew that Lavellan was enjoying this. She hated relying on him, and he knew it.

Lavellan persisted with his wanderings, apparently trying to draw out his revelations for as long as he possibly could.

'The stone belongs to the Keeper of the Northern Gate. So first we need to find the keeper.'

'I've never heard of a Keeper of the Northern Gate. I swear, Lavellan, if you're lying to me...' Sysa seethed, balling her fists against her thighs.

'Oh, for goodness' sake, not that again,' Lavellan said, turning to face her. 'All you need to know for now is that the keeper exists, and is our pathway to the stone. I'll tell you the rest when we get there. We don't have time for further explanations.' He darted a look at the mermaid.

'How much time *does* she have?' Sysa asked, seeing the answer written on his face.

'Very little,' he confirmed, holding Sysa's look until they were distracted by a flapping sound that signalled Three-Wings returning to his mantel on the window ledge.

Sysa looked round at the bird, and then the wolf, who peered back at her through expectant amber eyes.

'If you want to save her, we need to go now,' Lavellan

said, picking up Luna's limp body and moving her towards a nearby daybed. Sysa winced as she watched Luna's slack limbs hanging from Lavellan's chest as he placed her gently on the couch. His action held a tenderness Sysa hadn't expected, and she turned her face away, feeling shame and guilt rise up inside her. She thought of her mother and father, of Elva and of Brodie, the thought of being away from him almost as unbearable as the scene that lay before her in the room.

She squeezed her eyes shut and then opened them again, sweeping her gaze over the raven and the wolf until it finally landed on Lavellan.

'Let's go then. Back to Caithness.'

Around her, the candlelight blossomed, her words stoking an ember that was slowly coming back to life.

CHAPTER FIVE

Outside, the wind had picked up, battering their faces as they stepped out onto the gravel. Sysa looked over her shoulder to where Lavellan and Sirius followed.

'They're coming with us?' She gestured towards the wolf and then the raven, who was perched on a branch a little way ahead of them.

'Of course,' Lavellan answered. 'Where I go, they go.'

'And they can cross over? To the human world?' Sysa asked.

'It certainly seems that way.' Lavellan didn't offer any further explanation, and Sysa's returning sigh was lost quickly to the wind.

'There's a storm coming.' Lavellan lifted his nose to the air, which was laced with the tang of an ominous, salty fury. 'It's the sea. It gets angry when a mermaid dies. Or when one is dying,' he quickly corrected, shooting a look at Sysa from the corner of his eye.

Sysa heard the crash of waves against rock from somewhere in the distance. She paused to finger her starlights, still cushioned in their familiar home in the pocket of her cloak. She remembered how they had once helped her tame Modan, the kelpie, and wondered if they would be of any use to her on this journey. She was startled back into the moment when Lavellan's eyes followed her own downwards. She coughed, removing her hand from her pocket and yanking the hood of her cloak up. She walked a few steps ahead, and then turned back to him.

'So, where do we cross over? To get to Caithness?'

As she said the name of her old home, Sysa felt a prickle of emotion run up her spine and down again. Despite everything, she was excited to be going back.

'Well, we do have to go a bit further than the castle gates, my dear,' Lavellan said with a smirk that twisted Sysa's feelings of excitement back to anger. 'I believe there's a portal not far from Steel Castle – the one you yourself came through?' Lavellan's voice lifted with a mocking humour. The corners of his mouth twitched as he waited for Sysa to bite back.

'Find another,' Sysa said through clenched teeth as she narrowed her eyes at him. She didn't need to voice the explanation that hung in the air around them. *Somewhere that won't risk my family seeing me*. The skin on the back of her neck bristled with annoyance and a burning sense of shame.

'Luckily for you, there are portals into the human world all over Fyrish, Sysa.' Lavellan swept his arm around in the darkness. 'I like to travel through water tunnels, personally, but I know you're not much of a sea-babe.' He looked her up and down, as if checking for signs of a mermaid tail that had gone unnoticed until then. 'So we'll go another way,' he quipped, when Sysa folded her arms across her chest in answer. 'There's a mound not far from here. Come.' He gestured to her to follow as he made his way out of the gates that slid open with a flick of his pale wrist.

They rounded a corner onto a path edged with trees that bent over to meet each other in the darkness. The effect was of walking into a tunnel; not the water kind Lavellan had mentioned, but one that hung heavy with the smell of sap and the weight of pine-soaked air. Sysa blinked, glad of her faerie eyesight as she navigated the ebony darkness. It was as if a door had been closed, squeezing and shuttering the whole night into this woody round. She felt for her starlights then hesitated, realising with a strange feeling that the darkness didn't bother her. Behind her, the wolf's strides fell in time with his sticky breathing. Sysa felt his warm exhale as it licked against the soft flesh of her thigh.

She turned, wondering about the raven, but there was no sign of him. He must have taken another route, she thought, leaving the wolf to pad behind them on the leaves. Sirius startled slightly at her movement, a dark line of fur prickling along his back as he eyed her warily. Sysa lifted her chin in a small gesture of triumph. The wolf had obviously adjusted his expectations after their earlier encounter in the castle rooms.

Finally, they stepped off the path and into a clearing lit by a shaft of moonlight. The light fell, as if pointing, towards a small mound that grew up from the earth, giving the impression of a tiny mountain topped with snow.

'Here we are,' said Lavellan, twirling round to face her as Three-Wings descended to join them. 'It's not much to look at, but it does the necessary.'

Nearby, the circling trees seemed to shudder in the rising wind.

'Let's just get this over with,' Sysa said, stepping towards the mound and the small burn that trickled to the right of it.

She felt herself shiver involuntarily – the last time she had crossed between the human and the fae lands had also been the last time she had seen her grandfather alive in his human form. She remembered the pain, the awful shredding pain of leaving Na Trì Sìtheanan without him. And the noise. It had been like the screeching of birds and wind and rain. She closed her eyes as that terrible clamour came back to her, that sense of everything in the sky opening its mouth to scream in awful unison. She clenched her fists, steeling herself for the coming onslaught.

'It won't hurt as much this time.' Lavellan's voice was quiet at her side. 'It won't hurt,' he repeated, louder, and with more of his usual swagger when she didn't answer. 'Your powers hadn't been realised when you came here from Never Night. This time you're fae.' He paused to look at her and shifted his foot across the grass.

'Then why am I still hurting?' She spoke to herself, not expecting any kind of understanding from the man beside her. How could he know the physical, ripping pain of leaving someone you loved behind?

She pictured Grey, back on the hill at Na Trì Sìtheanan, and then Brodie, the two images blending to a blur of regret and shame inside her. She swiped at her eyes, burning with anger both at herself, and at Lavellan. How had she allowed herself to get into a situation where he might be the only hope she had?

'Would holding my hand help?' Lavellan's voice drifted over as he stretched his arm out in invitation. Sysa winced, remembering the way Grey's hand had slipped away from her when she left Caithness. Lavellan stood waiting, his eyebrows raised, blue eyes glinting in the dark.

'Are you serious?' Sysa turned away, pulling at the curtains of her cloak. She couldn't tell if he was joking.

'Suit yourself.' Lavellan strode off to the grassy peak above them, the raven and the wolf sweeping along behind him in obedient parade.

When Lavellan reached the top of the mound, he closed his eyes, awaiting the natural revelation that would lead them back to Caithness. Sysa dipped her head low against the wind and scrambled towards him, feeling annoyed that he hadn't waited for her, and at the same time annoyed that he now did. The wind was starting to howl around her ears, singing a song of return in rising shrieks and torrents. Beyond the trees, the sea was whipping itself into a frenzy, as the tale of the mermaid surged in swells that foamed and spat against the shore. Sysa thought of Steel Castle and the inhabitants who would soon be woken by rattling windows and falling branches. She imagined Ida, fussing around in small, hurried steps, barking out orders to servants to close the windows and reinforce the doors. She thought of her parents, and Elva – would they sense that she had done this? And she thought of Brodie, waking to find an empty space on the bedsheets next to him where she should have been.

She squeezed her eyes shut and then opened them again, trying to replace the images in her mind – right now, she couldn't think of them. All she could focus on was this, and fixing this, so she could get back to that awful Castle of Thunder and mend what she had done.

'We go to Caithness, we get the stone, and we get back here,' she said to Lavellan through clenched teeth when she finally reached him.

He peeked one eye open at her.

'And here I was thinking we were off to enjoy a lovely holiday.' Roughly, he pulled her closer with an arm that shot out like the tongue of a hunting snake. 'You'll need to stand closer, unless you want us to end up at opposite sides of Caithness.' His subdued manner of a few moments earlier was gone, replaced with an unreadable veneer that hung over his features.

Sysa sighed. He was right on that at least. Caithness was a vast county, and some of it was unknown to her. Her secluded life with Grey had not involved many excursions from the vicinity of their cottage, all part of her grandfather's attempts to protect her from the possibility of accidentally slipping back to Fyrish before her powers were fully grown. As much as she hated the thought of making this trip with Lavellan, the idea of ending up in some far-flung corner trying to find the healing stone without him was even less attractive. Her shoulder bumped his as she accepted his ungracious offer with an equally ungracious stumble.

A bolt like lightning shot down her arm, all the way to her fingers. As if realising it couldn't escape through her extremities, it made its way back up her limb and fizzled into the rest of her, lining every inch of her like a flame along a cord.

She looked over at Lavellan to see if he had also felt it. His eyes were closed, and he stood statue-like, the lifting of his white hair the only sign he was affected by the world.

The wind raged, lashing strands of Sysa's hair over her features. She looked up; rain was beginning to fall like angry pellets. A welt of lightning suddenly split the sky above her head.

Had that caused the feeling in her arm, she wondered? The storm around them began to rise in answer. Not far away, the wolf made a long whining sound. Above, the raven spread his wings, bracing himself against the onslaught. The world seemed to lift up around them, as if the earth itself was ripping from the ground.

The land ripped, thunder boomed, and Sysa heard that familiar noise like a finger on the rim of a water jug. The noise got louder and louder, until it felt like the world was going to smash to pieces and explode into flying shards like glass inside a closing fist. She looked up at Lavellan, who stood still and resolute as the dark air closed in around them.

Sysa smelled damp fur, pine, and the salty fury of a wave that was rushing towards the shoreline.

She took a deep breath.

The only thing she could do was close her eyes.

PART TWO

THE KEEPER
AND THE STONE

CHAPTER SIX

Sysa's feet were wet.

She came to this realisation as she opened her eyes and looked around at the filmy landscape. Her vision seemed cloudy, like she was peering out of a dirty window. She felt like someone emerging from a dream, trying to make sense of the waking world. With a shake of her head, her eyes cleared, and her senses readjusted. She looked down at her feet, pin-sharp again. She was standing on the bank of a river. Not just any river. She looked up, realising she was standing in the River Thurso. Not far away was the cottage where she had spent her childhood days with Grey.

'But… there's no faerie mound here.' Sysa's voice sounded desperate as she dragged herself up the bank, her shoes making sucking sounds against the water. She stood on the grassy riverside, her cloak heavy with the weight it had trailed in from the bank. Beside her, Lavellan stood, wiping his hair back from his forehead in a lazy gesture. If he had arrived in his rat-like incarnation, he showed no sign of it. As Sysa thought of his shape-shifting manifestation, she shuddered. This was the same place she had first encountered him, back on that Beltane, here, with Grey.

'I can arrive in Never Night anywhere near water,' Lavellan said, apparently unaware of her rising horror.

'And so you chose here?' Sysa spat out, feeling a sudden urge to strike him with a bolt of light.

'Well, yes,' he yawned, looking over at the rising sun, which was appearing over the steep bank on the other side of the river. 'I thought you might like to see the old place first, before we find the keeper.'

Sysa's fingertips tingled. Did they even have time for this?

All the same, now that she was here, she couldn't deny the longing that was stirring inside her chest, pulling her. Overhead, a heron flew, large wings beating over the snaking river as if following the path that was mapped out in her heart.

She looked out over the waking landscape and the sky that was tinged peach with sunrise. Ahead was the climb that would take them up to the cottage. Sysa breathed in the scent of gorse and morning dew and home.

'Yes, I want to see the place.' She avoided any note of gratitude.

'You stay here,' she ordered. 'Especially you.' She pointed at Sirius, who was standing nearby, pawing at some stones by the edge of the water. Three-Wings wasn't far away either, and alighted obediently on a fence post as Sysa turned and started to push her way through the long grass. She already felt traitorous being here with Lavellan; the last thing she wanted was him or his cronies following her. She kept her eyes forward as she left them, her mind returning to the memories that she had once forged in this place, the dreams she had trodden into the land beneath her feet.

She carried on, up to the rising crest where the cottage became visible. She stood for a moment, looking out over the place, which felt so familiar but strangely not the same. The cottage stood where it always had, still and lonely atop the hill that led down to the river's edge. Sysa smiled, thinking of the way she had run, almost flying down it, as a child. She pictured Grey, standing at the door of the cottage looking down at her. The hawthorn was still there, too, standing guard in the same way Grey had often done. Everything was there, and yet nothing was the same any more.

Grey's absence was like a wound, scarring the place. Sysa was looking for something she would never find again.

She strode up towards the cottage, where the wooden door sat ajar, inviting her. As she ran her fingers over its surface, startled birds flew from an open window and burst into the sky. As Sysa entered the old place, she saw the remnants of a hurried breakfast, a bowl atop a counter, a familiar porridge pot. The place was just as they had left it, the day they went to Na Trì Sìtheanan. She swallowed, understanding that Grey had never come back. She swung around, almost bumping into Lavellan, who had materialised behind her like a shadow.

'What are you doing here? I told you not to come.'

In an instant, all the anger and confusion she felt converged towards the young man in front of her. It was his fault Grey was dead, and here he was mocking her, just the way he always did. *How dare he,* she thought, *how dare he come into this place and sully Grey's home with his footsteps?*

'I hate you! I hate you!' She flew at him, raining her fists against his chest before he had a chance to speak.

'The place has been empty since you left.' Once Sysa had finished her tirade, Lavellan spoke quietly. He had remained still throughout the pummelling; they both knew it was the action of a child. Sysa turned away, swiping at her eyes, wishing she had released some of the fire inside her fingers. But, right now, she knew she needed him, so instead, she had vented her anger in the only way she could. Eventually, she turned back, exhaling her frustration and steadying herself against the table. Lavellan stood up straight, leaving her anger to hang in the air like the peat smoke that had once risen up towards the roof.

'But why, why wouldn't he come back here? Where did he die? Alone out there somewhere?' Sysa couldn't bear it.

'You know that whatever happened here, it wasn't his real death.' Lavellan swept his hand around to encompass Caithness. 'He died on a cliff as a unicorn. By the time you left him, the Grey in this world was a shell.' Lavellan paused for a moment. 'And when he died on that cliff, he wasn't alone.'

'No, you were there, and you killed him,' Sysa seethed, stepping forward and instinctively pushing her arm out.

Lavellan grabbed it, holding her loosely by the wrist.

'Your grandfather was a wise man. He knew what needed to be done.' Lavellan's words were gentle, his blue eyes made soft by the hushed light of morning. As he opened his mouth to speak again, his words were replaced by a thumping noise coming from the doorway.

'Who's in there? Show yoursel'.' A deep voice boomed from somewhere outside the door.

'Oh joy. The locals.' Lavellan dropped Sysa's wrist and rolled his eyes, dissolving his previous expression.

'What do we do?' Sysa hissed, her eyes widening to rounds like the spoons that sat upon the table.

'Sysa, he can't hurt you.' Lavellan cocked his head, the corners of his lips twitching. 'He can't even *see* you if you don't want him to. You're fae, remember?' Lavellan spoke as if Sysa had forgotten what she was.

'So, we just stand here? Do nothing?' Sysa whispered. 'How did they even know we were in here?'

'Ah, some of them are extremely vigilant. The birds, perhaps, alerted them.' Lavellan looked over at the open window and yawned, uncaring. 'They won't bother us. Just let them carry on with their little *inspection*.' He twitched his fingers in the air around him. 'Unless you want to have some fun with them, instead?' He raised an eyebrow and Sysa shoved him, wondering what his idea of 'fun' was.

'No, Lavellan, I certainly do not.'

'Well then, just remain still and quiet while they go about their business,' he breathed out in disappointment. 'That's assuming you can actually be quiet for a few minutes?' His lips curved as he shot her a glance from the corner of his eye.

Sysa said nothing in reply, instead crossing her arms and waiting for whoever was out there to make themselves known again.

There was an uncertain sort of shuffling noise from the doorway. Two men, who were mirrors of each other despite a marked difference in age, fumbled inside the cottage. They were both dressed in oatmeal-coloured gear, and possessed the same beady eyes and scraggy, unkempt beards. There was something in their respective gaits that suggested a familial relationship. The only difference Sysa could discern between the two was that one looked completely beige, and the other completely grey.

'I told ye, Father, there's no one here,' the younger one said over his shoulder as he crept his way along the floor, boots scraping against flagstone. 'Let's get goin' home. There's work to be attending to on the farm.'

'Aye, aye lad. But the *sìthichean* have been here all right. Ah can almost smell them.' The older man sniffed the air around them deeply. In his hand, he brandished a faerie dart, a small, flinty instrument that local folk believed offered protection from the fae.

'Well, they're not here now, Father,' the younger man said, looking around nervously. Beside her, Sysa felt the heat of muffled laughter, and saw Lavellan shaking his head as he pressed splayed fingers to his cheeks.

'There's been somethin' no' right aboot this place since that Grey Steel left, him an' that wee lassie of his,' the older man continued. Judging by the younger man's expression, Sysa guessed he had heard his father's reflections on the matter several times before. 'There was somethin' no' right aboot either of them, Ah said it from the start.' The man lifted his chin with an air of triumph. 'An' that Lavellan that goes aboot here, Ah'll catch him one day and kill him! They say if ye soak his skin in water, 'at water becomes all-healing. Ah'll use 'at for healing 'e livestock! Mebbe for healing folk too, let's make some coin while we're aboot the business, aye?' The old man chuckled, prodding his son in an attempt at shared conspiracy. The younger man looked down at the boot he was shuffling around the stone.

Sysa felt the air around her stiffen and glanced to her left, where Lavellan looked straight ahead, his expression a mask again. She felt strangely embarrassed. The feeling unnerved her, and she looked down at her feet, the stone beneath them as unreadable as Lavellan's eyes.

'We should'a set this place alight years ago, Hugh,' the man said, slapping his son on the back as they finally made their way out of the cottage.

Now it was Sysa's turn to stiffen as realisation poked her like an icy finger. It was Hugh, her childhood friend, and his faerie-fearing father, Geordie.

'You canna do things like that, Father, that's the way to anger the fae and set them on cursing us.' As Hugh spoke, Sysa's head began spinning.

'Aye, yer mebbe right, son,' Geordie murmured as the two men bundled their way out of the door. 'Ah'll get 'em yet, though!' Geordie spat out over his shoulder in threat to the empty doorway.

'I'd like to see you try. Pathetic little man.' Lavellan spoke to the open door as Geordie and Hugh tramped up the track, making for their croft. 'Old friends of yours?' Lavellan spun round towards Sysa, his eyebrows lifted in accusation.

Sysa nodded.

'Such delightful people. Are you sure I can't just kill them?' Lavellan stared out of the window, watching as the two men shrank away against fields that sloped up towards the sky.

'They don't like your kind.' Sysa shook her head, instantly regretting the words she had chosen. 'The Unseelie, I mean… they don't understand about the fae folk… it's not Hugh's fault, it's his father.'

'My kind?' Lavellan swivelled to face her, ignoring her qualification. His eyes narrowed to icy blue slits before he turned to the window again, resting his palms against the frame. He looked out, his gaze drifting over the landscape. 'Perhaps you and I are more similar than you think, Sysa. Judging by that conversation, they don't seem to like *your kind* much either.'

His words stung Sysa with a force she hadn't expected. She moved to the table, running a finger over the dust-lined counters as she walked.

'How long have I been gone from here? Hugh's a grown man now.' Sysa's voice trembled. She knew time meant something different in the fae lands, but she still hadn't quite expected it. The last time she'd seen Hugh he'd been a teenager. While time had touched her friend and his father, Sysa had barely changed since leaving Caithness. She looked down at her hands, turning them this way and that in the light that fell in through the window – she had no idea how old she was. Fyrish folk spoke little of age, and though they discussed time in human terms, the meaning was fluid – time was a moving, changing thing. Sysa touched a hand to her face, leaving a patch of dust on her cheek before making a final adjustment to her once-human expectations. The corridors of time would be different for her. She would never get old in the same way as Grey.

'You've been gone seven years. Seven of their years anyway.' Lavellan flicked his chin in the direction of the window. 'Didn't your parents explain all this to you? I thought you all loved talking, sharing your feelings, whatever it is you do to pass the time up at Steel Castle.' He waved his hand around the air.

'So, Hugh must be nearly twenty-five now, the same age I'd be if I was still here,' Sysa replied, choosing to ignore Lavellan's mocking question. 'He looked older.' Sysa thought back to Hugh's worn, tired-out features. She had become so used to the sharp beauty of the fae folk that the sight of a mortal human had been strangely shocking. She winced, ashamed of herself. In that instant, she had felt relieved that the dust of time would not settle on her in the same way it had done Hugh.

'The humans age poorly,' Lavellan said with a shrug, his tone unfeeling. 'All that hard work and complaining does them no good. You now,' he observed, wagging a finger at her as he moved a step closer, 'you'll age differently. You'll get older, but very slowly, like your mother and father. Time won't disturb you in the same way it does the human folk. It's all so graceless.' He made a face and drew his hand along the table. He blew on a dusty finger, dispersing the motes like faded stars into the air.

'And you... how old are you?' Sysa narrowed her eyes at him, irritated at herself for her own curiosity. She wanted to understand Geordie's comment about skinning him. She found it hard to believe that a dead Lavellan could foster healing. It reminded her of the lifeblood of Grey, and his death as a unicorn in a way that made her feel unhinged. Lavellan narrowed his eyes back at her, as if deciphering her intentions.

'Old enough.' He turned away, leaving Sysa feeling infuriated.

As she opened her mouth to speak again, Three-Wings alighted on the window ledge. He cocked his black head in Lavellan's direction, as if he was as curious about the conversation as Sysa herself had been.

'As lovely as this was, I think it's time to leave now.'

Lavellan spoke brightly, apparently welcoming the interruption. 'Do you need a moment to yourself?' he asked, gesturing to encompass the cottage, Sysa's old life, and her memories of Grey.

'Yes, I do.' Sysa frowned, wondering whether to thank him for his enquiry. She thought better of it, and made to turn, as Lavellan signalled his intention to leave with a quick nod.

'It's nice. This place of yours,' he said a moment later, standing with his back to her in the doorway. 'I can see why you were happy here.' He paused, then walked off, Three-Wings flapping behind him in the sky.

From the window, Sysa watched as Lavellan strode back towards the river, where Sirius was waiting patiently. She paused, grateful at least that the wolf was likely as invisible to the humans as her and Lavellan were – when they chose to be, at least. She didn't imagine Geordie would have shown quite as much bravado during his inspection had the wolf made his presence known around the cottage. She sighed, turning away from the window and scanning the empty home. She felt strangely alone all of a sudden. With Lavellan gone, it was as if the walls of the place expanded, reminding her of the vastness of its void.

She walked around, running a hand over this and that, feeling the memories in wood and stone and the scents her fae senses allowed her. She paused at Grey's rocking chair, wiping away the dust and cobwebs that now obliterated the carved brown wood. She could see Grey there in her mind's eye, rocking gently as he told her one of his stories. And then herself, sitting on the rug beneath him, wrapped up in their personal world of love. It was like watching someone else's life now, someone dim and distant, the child she had said goodbye to when she first met the unicorn. She was watching a past that had belonged to her, but was strangely not her own anymore. Since leaving Caithness, it felt like her life had become a raft of small goodbyes.

And now she knew it was time to say goodbye again. Her mind drifted back to the mermaid and the keeper – this time, right now, did not belong to her. She was grateful for the chance to gain closure in a way she hadn't been able to that day Grey had surprised her with the visit to Na Trì Sìtheanan.

She paused in the empty doorway before taking a final look over her shoulder and stepping out into the new morning and the sunrise that burned its way across the sky.

★

When she arrived back at the river's edge, Lavellan was standing on the bank, throwing pebbles while Sirius nosed around in the water. Three-Wings was perched on a nearby boulder, watching the playful scene with his usual beady stare. Sysa paused for a moment, surprised by their easy camaraderie. Somehow, she had imagined their friendship as superficial, something that existed only to benefit Lavellan. Yet up ahead, he was talking to the wolf in a lowered tone that sounded almost kind. As Sirius moved closer to his thigh, Lavellan stuck out a hand, stroking the fur around the wolf's muzzle. A prickle of heat darted up the back of Sysa's neck, running all the way to the top of her head. The emptiness she had felt on leaving the cottage was abating, being replaced with something equally uncomfortable. She frowned into Lavellan's back, feeling annoyed again, and announced her arrival behind him with a cough.

'Ah, there you are,' he said with a start, apparently unaware she had been watching him. Sysa thought about their fae senses, and narrowed her eyes, wondering if the scene was another of his little games. 'All done up there?' He gestured towards the cottage.

'All done.' She pulled her cloak tighter around her neck, noticing the bitter cold for the first time that morning. 'What time of year is it?' She looked around, trying to discern the earthly season. Until now, all she had thought about was Grey, the cottage, their old home.

'The morning before Samhain,' Lavellan replied with a shrug, apparently unbothered by the biting cold air that chafed their faces. Around his shoulders, the last remnants of the sunrise settled, framing his figure with a faded, peachy glow. Sysa thought back to the times she and Grey had visited the town around now for the fires that were lit to seek a return to sunlight. On Samhain's opposite, Beltane, similar fires would be lit in gratitude at the coming season of the sun. Never Night, as the fae folk called it, would stretch out into long days of near-endless illumination. For now, though, winter was creeping into Caithness in progressive steps of growing dark. The days would be short, and afternoons would soon feel like evenings. Perhaps time was fluid everywhere, Sysa thought, looking around at the rising morning.

'So, we had better get going. To the keeper.' As she spoke, Lavellan startled like he had forgotten why they were there.

'Ah yes, we should. But don't worry too much about the time. Fyrish is still on the fae clock, remember? We left

Luna but a moment ago. We've lost little by coming here,' he said, looking at her through blue eyes that matched the sweeping colour of the river at their side.

Sysa nodded, feeling like she had lost more than Lavellan realised. At the same time, standing here with him on the riverside, she felt she had also found something, something she didn't fully understand.

'So where do we go? Where do we find this person?' Sysa rushed out, keen to replace her unsettling feelings with movement. This was her way, she knew, replacing unwelcome feelings, finding a way to cover them like a veil. She thought back to the day she had left Brodie after their first kiss and the way she had launched herself into finding Luna and William.

This is nothing like that, she chastised herself inwardly.

Lavellan was still staring at her, as if waiting for her to process the inner workings of her mind.

'Come see,' he said, climbing back up the bank to where they could see past the trees that lined the further reaches of the river. Sysa followed behind him, leaving the wolf and the raven to linger at the bank. When Lavellan reached the peak of the small glen, he turned, pointing out into the distance at the headland.

'Dunnet Head?' Sysa looked up at him. She remembered looking out at the slice of headland that sat atop the sea like the great, pointing finger of the coast.

Yes, that's where she is – somewhere out there, anyway. The keeper, I mean.' Lavellan circled his hand in the air in demonstration.

'She? So the keeper's female?' Sysa's tone held the light pitch of surprise.

'Yes, female,' Lavellan said, shifting his attention away from the coast and back to Sysa. 'Like you,' he followed up after a pause that was long enough to make the contours of Sysa's cheeks burn red. 'The most powerful usually are.' He looked back at the coast, apparently unaffected by Sysa's reaction.

'And she lives out there, where the land ends?' Sysa hoped her line of questioning would deflect from the sense of embarrassment she felt.

Lavellan turned, studying her face for a moment that felt unfeasibly longer.

'What some people call the end, others call the beginning.' He carried on staring at her with the same intent blue eyes.

Sysa shook her head, dismissing him. 'Beginning, end, does it really matter? The point is, that's where we're going, and that's where we'll get this mess sorted out. Don't bother me with your riddles,' she snapped, surprised by the force of her own reaction.

'I'm just pointing out the matter of perspective,' Lavellan said, shrugging and making his way back down the bank.

Sysa trudged along behind him, frustrated that she seemed destined to spend the remainder of this mission following him. She looked around, wondering about the odds of finding this female by herself. She had never been alone in this place, save for the time when Lavellan had attacked her grandfather right at this very spot and she had thought that Grey was lost to her. She pulled her cloak tighter, instinctively seeking protection from the echo of the fear she had felt that day. Just then, Lavellan turned round, a strange, pleading sort of look on his face as the raven and the wolf converged around him.

Sysa sighed. 'Can we just go there now?'

'As you wish.' Beside Lavellan, Sirius tilted his head up to the sky.

Sysa made the final few steps towards them, entering the ragged circle of Lavellan's family.

Nearby, the water murmured softly, carrying Sysa's memories towards the place where the river met the sea.

CHAPTER SEVEN

Sysa blinked, casting her eyes around the beach that spread out like a gold and green blanket. Up ahead, the wintering sun hung like a huge orb, flooding the expanse of sand in a liquid yellow pool. At its edge, the beach was carpeted in marram grass-covered dunes that narrowed away to the far distance. Opposite, the sea swept towards the shore in salty crests, retreating away to leave long, dark whorls across the sand.

Sysa closed her eyes again, the action dispelling her confusion. When she looked out for a second time, she recognised the place she was standing as Dunnet Beach. She swept her eyes across the sea, where the shelf of headland loomed much closer than it had just moments previously. The time between leaving and arriving had been lost to her. That she had spent it with Lavellan and the others was confirmed when she turned and found them waiting behind her on the sand.

'Rather lovely, wouldn't you say?' Lavellan said by way of introduction to their new location. 'Fyrish has its charms, but the humans lay claim to some magic too,' he said, casting his eyes about the scene. 'You know it?' he probed, when Sysa didn't answer.

'I do,' Sysa replied, thinking of a childhood visit with

Grey when they had sheltered in the prickly dunes as he told stories. That day, the sky had been heavy with dampness and a haar that had covered the beach in its milky, misty film. That was the day Grey had held a shell to her ear, so she could hear the sound of the sea though she couldn't fully see it. She had grinned up at him, lifting her shoulder as her ear had tickled with the swirling, whooshing sound. Now, she thought back to the leaves in Fyrish, how they had once spoken to her, guiding her to find the piper Peter in the dark forest. She remembered Grey telling her about the trees that had once grown on this beach, and she looked around, wondering if they still spoke. She thought of the way the air had touched her face that day, as if it too belonged in Grey's story, speaking its part in a salty, briny chorus. She thought of the smell and the taste, the same ones that now kissed her lips and met around her nose. She picked up some sand and watched it fall through the spaces between her fingertips. She knew that everything Grey had told her about the world was true and constant. Everything was real, and all of it was alive.

She also knew that this beach was part of another story, the one Grey had told her about in the cemetery at Olrig. She lifted her head, looking for that place up and out towards the hill. These were the shores where Brodie's mother, the selkie, had been found as a baby. The place where the man who would become that selkie's father had walked, pacing the sand in desperation for a child. In that, Sysa could see that this beach was also part of Brodie's story, the place where he had begun; a series of steps that would finally bring him to her. She longed for him then, deep in the place where her heart lay. She angled her head towards the shoreline, trying to catch a taste of him on the wind.

'*Hmm*. Well, we've landed a little off course, it's over there we're headed,' Lavellan said once the lengthy pause made it clear Sysa had no plans to divulge any further information. He pointed out across the water, where the headland sat still and silent, like a waiting warrior on the sea. Sysa focused in, narrowing her eyes at the jutting clump of land, its sandstone cliffs hewn from the lashings of millennia. It rose up from the Pentland Firth like a giant sea mountain. Far below, waves swirled and foamed, attempting to climb its craggy peaks.

'So how do we get from here to there?' Sysa said, watching the raven, who, above, was making his own way across the water. Nearby, Sirius poked about on the shore, his huge paws sinking in the sand.

'We could jump over, the way we did between here and the cottage,' Lavellan said, studying Sysa's face intently. 'We'd need to wait a while first though, to collect our energies. There's only so much flitting about us fae types can manage in a short time.'

Sysa snapped her head round to face him.

'So, you have limits?' She laughed in a way she wasn't accustomed to. The noise sounded bitter and grating against her senses. Embarrassed, she turned her face away, fixing her gaze back on the sea.

'As do we all,' Lavellan said, following her eyes towards the headland. 'We could swim, if you'd like to.' Sysa knew without looking that the corners of his mouth were twitching as he spoke.

Swimming that current would mean holding on to him, or finding something else to cling onto, they both knew that. Sysa sighed, wishing that Modan and the other kelpies were here to carry them across.

'We'll walk. It won't take long. Not with our speed,' Sysa said, already marching away from him.

'Where you go, I follow.' Lavellan's voice floated on the wind behind her. When it caught up, she almost tasted it, his words like the tang of bitter apples on her tongue.

★

They walked silently along a rough track that stretched from the beach and up the incline towards the headland. There was something comfortable about the quiet, Sysa noted with a dull, guilty sort of feeling as they padded. There was something about the easy silence that reminded her of her relationship with Grey. Horrified by her own thoughts, she glanced at Lavellan, who had said nothing, save the odd murmured instruction to Sirius. As the three of them swept along at a pace which would have appeared a blur to outside observers, the wind licked against Sysa's face, pressing against her chest like a rhythmic, beating drum.

Now and again, they passed crofts and homesteads, where, unseen, Sysa would stop to watch the occupants bustle about, absorbed with the business of daytime. She wondered what they would think if they saw her, these folk of the county with their horseshoes overhanging doors. It was unsettling to think that she now resembled Lavellan more closely than she did the humans of her original homeland. Caithness felt at once near to her, and at the same time very far away.

They carried on walking until there were no more cottages and no more people. The land became quiet, falling away like dark seas to either side. There was no sign of Three-Wings; he must have found his own way across the water, Sysa thought, as she looked up at the darkening sky above them. Between inky patches of colour, the afternoon sunset sang out in red and orange embers, while at the coast, waves reared up, rasping against the clipped ending to the day.

They climbed a steep path along a track hemmed tight with bronze and purple heathers. When they reached the peak of it, Sysa felt breathless, not from exertion but from the sight of the coast spread out below. As they lowered towards the cliff edge, Sysa heard the rasp of reaching waves and breathed in the tang of sea spray. The cliffs wound next to the path, fingers of land stretching into the sea where they met with the calls of swooping gulls.

'We should stop. Find something to eat,' Lavellan said without preamble, as he followed Sysa's eyes towards a small beach that fringed the coast beside them. Ahead, the headland stretched out, appearing to recede forever to the night. Sysa blinked, awakening her keen fae eyesight – the last thing she wanted to do was stop here, with Lavellan.

'I'm tired,' he said, in answer to her silence.

As he turned towards the beach, Sysa noticed him cradling his arm, as if it were heavy. When she tilted her head in query he straightened, and was himself again, all trace of weakness gone.

'Can't we just carry on? The dark won't bother us when it comes,' Sysa said, without any effort to conceal her irritation.

'I said I'm tired.' Lavellan's voice was flat, his usual sing-song intonation seeming to drift off with the waning day. 'And Sirius needs to eat. As do I. It took energy, you know, whisking you back here, guiding you around the countryside.' His hand swiped air in demonstration.

Sysa stood with her hands on her hips, surveying him. She sighed and stomped off quickly up the hill.

'Fine, let's go hunt,' she shouted over her shoulder, as Sirius circled a patch of grass behind her, apparently unsure which master to follow.

'Wait,' Lavellan called into the growing darkness. 'Sirius and I will do it. You stay here and set a camp up on the beach.'

Sysa turned, narrowing her eyes before agreeing. 'Suit yourself,' she said with a shrug, passing him on her way back down towards the coastline. If she was being offered a break from his annoying presence, she wasn't about to argue or complain.

'I think there are deer up ahead a bit. We won't be long,' Lavellan said, motioning to the wolf to follow. Before Sysa had a chance to reply, they were gone, swallowed up by the folds of growing dark.

Sysa made her way down to the beach, picking over rocks that formed a stony staircase. The beach was small, a white strip that grew larger with the caress of the leaving tide. Above, the waxing moon hung like a twin, pulling the sea below it. Its light fell on the water in rippling crescents, painting the sea in silver, like a sky of dripping jewels.

To one side of the beach, a waterfall fell, soaking the rocks below in moon-drenched ribbons. Sysa stood for a moment, enjoying both the silence and the noise. She listened for the things that could not be heard without paying attention. She heard the song of selkies and mermaids singing softly in the gaps between the waves.

At last, she kindled a small fire on the beach, flicking her hand across air to lift stones from the shingled surface. The stones hung suspended in front of her before falling into a perfect circle that lit with flame in response to the rubbing of her palms. Magic came easily to her now, after many hours of practice with her father back in Fyrish. Emotions were more of a problem, she reflected, staring into the crackling embers. She pushed the thought away, busying herself with magicking blankets; a makeshift home to last them for the night.

When it was done, she paced the sand, feeling suddenly restless. The waves rasped in tongues beside her, sounding more and more like a goading chant. Why was Lavellan taking so long? She felt strangely adrift here on the beach without him. No, she was annoyed, she thought, annoyed that he had taken off like that, thinking himself able to command her. She strode off up the beach and across the dark land he'd disappeared to. She would set things straight, make sure he knew he didn't tell her what to do.

When she saw him in the distance, she thought at first that he was wounded. He was crouched over in the darkness, Sirius curved in like an echo at his side. As Sysa moved closer, she saw that they were looking at something on the ground, something Lavellan was murmuring to, his voice hushed and reverential. She peered over, registering with surprise that the object of his attention was a dying deer, obviously felled by either his wolf companion or himself.

Lavellan seemed unaware of her arrival, so she stepped

closer, shielding herself behind a clump of grasses. She watched silently as he comforted the animal, one of his large palms placed at its blood-stained throat. He was whispering small words of gratitude, his head bowed in respect and penance. When he saw that the animal was dead, he stood up, lifting it gently over his shoulders, the creature's blood dripping down his back and into the earth beneath them.

Sysa's anger dripped away too, transforming into something else as the deer's blood seeded in the ground.

She sprang out of the grassy clump, hoping to make her way back to the beach via a roundabout route while Lavellan was slowed down with the creature. As she launched, her foot caught in a twist of heathers, sending her flying a few steps and pitching up on the ground at Lavellan's feet.

'*So clumsy,*' she spoke to the ground in a sharp whisper, thinking of her graceless attempts at the things which came so naturally to other fae folk. She coughed, rising to her knees on the damp earth and brushing at pieces of grass which had attached themselves to the fabric of her cloak.

'Sysa?' Lavellan's voice drifted down from above like the watery ribbons of the waterfall. 'What are you doing here? I thought you were staying on the beach to set up camp?' He stuck a hand out, still managing to hold the deer with perfect poise. Sysa ignored the proffered hand and stood up, tossing her head in the way she had sometimes seen Elva do. Lavellan fixed her with a frank stare, his eyebrows lifted. 'How long have you been here?'

'Long enough,' she said, and marched off down towards the beach.

Once there, they busied themselves with preparing their meal, avoiding the incident on the headland in the same way they were avoiding each other on the sand they were now pacing. Sysa had taken her shoes off and was enjoying the feel of the cold against her toes, the way it silted through her feet and up towards her knees. Now and again, she glanced at Lavellan, who was ensuring Sirius had enough to eat before he cooked their portions. Sirius tore away at his huge share of the meat, obviously ravenous. Sysa supposed it could be some time before they ate again. When she caught Lavellan's eye, he turned away, looking at something out beyond the waves.

They ate quietly, picking at pieces of meat browned on the makeshift woody spit across the campfire. Sysa's face felt warm, flushed by heat and the crackle of the flames. When she looked over at Lavellan, his normally cold appearance seemed softened, more rounded. As he stretched out with one elbow against the sand, the light of the fire fell in golden streaks across his features and tiny orange flames danced in the blue mirrors of his eyes.

'So, where do you think Three-Wings is?' Sysa said eventually, peering over the piece of meat she held between her fingers.

'Oh, he won't have gone far,' Lavellan replied, leaning his head back and throwing a tiny stick into the fire. At the mention of the raven, Sirius popped up from his rest, nosing the air in deep sniffs before plopping back onto the sand, dejected.

'There, there,' Lavellan said, pushing out his bottom lip and running a hand across the wolf's coat. 'He won't be long, boy. Very close, those two. Wolves and ravens, *mmm?*' Lavellan gave Sysa a knowing look, his voice landing in its familiar mocking register.

He's an actor, pure and simple. Sysa remembered her father's words about Lavellan at her first ceilidh back in Fyrish. *So used to being someone else he has no idea who he even is.*

'Three-Wings will be out looking for the keeper,' Lavellan continued, seemingly oblivious to Sysa's wonderings on which version of him she was conversing with. 'He'll come back to us when he's found her. In the meantime, we should really get some rest.' Lavellan lay back, signalling the end of the exchange.

'Wait.' The word lurched out before Sysa had a chance to consider what would follow. All of a sudden, she wanted to know everything about this young man, where he had come from, what he had been before Rogart had taken him as a child. She had spent so long pushing him out of her thoughts, relegating him to some distant, imagined place where she would one day exact revenge on him. Now she saw that her thoughts had built a wall, a wall that was crumbling brick by brick around her ears. 'What was that, back there on the hill with the deer? You talking to it like that?' Sysa said, trying to distil the hugeness of her thoughts into a single question. All at once, it seemed essential that he rationalised his behaviour, point out the mistake in her perception. She wanted him to lead her back to the truth, which was that he was the monster she'd expected him to be.

'Can I not show compassion? Must I be so endlessly Unseelie? Is evil all you see in me?' Lavellan spoke to the stars, his face lifted skywards.

A sense of unease churned inside Sysa's belly. Lavellan was speaking to her, but it felt like his words were meant for someone different, someone out beyond the far reaches of the sky.

'It's just… you never seem like that. You never seem to care about anyone but yourself. It didn't seem like… you.' Sysa felt off balance, caught out by Lavellan's words, and the ragged, hoarse voice he was using. It had to be a trick, all part of his play-acting.

Across the fire, Lavellan turned his head to face her. He looked strangely vulnerable through flames that licked peaked orange knives across his skin. He laughed, a bitter kind of laugh that reached out over the fire and stung her. 'It didn't seem like me…' Lavellan echoed back at her, his words tailing off as he placed a finger to his chin.

'Stop! Stop it. Going back to – all that.' Sysa sat up straight, making a circling motion in the air with her fingers. The conversation was going all wrong. She was ruining everything – and he was ruining it too. She wanted to find out who he was, *what* he was, she needed to know everything about him. And here they were, arguing again. Yet, across the fire, she felt like she had seen him – really *seen* him – for the first time since they'd met.

'All what?' Lavellan finally addressed her, his eyes narrowed as he lifted himself up from the sand in a heartbeat. 'All this?' He gestured to the area around his chest, sweeping his arm up and down in front of his body. 'You mean exactly what I am? Everything you hate, everything your old pals here hate, everything the whole world hates!' He spun around, lifting his head to the sky, half-crazed in the darkness. 'This is what I am. All of me.' He stopped to face her, his eyes burning in the space between them. He lowered his head, then looked up, his expression filled with unspoken challenge in the night.

'It can't be! You can't do the things you do, and then

behave the way you did back there, and expect people to understand you.' Sysa felt an uncomfortable sensation begin to spread inside her stomach. She couldn't accept this, couldn't accept *him*, if he was really that monster he reported himself to be. As they stared at each other across the firelight, Sysa saw the slackening in his features, the drop of his shoulders, the pleading look that lay behind the challenge. He wanted her to accept him as he was, and she couldn't.

She stood up and turned away, arms crossed over her chest as if they could stop the spread of what was growing inside her, like a stain across fabric. She paced the sand, wanting to get as far away from him as she could. 'Why can't you just…?' She rubbed at the space between her eyes, not sure what she was even asking.

'Be perfect? Be Seelie? Be more like you?' From somewhere behind her, Lavellan's voice gathered like the waves that were reaching to the shore with moonlit hands.

'Yes!' Sysa fumed, feeling her hands close into fists. 'You could change, if you really wanted to.'

There was a long pause before Lavellan spoke again. She heard him sigh, not his usual kind of sigh, but one that sounded like he was readjusting something in his mind.

'It's not as simple as that,' he finally said, as Sysa turned round to face him, realising her cheeks were wet. She scrubbed at them with the heels of her palms, rubbing away her frustration.

What was left was a strange sort of sadness, like someone had taken a jug of something from inside her and poured it on the sand.

'All right, you win. Be *you*. See if I care,' Sysa muttered, knowing that she cared a lot more than she was willing to admit right now. How had this happened? How could she have let herself fall under whatever ridiculous spell Lavellan was weaving in her head? 'And by the way, I'm not perfect,' she said, determined to remind him how little he knew about her.

When he answered, it was in a voice she didn't recognise, one that would later make her wonder if she had imagined it.

'You are to me.'

He shook his head and turned away, returning to his place by the fire where Sirius awaited him. He dropped to the sand, covering himself in his blanket.

Sysa was left standing, blinking disbelief into the night.

CHAPTER EIGHT

By the time Sysa awoke, Lavellan had left her.

She knew this before she rolled over on her side, before she saw the empty nest of his blanket, before she realised Sirius was gone too, his absence signalled by an indent in the sand. She knew Lavellan was gone because she felt it in her bones, inside her chest, and in every part of her that had woken. The sense of absence seeped out of her like a song, the kind the selkies sang when one of their kin was lost. And yet her song made no sound that she could decipher. It just drifted off like a cloud or a snowflake, and was swallowed without question into the frigid morning air.

They hadn't spoken after Lavellan's admission – was that what it was? – in the dark last night. Instead, Sysa had stumbled under the veil of her blanket, hoping its warmth might somehow distort his shocking words. She went over and over them in her head – four words, ten letters, all familiar to her, yet now as unknown as an ancient language. She rearranged them in her head, turned them this way and that, but could find in them no other meaning. *You are to me*. Perfect.

Perfect. Like that word *before*, it seemed to belong to another universe, part of the darkness into which it had been born.

As she'd thought all of this, she had listened to Lavellan's breathing until it had fallen away into something soft, like the sound of the waves that arrived and retreated on the shoreline. She had thought of Brodie, in pangs of hurt and longing that seemed to tear away at the membranes of her soul. Being away from him was unbearable, like stepping out of herself and watching the world from somewhere distant. Yet she also felt something new and intangible inside her. Something that could pull that other self back to her.

Something that had always been there without her even knowing what it was.

She rolled over onto her back, pulling the blanket from her face and then draped a hand, like a shield to it all, over her forehead. Above, gulls cried out in the sunrise, reminding anyone who listened that they owned the morning sky. Sysa stood up, shrugging off the blanket and making the few steps towards the water. She pulled off her cloak and her garments, slipping into the silky wetness with a brief exclamation. The sudden cold surged up her body, dispersing her thoughts into the air as she waded further in. As she dipped her shoulders under the water, the cold momentarily took hold, wrapping itself around her chest with an icy fist of sensation. She looked over at the ragged coastline, the Coast of Widows that Grey had told her about when she was young. She shivered, thinking of the fishermen who had lost their lives around these waters, swept away by the meeting of the North Sea, the Atlantic and the Pentland Firth in this watery cauldron. Around her, gentle waves licked at her body like an enchantment, and the rising sun lit streaks of gold across the sea's surface in a path.

As she stood there in the water, Sysa's senses sharpened, brought back to life by the cold and the new morning. Suddenly everything became clearer, like the top of a bottle had been screwed on tight inside her mind. The sharp air honed and renewed her, until she could see every insect in the sky, every ridge of the cliff's striated surface in the distance. She smelled salt, mixed with the fresh, damp tang of sea air. Overhead, she heard the flap of a wing, followed by a distant sort of settling noise somewhere on the rocks. On the shore, Three-Wings had alighted, offering her the expectant gleam of a black eye as he swivelled his head towards her. Sysa sighed, padding her feet up and down before beginning her way back to the beach. She pushed through the blue water, the waves falling away like an icy, silken gown dropping slowly down past her waist, her thighs, her ankles. When she reached the beach, she became strangely aware of her own nakedness, and cast a glance at the raven, who turned his head away, as if he had felt her vulnerability too. Sysa remembered what Lavellan had said about his companion – his sky seer – and felt a prickle of heat make its way along her spine as she reached for her cloak and garments, quickly covering herself. She wondered what sort of messages Three-Wings was in the habit of conveying to his master.

Pulling her gown and cloak over still-damp skin, she made her way towards the rocks, where she stood, arms folded, and fastened the raven with her own expectant stare.

'So, where is he?' she said after a pause, in which it had become clear that she and the bird had no established mode of communication. In response, the raven tilted his head out towards the sea, where the coast rounded towards the very edge of Dunnet Head. Sysa followed the line of his beak, which pointed like a hooked arrow towards either the sea, or the cliffs that rounded away from it. Finally, she exhaled loudly, frustrated.

'So, he's in the sea? Or on the cliffs somewhere?'

The raven stared back at her, apparently also aware that their conversation had reached an impasse.

Sysa shook her head, and made to turn away, noticing as she did that the raven had raised his stacked wing in her direction. She stopped, surveying the appendage, which stuck out like rough branches on a black, unusually feathered tree. The bird appeared to be offering the wings to her in invitation, so she stepped forward, reaching her fingers out to touch them.

My own sky seer. Lavellan's words rang like a bell inside her head as she made contact with the stiff black mass of feathers. In the next beat, her vision flooded with a flash, as if she was tunnelling through glass and hurtling into blue as something smashed behind her eyes.

She saw the sea, rushing up towards her as she flew over it, the water so close that she felt its salty spray against her jawline. She – or at least the Sysa inside this vision – was careering towards the cliff edge, which loomed above her like a sandstone mountain, bearing down on the sea like a threatening, waiting wall. Sysa flinched, finding that just as she was about to crash into it, she stopped, hovering above the rolling water. She understood that for now, she was both the raven and herself, although she seemed to exist in neither form. Her physical self was standing on the beach, holding the raven's wings, while another Sysa

82

floated above the Coast of Widows. With the clarity she had forged in the cold water, she understood she was seeing through the eyes of the raven.

And with the eyes of the raven, she saw something more beautiful than she had ever known.

Ahead of her, wading out of the water, was Lavellan, leaving the sea just as Sysa had done herself a few moments previously. He was approaching a scrap of sand, where rocks coiled upwards towards the mouth of a golden, glittered cave. Sysa wasn't looking at the cave, though, she was watching the flecks of gold and silver that fell from Lavellan's body like salty stars as they met with sea spray. She was watching the long lines of his limbs and his torso, which were covered in iridescent blue and green patches, like the colours of the sea and sky had been tattooed across his skin. As he left the water, the colours paled, each one receding like the inward bloom of an ink stain. They were absorbed into his flesh, while on the outside, the stars fell away, belonging only to the sea.

Sysa swallowed, thinking back to the only shape-shifting form she had previously seen Lavellan in – the shrew-like character that had attacked Grey at the river all those years ago. He had been abhorrent to her then, yet the Lavellan ahead of her could not have been more beautiful if he tried. His snow-white hair clung to his head in a slick curve, ending at the nape of his neck and sending final shards of starlight down his spine and into the bed of the shoreline. Sysa felt herself flush as he stood, uncovered, on the shingle. Whether her cheeks burned pink above the sea, or back on the beach with Three-Wings, she couldn't tell.

There was a flash, and a series of pictures rushed

towards Sysa's racing eyeballs. She saw a butterfly, a blue one, like the winged creature that had crossed her palm in Fyrish when she had said goodbye to Grey. She saw Lavellan, clothed and transformed to the familiar Lavellan she knew, entering the cave and being swallowed by the shimmering darkness. And then the flash of a female, a wisp of grey hair that fell across a shoulder, a pair of green eyes that shone like sea-jewels.

And then the vision broke, like shattering glass across the screen of her closed eyes.

Sysa opened her eyes, then blinked, trying to reset her senses. The raven was still staring at her, his black eyes bright with their usual polished gleam. She looked down at her hand, drawing her fingertips away from the dark clump of Three-Wing's feathers.

'I saw him,' she said unnecessarily to the raven, who cocked his head at her. 'So, what do I do now?' Sysa looked out to the horizon for an answer that might be forthcoming from the sky.

She turned her thoughts over in her mind, like the white edges of the waves that rolled and curled towards the shoreline. At least she knew where Lavellan was now, although in itself that didn't help her very much. Lavellan's appraisal of her back in Fyrish had been right – she was no mermaid. She was unused to crossing bodies of water unassisted, and the only access to the scrap of beach she had seen him on appeared to be by sea. For the second time since arriving back in Caithness, Sysa wished Modan and his kelpie friends were with her.

But, for now, it was just her and Three-Wings. She turned back to him, the tilt of the raven's head seeming to convey a new affinity forged by the revelations they had shared. Grey had told her about seers, how touching a part of their body could give non-seers access to their visions, so long as that access was invited. In the same way, Sysa knew, Arno had once offered childhood images of her to Elise. She wasn't sure why the raven had chosen to help her now, but she was grateful for the sense of intimacy that suddenly appeared to exist between them.

As if thinking the same thing, the raven swivelled his beak towards the pocket of Sysa's cloak, his dark eyes fixed on the velvet pouch. Sysa put her hand inside the pocket and felt the starlights, a smile of realisation spreading across her features.

Lavellan had been right – she was no mermaid. But she was fae, and magic lived inside her bones.

*

Sysa pulled the line of starlights out of her cloak, pooling them on the palm of her hand, where they sat waiting in sparkling anticipation. She looked out over the sea, tracing a pathway to the cave inside her mind. If Lavellan wouldn't come to her, she would go to him, she thought, with a sense of satisfaction. Not having to ask for his help, even when he wasn't around to notice the absence of her plea, felt good to her. She threw the starlights into the air, calling out to them as they rose skywards.

'A star horse.'

She held her arm up, painting the image of a sea stallion with her outstretched hand.

In response, the stars began to curve and bend, twisting

themselves this way and that like a starry mirror to her fingers. They sparkled and shone, forming themselves into the curve of a belly, a muscled shoulder, a hoof, a chest, a mane. The creature slowly came to life, a steed born of magic and the starry peaks of Steel Castle. Complete, it hung in the sky for a moment, as if showing off its silver-backed beauty to the world.

Sysa watched, pausing only long enough to glance back at the raven. Three-Wings dipped his beak, which she took to be a sign that he was quietly impressed. In the instant her head was turned, there was a loud cracking noise, and the sense of something large pressing down on the air around them.

When Sysa turned back, the horse had grown a pair of starry wings, which it was holding out from its body in demonstration. Sysa nodded, signalling her approval.

'Welcome, Star-Steed.'

With a flick of its mane, the starry mount floated down, its glittering hooves meeting gently with the sand.

Sysa stepped towards the horse, reaching her arm out in cautious enquiry. In response, the horse dipped its head downwards, sending a flurry of stardust floating from its mane. Sysa touched the sweeping mass, feeling a crackling sensation that was not dissimilar to the fizz of her powers when they emanated from her fingertips. This was nothing like taming Modan, she thought briefly, remembering the kelpie's struggle as she'd constrained him with a bridle forged from these same stars. No, this horse was born willing, born of the obedient starlights that now lived constantly around her. And now, her magic had extended to shape-shifting them into this living constellation of stars and light. Sysa thought of her father then, how proud he would have been to see her powers enlarge, and she felt a dull ache grow inside her stomach.

In the next breath, she thought of the mermaid, lying prostrate back in the Castle of Thunder. Would Bruan really be proud, she wondered, or ashamed of what his daughter had become?

With a sweep of her leg, Sysa climbed atop the star-steed, Three-Wings watching patiently behind them. As she settled herself on the creature, tiny stars fell away, floating in the air like grains of sand. The horse rose up to its full height, wings beating softly in the sunrise as it announced itself to the morning. Above them seabirds hovered, calling out curiously, momentarily confused by the melting of morning and the starry world of night.

'To the cave. To Lavellan,' Sysa finally said, dipping her head to the horse's ear and rubbing at its neck, which shone like a glittering, twinkling rainbow. She turned and inclined her head at the raven.

'You're coming?'

Three-Wings rustled his wings, signalling his intention to lead them to the cave.

In the next beat, he lifted himself off the rocks and soared overhead, his large wings black against the morning. Sysa couldn't help thinking that Three-Wings wanted to put his dark beauty on display in response to her mount's impressive presence. She stifled a smile, realising that the raven and Lavellan were more alike than she had thought.

'Very well, then, let's go,' she said, as Three-Wings made a series of loops and turns in the air above them. Sysa rolled her eyes, pressing her thighs against the star-steed's sides in instruction, at which the raven stilled, stretching his beak out like an arrow pointed above the beach. Star-Steed lifted onto his back legs and then thumped back to the sand, his mouth open in silent declaration. As Sysa clung to his silver mane, he rose up, his wings beating once as his hooves skimmed the surface of the waves and pounded above them. Sea spray and sparkle mingled against Sysa's cheeks, and her hair flew back like a dark ribbon in the wind.

Soon, they were flying low over the sea, the star-steed's hooves thrumming just above the surface. Sysa angled herself forward on his back, holding onto the horse's drenched mane as the wind whipped up small starry planets in the air. Ahead, Three-Wings was leading the way, curving around the cliff in a flash of wings and feathers. Behind them, a chorus of gulls followed, curious to discover the reason for their procession across the firth.

As they rounded the cliff, a colony of seals on a rocky outcrop peered from moist black eyes and whiskered faces. Sysa lifted her arm in greeting, as unperturbed, the seals plopped gently into the sea. Further out among the waves, a pod of dolphins cut through the water, leaping out now and then in grey arches. It was as if all the creatures of sea and sky had come to witness them. As the sea rolled below Star-Steed's hooves, Sysa gulped down air, wondering when she had ever felt more alive than this.

Finally, they were heading towards the cliff, the same cliff Sysa had seen in her vision. Blinking, she lifted her face to where the huge mountain of sandstone loomed above her head. People called Caithness flat, but she wondered if that particular observation was another matter of perspective. The hulking cliff stared back like some sort of rising guard in response to her examination. Against its endless battle with winds and tide, Sysa felt small and insignificant. She dipped her head, pushing against gusts that protested against her face.

Forcing through the wind behind Three-Wings, Star-Steed found his way to the patch of sand that stretched protectively towards the cave mouth. As they drew up, Sysa dismounted, noticing that Three-Wings had alighted onto another rocky perch. Sysa rubbed at the horse's side, murmuring words of thanks as sparkles flew from her hand like dust motes.

'Wait here,' she said, twisting away from the star-steed. As she turned, she saw Lavellan standing against the rounded lip of the cave, his arms folded across his chest as if he had been waiting there for quite some time. He tilted his face towards her, one eyebrow arced slightly upwards in a manner that suggested he was impressed with her. Sysa turned towards the starry horse, realising Lavellan had been watching their parade across the sea.

'I see you have a new friend.' Lavellan tipped his head in the direction of the horse and stepped towards her.

It felt as if the movement had sent a wall of air ramming against her chest, and Sysa's words escaped in a tangled, high-pitched blurt.

'Oh, the horse... that's Star-Steed... my starlights...' Sysa waved her hand around in explanation.

You are to me. Perfect. Their conversation from the previous evening swam around her mind, like a cloud interrupting her normal verbal poise.

Lavellan nodded and dropped his eyes to the sand before looking up at her.

'I was coming back for you. I wasn't going to leave you.'

'Oh?' Sysa heard that strangled voice again, and realised it was her own. All the assurance of her passage across the water seemed to have slipped away in the course of Lavellan's few steps across the beach.

'After last night...' Lavellan raked a hand through his slick hair, looking uncharacteristically nervous. 'After last night, I needed some time to think,' he murmured, looking around vaguely. Sysa noticed he was having trouble meeting her eye, and realised she had the upper hand.

'So, you left me?' she said, regaining her composure.

'No. I couldn't sleep, so I decided to see if I could find the keeper myself,' he said, tossing a glance over his shoulder. 'I planned to come back for you before you woke up this morning. But I see that you've been managing fine by yourself, as usual.' Lavellan jerked his chin towards Star-Steed, who was snuffling starry motes along the sand.

'Well, how did I know you were planning to come back for me? Did you just expect me to sit and wait, twiddling my thumbs until you graced me with your presence?' Sysa folded her arms across her chest, easing back into their combative mode of conversation. Somewhere in her mind, she knew that this was all a distraction, a way of avoiding discussion of what Lavellan had said last night.

'No, that would have been dreadfully silly, to think that you might have waited for me, or trusted me. I can see that now.' Lavellan looked out to sea and made a defiant sort of sniffing noise. 'Anyway, what does it matter now? You're here, and all is well again.' He flung his arms up in the air, twisting himself around in his familiar grandiose way.

Sysa sighed loudly. 'Where's Sirius?' Until now, she had

all but forgotten about Lavellan's wolf-friend. She looked around the beach for any sign of him, but all she saw was the star-horse, and Three-Wings, who had been observing their conversation from his rock.

'He's not here,' Lavellan said, looking around the nearby coastline. 'Probably off hunting somewhere.' He flicked his head upwards, indicating the huge expanse of Dunnet Head. 'Don't worry about him – he'll find his own way here. I don't feel the need to keep tabs on him.'

'I didn't say I was worried,' Sysa said, realising with an odd feeling that she had actually felt a pang of concern over the wolf's well-being.

'No, you didn't.' Lavellan was looking at her from under raised eyebrows, a quiver of a smile tugging at the corners of his mouth.

'You said you couldn't sleep last night,' Sysa said, hoping to turn the conversation back onto Lavellan, although she wasn't sure that could be any less awkward than him highlighting her transparency. 'I thought perhaps we should talk about that. About that thing you said. About me.' She offered him a searching look, but he cast his eyes away.

'I don't think this is quite the time to discuss that, actually,' he said, talking to the sand, as if there was something of great interest around the area of his foot, which he was using to nudge a piece of seaweed.

'Why not?' Sysa said, looking around the empty beach, and the waves that were lapping the shore like kisses. 'It's not as if there's anything else going on, is it?'

Lavellan carried on poking the seaweed with his toe.

Sysa sighed, feeling impatient, and opened her mouth

to speak – perhaps she could ask about what she had seen in her vision. She felt a prickle of something uncomfortable run up and down her spine as she thought of him, covered in blue and green and looking so strangely beautiful as he'd left the water—

'That's not quite true,' Lavellan said, interrupting her thoughts as he finally lifted his head in exactly the same moment that another question was about to leave her mouth. 'There is something going on. Or rather someone. I found her,' Lavellan said, as Sysa stood with her lips still slightly parted.

'She's here?' Sysa whipped her head around, expecting the mysterious woman to materialise somewhere on the beach.

'She's in the cave.' Lavellan turned around very slowly and looked at the cave mouth, which gaped open in glistening invitation.

'Well, let's go and speak to her then,' Sysa said, marching towards the opening.

As she made to pass Lavellan, he caught her gently by the arm.

Sysa looked down at his hand, his long fingers curling over her cloak, encircling the folds of velvet. There was something protective in the gesture, something that made Sysa feel very strange, and safe.

She looked up at him, her eyes a still, green question.

'There's something you need to know,' Lavellan said, darting another glance towards the cave.

As he did, a woman emerged, a woman who seemed to Sysa both known and unfamiliar. She stood at the cave mouth, her silver hair falling like ribbons that pleated in around her waist. A green dress fanned out at her feet and wrists, skimming her skin in silky caresses. Around her whole body, a faint glow traced her outline like a small echo of the sun.

Sysa narrowed her eyes – the woman was fae, of that she was certain. There was something else about her, too, something Sysa recognised in the natural grace the woman emanated as she stood there by the cave. She wasn't young, but she was beautiful, with high cheekbones and the suggestion of long, toned limbs under her silken garment. Her green eyes shone like emeralds. It felt to Sysa that they could see through and beyond her, their vision reaching to an entirely different place.

When the woman finally moved towards them, Sysa felt herself move too, racing across the sand as if pulled by some sudden magnet. She felt Lavellan move too, keeping pace behind her as Three-Wings and Star-Steed watched from the far side of the beach.

As the space between them closed, the woman held out her hands, her fingertips outstretched, her expression one of joy, sadness, welcoming, apology.

In that instant, Sysa knew where she had seen the woman's face before. It was a reflection of her father's. She grasped both of the woman's hands, squeezing them like she never wanted to let go.

As she looked into the woman's eyes, she understood most of what Lavellan was about to say before he said it. She didn't turn to him as he stopped on the sand beside them, but remained fixed on the woman, a meeting of green eyes across clasped hands.

'This is Brigid, the Keeper of The Northern Gate,' said

Lavellan, his voice sounding distant as Sysa felt the sweep of air that accompanied his gesture between them. 'And, your grandmother.'

But Sysa didn't need him to tell her that. She closed the space between herself and Brigid, both of them accepting the damp tears of reunion that mingled on their cheeks.

CHAPTER NINE

By now, Sysa thought to herself in the cave a few minutes later, she was getting used to surprises.

She sat down next to Brigid on a shelf of rock that protruded from the cave wall, their hands clasped in the space between them. After embracing on the sand for several long moments, it seemed that neither of them had wanted to let the other go. Brigid had finally pulled back, cupping Sysa's face in her hands and drinking her in, before nodding and saying, 'Yes, I see him in you.'

'My father?' Sysa had asked, watching Brigid's eyes cloud to another shade of green in a flicker of memory.

'Him too. But I was actually thinking of Grey,' she'd said, stroking Sysa's face with a feather-light touch that ran the length of her still-damp cheek.

Sysa had nodded too, with a sense of simple understanding. She had asked Grey to help her and, as always, he had found a way to come back into her life. She might never truly have her grandfather again, but she had *this*, this connection with Brigid, the only other person who had probably really known him. As soon as that thought came to her, her brow wrinkled with a thousand different questions.

Brigid had seen it all, and had pulled Sysa's hand closer.

'Come,' she'd whispered, gesturing towards the cave mouth. 'I'll explain everything.'

And now here they were, inside the cave, with Lavellan hovering awkwardly beside a nearby shadowed arch. 'Perhaps I should go, leave you both to it,' he offered finally, when it looked like Brigid was about to begin her story.

'Sysa, do you want your friend to leave us?' Brigid swivelled towards Sysa, one eyebrow lifted in a kindly curve.

Sysa opened her mouth to protest Brigid's assessment of *friend*, but something in the older woman's expression stopped her. Brigid was right – despite everything, Lavellan was no longer Sysa's enemy. Then again, she wasn't quite sure *what* he was, or how much she could trust him with whatever information her grandmother was about to divulge. As these thoughts arrived, Sysa thought back to the way Lavellan had introduced Brigid on the beach and she sighed, realising he already knew more about the background to this situation than she did. She cast a look at the rocky arch where Lavellan awaited her answer, small drops of moisture falling like tears in rhythmic drips around him.

Eventually, Sysa let out a long breath and turned back to Brigid.

'He can stay.'

Sysa sensed a sort of lifting coming from Lavellan's direction, as if a small light was blooming somewhere in the cave.

'Very well.' Brigid nodded and pursed her lips together in what looked like approval.

'I'm a seer, Sysa. I think you know about seers, don't

you?' Brigid lifted her chin in the direction of the raven, who was still perched somewhere on the rocks outside.

'I do,' Sysa said, glancing towards an unseen Three-Wings before turning back to Brigid. She realised that her grandmother had probably been watching her for some time and felt a burst of tenderness rise up inside her chest.

'I always had the sight, even as a young girl,' Brigid said, her green eyes misting over. 'And then I fell in love with, and married, your grandfather.' Brigid squeezed Sysa's hand in remembrance. Sysa felt tears pricking against her eyes then, as she thought of Grey, and the way his own eyes had misted over when he told her stories about people falling in love. Grey had loved once too, and Sysa was so glad of it. She squeezed Brigid's hand back, curling her fingers tight, a seal of that love held close between their palms. 'But it was when I had your father that the strength of the sight really grew in me,' Brigid said, her eyes now clouded over with sadness. 'Childbirth strengthened me, made my visions more powerful. That power came with a price, though – I saw something that would change our lives for good.'

'Go on,' Sysa said, feeling a spark of the child inside her, the one who had prompted and prodded Grey's stories, the child she'd believed was lost to her.

Brigid's gaze drifted to the drops of water that were falling to the rock and pooling on the surface in puddles.

'That was when I saw the Young Trinity,' she continued, squeezing Sysa's hand again. 'And that was when I knew I had to leave, to come here and protect the Steel family and the fae lands.' Brigid gestured around the cave as if it had transformed into some sort of rocky fortress.

Sysa squeezed her eyes shut, conjuring a memory.

'Wait. I know about the Young Trinity. Wasn't that some old prophecy Rogart believed in, about the three who would one day be all-powerful?'

'Indeed it was,' Brigid said, casting a strange look across the cave.

Sysa was thinking about the story Krystan had once told her; how Rogart had believed the Trinity had been Luna, Krystan and Lavellan until his convictions on their power had proved unfounded. Krystan was now happily installed on Selkie Island with Frode, and Luna... well, Sysa didn't want to think about that right now. As for Lavellan, he was still listening to Brigid's story with an anxious-looking expression; hardly the demeanour, Sysa thought, of the all-powerful. She reminded herself she would need to resume her enquiries about the shape-shifting form she had seen him in in her vision before meeting Brigid had scattered her questions to the wind.

Sysa swivelled back towards Brigid, forming another question that for the moment, at least, seemed far more pressing.

'But what on earth did the Young Trinity have to do with us?'

Brigid rubbed the back of Sysa's hand, letting out a long breath that mirrored the soft passage of her fingers. When she spoke, her voice was slow and steady, her words entering the cave in wheels and falling gently to the rocks.

'As soon as I had your father, I received a vision, one that told me my son would sire a child of the Young Trinity,' she said, her eyes again veiled with the mist of recollection. 'That child would be you, Sysa, and right then Grey and I knew your life would always be hunted. Hunted by those who sought to claim you, to bring together the Trinity for themselves. Grey and I needed to scatter – to protect the parts of Fyrish and Never Night through which these hunters would seek to penetrate our family. I knew that if the vision of the Trinity had been offered to me, it would also have been shown to others – those whose intentions would be to one day gather the children of the Trinity and use you as a force for their own ends. And so, I came here, leaving Grey alone to raise our son, a son who would never know me.' Brigid paused, the smooth timbre of her voice cracking on the last few syllables. 'Love almost always requires sacrifice,' she said, offering Sysa a placating smile and waving away her expression of regret.

'But, why here?' Sysa asked, gesturing around the cave, the thought of Brigid's departure fleetingly dulling the revelations about her own part in the Trinity.

'This is the gate to the north, Sysa, where, as you know, fae folk abound, moving between Never Night, Fyrish, and the other fae lands. It was up to me to guard the Northern Gate against those who could find a way in through the thin spaces that exist between worlds here.' Brigid looked out of the cave with a faraway expression as waves rolled towards the shore and curled like ominous tongues against the sand.

'And did they come? These others?' Sysa looked out at the beach, half-expecting an advancing army to emerge from the foaming water.

'A few tried.' Brigid shrugged their attempts away as inconsequential. 'But never the one I expected.' The old woman pressed her lips together, casting a strange look at Lavellan, who just lifted his eyebrows in response.

'And you've lived here... all this time?' Sysa asked, glancing between the pair and trying to form a question that wouldn't quite emerge from her.

'You mean, how have I stayed alive so long?' Brigid smiled, her lips curved in an understanding line.

Sysa nodded. Fae folk could not normally survive in the human world for long – even Grey, whose powers had been exceptional, had waned against the advance of mortal time when Sysa had returned to Fyrish. How had Brigid survived here all these years, with only this cave to shelter her from the sea? All this isolation – all those years of separation for Grey and Brigid. At its core, Sysa knew this was all because of her. And now she was here, about to ask for help for another problem she had caused.

Sysa's chest felt weighed down, as if something was pressing against it. If she was so powerful, why couldn't she just wave this all away?

Across the gap, Brigid studied Sysa's face intently. She patted Sysa's hand, and when she spoke, her answering voice was as gentle as a song.

'I've survived here so long because my powers were greater than Grey's,' she said, without any trace of self-importance. 'The women of fae almost always outstretch the males, and so it made sense for me to come here, knowing how long it would be before our own son sired a child. Your grandfather stayed in Fyrish, raised Bruan—' Brigid stumbled momentarily over her son's name— 'and I remained here... for protection. It was imperative that our only child was guarded, knowing the future he was bound to. And, of course, like all parents, we lived only to keep him safe, no matter the reason. We loved him.'

Sysa remembered her father's words when she had once asked about his mother: *I don't remember her.* And then the words Brigid had just spoken: *love requires sacrifice.*

She looked out to the waves beyond the cave mouth, wondering what her own sacrifice for love might one day be.

'So, you never saw each other? All those years, when you were separated?' Sysa was still thinking of Grey, raising a child alone back in Fyrish and then repeating the whole thing here with her in Caithness.

'Not for many years… in the physical sense, at least.' Brigid smiled again, her eyes moist with remembered love. 'What Grey and I had went beyond that, though Sysa – our nearness was never measured by distance. He was here with me, always.' Brigid looked around the cave as though Grey still existed in every rocky crevice of the walls.

Sysa thought of the cottage then, the slice of Dunnet Head they could see from the track and the way Grey used to look out into the sky as if it held the answer to all his questions.

And, of course, it had, Sysa could see that now. Brigid had been Grey's answer. She had been all of his answers.

Brigid leaned in close to Sysa's face, her body twisting in reassurance. 'Grey was exactly where he wanted to be. First with your father, then with you.'

Brigid wiped at a tear that was tracking its way across Sysa's cheek and then pressed her forehead against her granddaughter's. From somewhere across the cave, Lavellan made small shifting noises in the dark.

Sysa pulled back, swiping at her nose and shaking her head, displacing her emotions into the heavy, cloaked air of the cave mouth. She sat up straight and took a deep breath, gathering herself for whatever Brigid would tell her next. It felt like Brigid's words had pulled her into the warmth of summer, before pushing her into the swirling air of a storm-filled winter. She needed to ask Brigid about the Young Trinity, about the stone, and about helping Luna. But for now, all she could think about was Grey.

'He took me to Dunnet Beach once,' Sysa said, thinking back to her childhood visit with Grey and the memory of listening to watery secrets in seashells.

'Why didn't you come to us then? Why didn't we go to you? We could have been together.' Sysa's voice lifted with a hint of desperation. It seemed so wrong that Grey and Brigid had been so close, and yet so horribly separate.

Brigid smiled, accepting all of Sysa's bundled thoughts.

'I understand why you would ask that, Sysa. But we couldn't risk it. We both knew it would be safer for you if we kept our distance. Being together could have exposed us, left some of our defences open.' Brigid waved her hand around to encompass the sea that lay below the cave. 'And anyway, I found my way to you that day. Who do you think sent the song in the seashell?' Brigid smiled again, a hint of mischief glittering in her eyes, while outside, waves seemed to murmur in collusion.

'And I was never alone here. I had the sea and the sky, the sun and moon, all the creatures who live here. They were my company.' Sysa thought of the procession that had followed her route on Star-Steed and smiled to herself, finding comfort in the thought of Brigid's connection to the earth. But now she knew that Grey had given up his love as well as his life for her, that feeling was quickly followed by a racking sense of responsibility.

'You and Grey were always here with me,' Brigid whispered, tugging at Sysa's hand and pulling it towards her heart-space. 'And, at the end, I took Grey back to me.'

Sysa's eyes flickered up to meet Brigid's.

'You were together... at the end?' Sysa thought of the cottage, how it had been clear that Grey had never returned.

'Yes.' Brigid nodded reassuringly. 'Once I knew you were safely gone, I went to him, at Na Tri Sitheanan, and took him here. We spent his last days here together. Until his spirit lifted up towards the sky, and drifted back to Fyrish, finding a new shape as a unicorn as it made its way across the sea. The shell of him remained here with me, in my arms on the sand out there, until I was finally able to say goodbye to him.'

Brigid looked out at the beach again.

Sysa turned her head, thinking of Grey's body, out amongst the shingle, his spirit seeping out of him like the songs escaping from the shells.

'What did you do with him? With his body, I mean.' Sysa's face flushed at her own question, but she needed to know if Grey's bones lay underneath the beach here.

'I sent him off to sea, to meet the horizon, on a wooden raft lit with a flame like sunrise. He became part of it all.' Brigid inhaled deeply and moved her hand in a circular motion, an arc representing the sun, the moon, the curling finger of a wave.

'So, he's everywhere.' Sysa spoke almost to herself, confirming what she really already knew – that Grey still existed wherever she was, that the world carried him beside her, that he would never really be gone – because she loved and remembered him.

And now she knew Brigid loved him too, and he hadn't been alone, and she felt like the whole world was smiling down on her. She dropped her head and sobbed with the kind of racking gulps she had never let escape before.

Brigid leaned forward, enveloping her with a warmth like the rays of a waiting sun.

★

'Nothing ever really dies. It just becomes part of something else,' Brigid said some time later, breathing her words into the warmth of her embrace with Sysa.

'I know,' Sysa said, pulling away slowly. At the other side of the cave, Lavellan caught her eye, his blue stare dark with shadows. There was something pained in his expression – Sysa wondered if he was thinking about Grey's final moments as the unicorn. More than that, she could hardly believe he'd managed to stay quiet for so long.

'But you have so many other questions for me.' From the corner of her eye, Sysa became aware of Brigid sweeping across the cave as her voice drifted back into focus. Finally, she planted herself in front of them, her back to the rear of the cave, the silky hem of her dress brushing against the slippery green algae on the rocks.

'Yes, I do. I have so many questions for you, Brigid.' Sysa's eyes traced the triangled shape between herself, Lavellan and her grandmother. She didn't know where to start, but she knew she had to ask about the Trinity soon. She shot another glance at Lavellan, who was now standing with one elbow cradled in a palm, his other hand lifted to his chin, as if he were holding his own thoughts up. When he caught Sysa's look, he offered a brief nod of encouragement, so far his only perceptible contribution to the discussion. Sysa exhaled sharply, squeezing her fingers into the space between her eyebrows before waving her hand around.

'So, I'm one of the Trinity, but where are the other two?'

'That I don't know, Sysa, at least not for certain.' Brigid looked at Lavellan warily. 'Visions are abstract, they don't tell us everything. Can you imagine someone looking through a spyglass?' Sysa's head filled with the thought of old explorers, and she nodded in the affirmative. 'Visions are a bit like that. I can see one piece of the thing, but not all of it. My visions didn't tell me about the other members of the Trinity, they only told me about you.'

'I see.' Sysa's thoughts trailed off, wandering back to another time. 'So, what about Rogart? How did he fit into all of this? Did he see a vision of the Trinity like you did?'

'Rogart was no seer, Sysa.' Lavellan's voice crept into the air like a cloud escaping into darkness.

'He's right.' Brigid made a scoffing noise, dismissing Rogart's capabilities. 'Rogart happened, became what he was... because of his jealousy of your father and mother. His powers grew out of darkness, but he never had the sight. He must have pieced things together, things he heard, information that came from those spotters of his.' Brigid looked around the cave, pondering the source of Rogart's intelligence. 'But he was wrong. And Sysa...' Brigid pursed her lips together before speaking again. 'I have to be honest with you... Rogart was only just the start.'

Sysa dropped her head, looking at the dark sand under

her feet, wondering how this situation could get any worse than it was already. After all that had been lost in defeating Rogart, she now had to face the possibility that there might be more to come. All this before she had even asked Brigid about the healing stone and Luna. She felt the spark of a lighting flame within her fingers, but whether she was upset with herself, or someone else, she wasn't sure.

'What I do know, Sysa,' Brigid said, glancing at the hands Sysa was now bunching at her sides, 'is that when you and the other Trinity members come together, your powers will be truly realised. You – what you are right now – you're only a fraction of what you will become. I know too,' Brigid hurried on, as Sysa slowly uncurled her fists, 'that you are at the centre of the Trinity, the one on whom all of it rests. The others will not fulfil their destinies without you, yet you could still be a powerful force without them. Together, though, the three of you could be something very special.'

Sysa thought back to her arrival in Fyrish, when her parents had told her of their belief that the fate of the fae lands rested on her.

'How do you see it all, Brigid?' Sysa asked with a note of hopelessness, thinking of the mermaid. What if she was destined to use these powers for evil, not for good?

'I have a stone,' Brigid answered, fishing in a pocket and drawing out a polished stone with a hole at its centre. She held the stone up in front of her, raising it to eye level, so that only the flash of a green eye was visible through the perfect, open round. 'Remember the spyglass? This is my version of that,' Brigid said, sweeping the stone from side to side in demonstration as she peered through it. 'I was given this stone by my own mother, and I see the visions through it. As I told you, those visions became stronger after I had your father. The stone itself also became stronger. After your father was born, it became a force to heal.'

'A healing stone,' Sysa said, her thoughts converging back towards the matter of Luna.

'The stone is many things, my dear,' Brigid replied, the corners of her mouth curving very slightly upwards. 'But yes, one of its powers is to heal.'

'I need your help with something,' Sysa said, shame lighting its way across her cheeks as she began speaking. She glanced between Lavellan and Brigid, wondering if the two of them had already discussed the mermaid, or if one of Brigid's visions had already explained why they were here.

'We need the stone,' Lavellan's voice cut in when it became clear that Sysa was struggling to get the words out.

'You do?' Brigid swivelled her body towards him, tilting her head in a sharp, enquiring line.

'Sysa hurt someone. The mermaid Luna, back in Fyrish.' Lavellan flapped his hand in the air impatiently. 'We came here for the stone, to take it back to Fyrish. We need it to heal the mermaid.'

As Lavellan spoke, Brigid watched him, her eyebrows lifting towards the sky.

'We need you to help us.' Sysa heard her own words bouncing off the cave walls like an echo, reshaped to something softer. 'I need you to help *me*.' She stared at Brigid, her eyes burning with the same flame that still lit her face.

'I understand,' Brigid said, curling her hand around the stone and nodding.

There was something kind in Brigid's expression,

something that made Sysa want to run to her in gratitude. She had expected her grandmother to recoil on hearing about Luna, but instead the older woman surveyed her with an acceptance of everything she was. It reminded Sysa of Grey, the way he had understood all the different parts of her, and loved her regardless. The colour across her face receded, and she nodded back, lighting up with a different kind of glow.

'Thank you, Brigid.'

From across the cave, Lavellan spoke again, his words tumbling out in a hurried, clumsy question.

'So, you'll give us the stone?'

Brigid cast him a sharp look, her green eyes narrowed. Sysa wondered how much her grandmother knew about Lavellan and the unicorn – and if Brigid did know, why was she tolerating his presence now?

As if in answer to Sysa's thoughts, Brigid's expression cleared, and she replied to Lavellan with the grace Sysa had already come to expect of her.

'It's not quite as simple as that. The stone and I are bound together, our powers entwined as it were,' Brigid said, rolling the stone like a jewel inside her palms. 'Where it goes, I go. And so, of course I will help you. But that means I will have to come with you. Leave this place.' Brigid looked around the cave walls, her eyes misted with the wash of a thousand different memories.

'But won't that mean leaving it… unprotected?' Sysa asked, thinking of the years Brigid had spent here because of her, because of the Trinity. And now here she was, asking her grandmother to give up something else.

'If you need the stone as much as you seem to, that's

a chance we're going to have to take,' Brigid said, stepping towards Sysa and placing a palm against her cheek in reassurance. 'And I see you have someone else you need to get back to.' Brigid tilted her head slightly, as if something else of Sysa's story had seeped through to her, traversing flesh and bone and skin.

Brodie. Sysa felt his name inside her head with an ache, her chest as much a cavity as the cave they stood in. As soon as she felt that longing in her chest, she turned to Lavellan, pulled by a cord that seemed to run between her heart and her head, taking no mind of her free will on its way.

Lavellan stared at her for a long moment, before flicking his eyes away, his expression as full as it was empty.

'Yes, I have Brodie back there – my fiancé. And my family, of course.'

'*Mmm.*' Brigid nodded with a strange sort of understanding. 'Family has a way of sneaking up on you.' She looked around the cave, taking it all in, all the cracks and corners, the creatures who scuttled about in the half-darkness. As Sysa and Lavellan followed her out of the cave mouth, Brigid cast her eyes around the vista, peering up at the gulls who cried out her leaving to the morning, their longing blending with the sad chorus of the sea.

CHAPTER TEN

'Brigid, before we go, there's something you should probably know – about Lavellan,' Sysa said as her grandmother stood on the sand, taking a last look across her earthly homeland. Above the water, patches of cloud hung, while not to be outdone, the sun drifted in and out of vision, sending bright rays towards the sea in a celestial display.

From the corner of her eye, Sysa saw Lavellan walk away, something in his gait suggesting pain, an idea borne out by the way he held his arm just as he had when they arrived on the headland. Sysa felt pain, too, as if she were betraying him. Yet the alternative meant betraying Brigid, and by association Grey, and that notion was impossible to her.

Across the beach, Lavellan was reacquainting himself with Three-Wings and casting admiring looks at Star-Steed, who was still standing snuffling on the sand.

'I know, Sysa. He killed your grandfather,' Brigid finally answered, her eyes still locked on the horizon. 'I know that,' Brigid repeated, turning and taking Sysa's hand in her own. 'It's all right. Grey knew what needed to be done.'

Lavellan's words from the cottage swept back towards Sysa, as if carried on the distant waves Brigid had been staring at. Lavellan had also said that Grey knew what needed to be done, and now Brigid's answer confirmed that. It suddenly felt like something had opened up in Sysa's heart, a place where forgiveness was finally allowed to flourish. All at once she realised how much she had wanted that opening, even when it had felt intolerable to her, and she breathed out a sigh of relief towards the sand.

'But what does that mean? Why would Lavellan have done that? What's going on, Brigid?'

'I think perhaps you should talk to Lavellan about that,' Brigid replied, the wind rippling the silk of her dress across her body. 'In fact, I think you two need to talk about a few things before we go back to Fyrish, don't you?' Brigid said, as strands of silvered hair criss-crossed their way across her cheeks.

'I've tried talking to him, Brigid… it gets me nowhere,' Sysa murmured, her voice coated with frustration.

'Well, something tells me he might be ready to talk to you now,' Brigid said, casting a knowing look across the beach.

'I'm going to say goodbye to my friends here,' Brigid announced, gesturing around the beach and out to sea where the seals stared back in glossy columns. Beyond the waves, the backs of dolphins arced in melody, joining the gulls in an orchestra of farewells. Up on the cliffs, seabirds tumbled from the ledges like falling, feathered stars, keen to join the valediction. Sysa took it all in, understanding Brigid's earlier comment about never being alone here.

'Take as long as you need,' Sysa said, leaving Brigid to her companions.

She turned away, pulling at the hem of her cloak as

the wind whipped up in frenzy around her head. 'The weather's turning,' she said, once she had reached Lavellan, who was sprawled out on a rock, still talking to the raven. It reminded Sysa of the way Brodie spoke to Arno, and she felt a small lifting feeling in her chest.

'Fenja and Menja are grinding hard,' Lavellan said, jerking his head in the direction of the horizon.

Sysa turned, thinking of the stories Grey had told her of two giantesses who ground the salt to feed the ocean. Out there, in the distance, they swirled a magical quern-stone, pushing salt into the water and forcing a tidal whirlpool known as 'the Swelkie' in its wake. It was said that the women could sink ships by grinding more salt, turning whatever emotions they felt to either calm or ignite the mood of the firth around them. Sysa could see the ominous swirl of white-tipped waves in the distance and wondered what had come to anger Fenja and Menja. The wind was rising, too, and Sysa felt tiny grains of sand blast against her face like a thousand flying suns.

'Before we leave, we need to talk – about everything,' Sysa said, turning her attention back to Lavellan, her fingers lifting involuntarily towards him.

'Everything?' Lavellan said, his eyes darting momentarily to her outstretched fingers. Sysa dropped her hand, not sure how to bridge a way across this gap.

'I need to know why you killed Grey. I need to forgive you,' Sysa said, not understanding why this need was so important to her.

'I need you to forgive me too,' Lavellan answered, standing up and rolling the skin between his eyebrows with a finger and a thumb. 'When we were up on that cliff, the day it all happened…' His voice trailed off. 'You know what day it was.'

Sysa nodded, urging him on in the only way possible to her. Her memories had silenced her, as if she had been cut with the same blade that had seared the unicorn that day.

'Your grandfather found a way to tell you things, about Brodie—' the name dripped from Lavellan with unwillingness— 'but he also said things to me too, that you needed Brodie, that you wouldn't be able to do all this without him. Nor he without you. Especially he without you.' Lavellan's head dropped, and he squeezed at his skin again. 'So, he told me I had to do it, to get my blade and kill him, to save Brodie, for you, because he wanted me to.' Lavellan's words rushed out in an uncharacteristic tumble.

'But I needed Grey too! Why would he sacrifice himself for Brodie?' Sysa cried, finding her voice again. The idea of this choice between the two people she loved most was impossible to her. She felt guilty, horrified and angry all at once.

'Why do you think? Why do you think he would do that, Sysa? His whole life was about loving and protecting you!' Lavellan spun round, flinging his frustration to the sky in an angry gesture.

When Sysa spoke again, her voice was quiet.

'And protecting the Trinity. Brodie's one of the three, like me, isn't he?' She dipped her head under Lavellan's, challenging him.

'Yes, he is, Sysa. And that's why Grey asked me to kill him, to protect that. To protect you. And so, I did it.' Lavellan turned away from her, holding onto his arm, pain etched across every fibre of his flesh. Sysa understood now;

that pain was a remnant of what he had wielded, his body's warped attempt at retribution for the killing of another being. All at once, she wanted to envelop him in her arms, surround him, pound at his chest for taking away the thing most precious in the world to her.

But all she did was lift her fingers again, this time reaching out and pressing them gently to his back.

She didn't know what to say or how to feel, except to understand that when his head lifted and he stood staring into the rocks, he knew she had forgiven him. She knew that there was something in her touch that spoke to him, that healed him, and she felt the pain inside his body begin to uncurl, finding a way to bloom as something else. She thought of Brodie and felt a rush of guilt, tempered with a sense of something else, a question that hung around her like a dull fog descending over her reason. Had she really chosen Brodie, and he her, or had they just been drawn together like a pair of magnets? She railed against the awful clawing in her chest, the possibility that they had both been cheated into a love that was merely biological. And now, Brodie was also in some way to blame for Grey's death, and without either of them here it all seemed so confusing and unreal. She was tired, and all of it swirled in the air around her. Without fully realising what she was doing, she placed her forehead against Lavellan's back, feeling something surge like lightning inside his chest. She quickly pulled back, turning away so that they faced, like two different worlds, away from each other. She hugged her arms around her body, clinging to herself with the only comfort she could find.

'So that's why Brodie's powers started to grow after we

met,' Sysa said, piecing together Lavellan's words and the things that Brigid had told her.

'That's right. He needed you. You're the spark, the source of it all. Without you, the Trinity would be nothing.' Lavellan's voice drifted over her head and crept in towards her face.

'But why did you help? It makes no sense. You were with Rogart.' Sysa tugged at the collar of her cloak, seeking out warmth wherever she could find it. There was a long pause before Lavellan spoke again, then a shifting sound, and the feel of his breath falling like soft air against her neck.

'Sysa. You need to know that whatever happens between us, what I said on the beach back there was true. I meant it.'

You are to me. Perfect.

Sysa turned round to him, looking up into blue eyes that seemed to recede to a thousand different skies.

'You can tell me anything,' she said at last. 'I want to know all of it. I know you're not what I thought. I saw you – in a vision I had. You were beautiful.' Sysa reached up and touched her finger lightly to his cheek, realising it was wet.

'That's all because of you.' He took her hand and moved it slightly, so that her fingers rested on his lips, and he closed his eyes, inhaling deeply. When he opened his eyes again, they stared at each other, and Sysa forgot about Brigid, Star-Steed, Three-Wings and the beach. The world around them fell away, and it was just them, and the sound of a distant rumble from the horizon. Sysa felt her hair lift up towards the sky, mirroring the lifting in her heart.

She was the spark, the source, of course she was.

As the world started to shake around them, she spoke to him, her voice steady and paced with certainty.

'You're the third.'

'Yes.'

She reached her hands to the collar of his jacket, twisting the leather between her palms, not sure whether she wanted to kiss him or curse him.

As the storm grew, she leaned in to him, settling on the first.

★

When she pulled away a few moments later, she wiped at her lips, trying to erase it. Lavellan's kiss had been soft and searching, the opposite of everything she had expected of him. She fisted her hands, feeling angry at both of them for being pulled together by this ridiculous, unyielding force that seemed to overrule their own reason.

Who did she love? Were her feelings all some sort of trick?

'I'm supposed to be getting married. To Brodie,' she said finally, hardly able to look up into Lavellan's face again.

'I know that. Is that what you want?' His voice was choked with the act of kissing her, and a strange tone that might have been hope or something else.

'I don't know what I want. I thought I wanted Brodie, but now I don't know if that's love, or some sort of… magnetism.' Sysa circled her hand around. 'Right now, right here, I wanted you.' She saw a burst of warmth cross Lavellan's features as she spoke.

'But none of this makes sense. You led Rogart to us out in the woods, you had a spotter drop Brodie over a cliff, you wanted to kill us. Why would you do that, if you were going to help us in the end? Why would you do all that if you were one of the Trinity?' Sysa was shouting over the wind now. 'Did you know before the battle with Rogart, Lavellan? You need to tell me – now.'

'I knew.' When Lavellan spoke, his face was clouded. 'What if, all that time, I was actually trying to keep you safe? That day in the woods with the piper – I didn't lead Rogart to you. I led your sky seer to you. Who do you think told Arno and the eagles to save you all that day? And the cliff – believe me, I would have loved to have thrown Brodie over it properly,' Lavellan said, shaking his head at the remembered agony. 'I had the spotter drop him in exactly the place where I knew you'd be able to pull him off that ledge. I did everything I had to to let Rogart think I was doing the job he wanted from me. And when Rogart cast Brodie out to sea before the final battle, of course I knew the seal-folk would rescue him.' Lavellan let out a long breath, his cheeks hollowing with relief at getting his story out.

Something in Sysa's chest felt like it was leaking then, a release of all the anger she had once felt towards this cool-eyed shape-shifter. It seemed to ball in the air before being blasted off to sea on the rising wind. She stepped close to him again, peering into his face as if she had never seen that mouth, those eyes, that elegant nose before.

'But what about the day you attacked my grandfather and me at the river? Why did you do that? Why would you have ever wanted to hurt Grey?' Sysa's words were pleading.

'I didn't want to hurt your grandfather. Not really.' Lavellan cast his eyes away, looking down at the sand as if his shame reflected it. 'I only did as much as I had to, to convince Rogart I had tried. Remember, Sysa, your grandfather's powers were starting to fade by that point and yours weren't fully realised. I did just enough to persuade Rogart – the old fool – that I had attacked Grey, but he'd managed to overpower me. And like the fool that he was, the giant believed me. Sysa, if I'd really wanted to, I could have killed both of you that day.' Lavellan peered up at her from his hunched position, his blue eyes flashing with a desperate kind of look.

'But this still doesn't make sense,' Sysa said, turning herself around in small circles of confusion. 'If you've been protecting me all this time – protecting this *Trinity* – then why were you with Rogart? And if you were with Rogart, why were you trying to help me?'

Sysa thought back to something Brigid had said – *Rogart was only just the start.* The start of what? And what did Lavellan have to do with it?

Beside her, Lavellan's face fell, and he squeezed his eyes shut. When he opened them again, he turned to her with a long look, and an expression Sysa could only read as lost.

'Sysa, when I tell you why, please know that somewhere along the line, my feelings for you changed, the way I change into another body – you saw what you did to me.'

Sysa nodded, thinking of the blue-inked Lavellan she had seen from the sea in her vision. Her thoughts flooded with memory – the image of the blue butterfly that had fluttered around her palm the day she said goodbye to Grey. She knew that whatever Lavellan was about to tell her, they were bound together by some force that might be love or magnetism or friendship. But there was also something between them that meant rebirth, like the caterpillar emerging into its new world with fragile wings. She lifted Lavellan's hand, and the wind swirled around them, like an echo to everything she was feeling. When Lavellan opened his mouth to speak, she tilted her head to hear him, her fae hearing overcome by the storm-tossed clamour.

But the sound she expected to hear did not come from him.

Instead, she heard the howl of a wolf, and the cry of a raven.

And all of a sudden, it felt like the walls of the world came falling down.

CHAPTER ELEVEN

Sysa and Lavellan sprang away from each other and turned to the cliff, where Sirius was roaring down the ledge, his grey form almost vertical against the cliff face. Above them, Three-Wings had begun to circle, crying out some sort of protest, a winged foretelling of a coming ill. At the shoreline, Star-Steed was rearing up onto hind legs as white lips of foaming waves pounded the strip of silvered sand around them. From across the beach, Brigid hurried over, her hair flying out in all directions, as if a spinning wheel had been placed in the space atop her head.

'Brigid, what is it? What's happening?' Sysa called out, the wind pressing against her mouth and bouncing her own voice back to her.

'Something's wrong, but I can't see it,' Brigid said, looking around the beach, as if the blasting wind and waves could offer some kind of clue to what was going on. Sysa wondered briefly if Brigid had seen the kiss between her and Lavellan, but the way Brigid glanced at them suggested she had been too absorbed with her farewells to notice. Sysa flushed, thinking how lost in that moment she must have been not to consider her grandmother's closeness. With the next blast of wind, she swept the thought away – they had more important things to worry about right now.

'Lavellan, what do you think?' she asked, startling herself with the realisation that she suddenly cared about Lavellan's opinion. The knowledge that they were both part of the Trinity had forced a shift in her, one she knew could never be dissolved. Something had seeded in her, some sort of bond that would link them together always. For a second, her mind drifted to a memory of Grey plaiting her hair, separating the strands into three links that came together, twining over and around each other, like the three of them – Brodie, Lavellan and herself. But, right now, that bond meant that she could see Lavellan wasn't as surprised by the turn of events as she had expected him to be, and she felt a prickle run the length of her spine like a cold finger.

She tilted her head, pushing against the wind and looking up at him. 'Lavellan. What's wrong?'

In answer, Lavellan jerked his chin out to the horizon, a slow movement that looked both hopeless and accepting. Sirius was curling around his master's legs now, his wolfish gaze following Lavellan's out to sea. Three-Wings was still crying out to the sky in a way that sounded strangely triumphant, making Sysa shiver again.

Lavellan wasn't going to answer, but it seemed the sky was getting ready to do just that.

In the next breath, the sky sucked in on itself, pulling backwards, reaching further and further away from them, making that sound Sysa had heard before in Fyrish – the sound of a finger around a glass rim. The noise grew louder and louder, until the sky ballooned back at them, pushing its way out to meet the horizon and the sea. As it did, a dark shape catapulted from its middle, propelling itself forward on the wind and hurtling towards them.

As the thing got closer, Sysa saw wings, amber-coloured eyes, a face she had seen so many times before.

'Arno?' she called out, dropping the hand she had been shielding her face with. 'Arno, is that you?'

The eagle responded by flying at Three-Wings and entering into a skirmish of feathers, shrieks and cries.

'Arno, what are you doing? Stop it!'

Before Arno had the chance to comply, the sky spat out something else, dropping it like an anchor on the beach. Diverted from the ongoing avian battle, Sysa walked towards it. As she got closer, she saw it was a person, curled up in a way she had seen before, like a question mark in the sand. The identity of the curled shape ballooned towards her, just as the sky had moments previously.

'Brodie, what are you doing here?' Her hand flew to her face as Brodie scrambled to his feet, grey-rimmed eyes blazing like steely weapons.

'Sysa.' He stared at her just long enough for Sysa to see that grey bloom in his eyes again.

Before she had a chance to answer, he swept past her, focused on Lavellan.

'I'll kill you!' he raged, reaching Lavellan and grabbing him by the shoulders, before ramming him into the waiting rocks.

'Brodie, Brodie stop!' Sysa rushed to the other side of the beach, where Lavellan, his back to the rocks, was holding his arms up in a conciliatory gesture. It did nothing to appease Brodie, whose hands were now fisted around Lavellan's collar, while the muscles in his neck twitched in lines of rage.

He must have heard about the kiss, Sysa thought, wondering how on earth Brodie had managed to find out so quickly, and for that matter, from across in the fae realm. Her face burned with shame and frustration, knowing she was at least partly responsible for her fiancé's pain.

Just as that thought swam over her, Lavellan leaned his head to one side and then flicked it back up, signalling the end of his patience with Brodie's offensive. His eyes grew wide, and he pushed back at Brodie with a dart of bright blue that sprung from his fingertips.

Brodie went sprawling backwards to the sand, before lifting himself up and charging at Lavellan with a spark of his own light, and exactly the same vigour as before.

Sysa looked over at Brigid, who just raised her eyebrows at this strange introduction to Sysa's fiancé.

'Stop it, both of you!' Sysa flew towards them, pushing them apart with a subdued dart of her own lightning, so that they both fell, panting, to the beach. They sat there, like mirrors of each other, their fingers spread out on the sand to either side of them. Sysa entered the gap, lifting her arms and feeling the force of the two glares, which were now halted by her palms.

She turned her head towards Brodie.

'You can't hurt him, Brodie. We all need each other. You need to listen, to understand what he is... what we are.'

Brodie's eyes narrowed back at her.

'I know exactly what he is, and what he's been up to.' Brodie gestured with his hand, indicating Lavellan's form at Sysa's rear. In the air, Three-Wings and Arno took leave of their avian combat and circled, apparently keen to keep abreast of developments.

Sysa jolted at Brodie's words. *What he's been up to.* She was convinced now – Brodie was talking about the kiss.

'Brodie, it was just a kiss, a moment we got wrapped up in. I can explain this.' Now that Brodie was here Sysa felt less sure about what had happened with Lavellan. Behind her, she heard Lavellan make a small noise, a shattering sound that he breathed into the air.

'You kissed him?' Brodie spat back, his voice also conveying the sense of something breaking. The rims of his eyes pooled, swelling into rounds of grey betrayal.

Sysa cursed herself under her breath – Brodie obviously hadn't been aware of her entanglement with Lavellan after all. She flashed a glance at Brigid, who was observing events with a half-sympathetic, half-embarrassed look. As Sysa turned back to face Brodie, he charged, swerving past her and ramming Lavellan into the rock with streaks of light that burst like grey shoots from the centre of his hand.

In response, Arno and Three-Wings joined with the melee, reflecting their masters' battles in swirling shapes and wing beats.

'Males!' Sysa breathed out in frustration to the air – even fae men, she decided, were not immune to these nonsensical honour-bound displays. It appeared Brigid felt the same way, and she stepped forward and lifted her chin up.

'Enough!'

Her voice reverberated around the beach, arriving and leaving with the tide in windswept peaks.

It was enough to part the men and the birds like curtains, and Brodie and Lavellan drifted away from each other, shrugging and sniffing. Nearby, Sirius – who had remained surprisingly restrained through the proceedings – looked on like a grey-furred, watchful judge. Out at sea, the waves receded, temporarily bowed, it appeared, by Brigid's proclamation. Every eye on the beach turned to her as she began to talk, her form a silken beacon on the sand.

'Forget this for now – it is clear that other, more pressing matters are at hand than you bartering over the matter of my granddaughter. And may I remind you that Sysa belongs to neither of you. She belongs only to the world, and to herself. As Sysa was trying to tell you a moment ago, Brodie – you are my granddaughter's betrothed, I assume?'

Brodie nodded quickly, cowed into shameful silence.

'Well, I'm pleased to make your acquaintance. But you obviously arrived here in that manner because of something important. So please explain yourself.' Brigid's voice was clipped, brooking no offer of appeal.

Brodie coughed, as if rattling himself out of his stunned silence. 'Pleased to meet you too,' he rushed out, as Brigid eyed him. 'And yes, we'll come back to that other matter later,' he growled, his eyes tracking Lavellan with an ominous grey glint. 'He tricked you, Sysa, brought you here so that Fyrish would be exposed, left without the most important part of the Trinity.'

'So, you know about the Trinity?' Sysa asked, struggling to keep up with this flurry of revelations. Not far away, Lavellan's head was bowed, and he was rubbing his finger against his brow in an up and down motion. Brodie cast a disgusted look in his direction before continuing.

'I do now. A few things have become clear since you left me.'

'I didn't leave you… not in the way you mean,' Sysa rushed out, containing the urge to run towards him and wipe the look of betrayal from his face. 'And what do you mean, he tricked me?' Sysa asked after a pause, in which the other part of Brodie's statement had come crawling towards her like a spider. Lavellan's head was still lowered, and he was doing everything he could to avoid making eye contact with her.

'He wanted to get you out of Fyrish to make room for whoever's taken residence at the Castle of Thunder. They made sure Rogart was out of the way, and then he brought you back here. It was all part of his perfect plan, Sysa. Arno was there, when you left, he saw what happened.'

Sysa looked up at the sky seer, felt a vague memory of hearing something in the trees around the Castle of Thunder on the night they'd left.

'But what about Luna… that can't be right… I hurt her.' Sysa's voice was hoarse with a sense of rising understanding.

'She was all part of the trick, Sysa. He did something.' Brodie pointed in Lavellan's direction, his voice thick with fury. 'He used some sort of glamour to make it look like you had really hurt her. You hadn't – it was a ruse, to make you feel like you had to come here and… do whatever you've been doing.' Brodie sent an apologetic glance in Brigid's direction, obviously seeing her as some sort of unwitting accessory to it all. 'He's working with them – the one who's in the castle – the one who's – Sysa, there's something else you need to know about what's happened since you left Fyrish.' Brodie brushed a sweep of dark hair back off his forehead.

'Go on,' Sysa said, her voice laced with trepidation.

'They've unleashed something from the castle – some sort of sleeping sickness.'

Sysa's heart lurched as she remembered the fae lines on which the castle was built, the powers for good or bad it could draw up like water from the magical roots beneath it. And now, those powers were obviously booming into Fyrish under the orders of some new force there.

Brodie continued speaking, but Sysa's eyes drifted to Lavellan – she knew what was coming, just as he did.

'Your parents, Elva, William, the people of the kingdom – they're all sick, Sysa, and they're all sleeping. You know that their powers aren't as great as yours, they just weren't able to withstand it. The only one who did was me. And I know why that is – what we are.' He licked his lips, his eyes tracing a triangle between himself, Sysa and Lavellan, the three points of the Young Trinity. 'They wanted you out so that they could take over – you're the central force in it all. And whatever they're up to, he's in on it.' Brodie turned towards Lavellan in accusation.

Sysa felt her fingertips light up like the starting embers of a fire.

'You brought me here so that someone could hurt my family, my home, Lavellan?' Sysa turned towards him in disbelief, her body rigid with pent-up fury. It was coming to life inside her flesh, across her chest, and trickling through the blood vessels in her limbs. She glanced at his arm, which he was no longer holding in that awkward curve of pain – *because she had forgiven him*. She struck out to each side of herself with her hands, blasting green darts into the air around her. Then she walked towards him, that same surge of furious desire she had felt towards Luna at the castle rising up in her like a flame.

Lavellan's eyes sought hers, and they were blue and huge and hopeless.

'I'm so sorry, Sysa. Please, let's talk about this,' he said, lifting his palms and flashing a wary glance towards her hands.

The look in his eyes seemed to clear something in Sysa's vision and she turned away from him, blasting a piece of rock, her anger dissipating in the process. She was left with the feeling of emptying, of something pulling out all the warmth inside her core.

She wrapped her arms around herself, rubbing at her skin as if she could erase the parts that had been reached by him kissing her.

'Get him out of my sight,' she said, eyeing Brodie from under dark lashes.

'It would be my pleasure,' Brodie said triumphantly, manhandling Lavellan across the beach and pinning his arms behind his back.

From the corner of her vision, Sysa could see that Lavellan didn't fight back, except to shrug Brodie off in repeated gestures of small defiance. She knew that if he wanted to, Lavellan could match Brodie blow for blow. She watched the two of them curve along the beach, until at last Brodie pushed Lavellan down on his knees, his eyes facing out towards the water. She could see that Brodie was getting some sort of satisfaction from the experience, and wondered if he was enacting his vengeance for more than just the kiss. Lavellan, of course, had been chosen by Rogart as a sort of son – and yet Rogart had tried to kill Brodie, his true son, on more than one occasion. She could hardly blame Brodie for hating Lavellan – just as she once had. And yet here they all were, in this strange triangle of dependence, betrayal and distrust.

'Don't hurt him.' Sysa spoke to the sand, but Brodie had heard her, and shuffled backwards.

'We need to go back. All of us. And, right now, we need him—' she found that she could barely say Lavellan's name again— 'we need him to get us into the castle and find out what's going on.'

'Might I suggest…?' Lavellan began, retreating to that older version of his voice, that cool, crisp intonation that fell from his mouth like a pointed icicle.

'No, you don't get to suggest anything right now,' Sysa interrupted. She couldn't bear to look at him, much less converse with that other version of him. Instead, she stepped towards Brigid.

'We need to go back, not for Luna, but for my family – my people. Will you still come with us – bring the stone, see if that will help them?' she asked, looking at her grandmother with pleading eyes.

'Of course I will. They are my family, my people too, remember Sysa.' Brigid nodded once, sweeping her eyes over the assembled party. 'We must move quickly. And however much you might dislike it, whatever he's done, Lavellan is our route to finding out what's happening.' Brigid flashed a minatory glance at the two males, and a more sympathetic one at Sysa.

'Come.' Brigid wrapped an arm around her grand-daughter and pulled her gently towards where Lavellan was still kneeling on the sand.

'Creatures, join us.' Brigid gestured towards Sirius, Three-Wings and Arno, who dutifully followed. From his place at the edge of the water, Star-Steed joined the circle, his glistening hooves sending ribbons of sand and shingle scattering around the beach.

'Who will protect this place now, Brigid, if you leave?' Sysa asked, suddenly thinking back to Brigid's words about leaving the Northern Gate unprotected.

'The time for protecting this place has passed, Sysa. The threat to you and the Trinity has slipped in by another means. I wish I had seen – I wish I had been able to see – what was occurring when you left Fyrish to come here.' Brigid loosed a long sigh, her eyes misting over as she stared out to where sky and sea merged along a dark line of horizon.

'Do you know who it might be... who might be at the Castle of Thunder?' Sysa pressed on, noting the thoughtful planes of Brigid's face.

'I have my suspicions,' Brigid answered, before swivelling on her heel, sending small clouds of sand blooming around the fine bones of her ankle.

'So, tell me,' Sysa said, grabbing Brigid's arm and pulling her close again.

'Soon,' Brigid said, her wary glance at Lavellan suggesting she too was feeling a quiver of distrust. 'Soon,' she repeated, patting Sysa's hand in reassurance. She made to move again.

'Brigid, before we leave,' Sysa spoke in a hushed tone, and turned Brigid away from the circle. 'When Lavellan came to you, before I met you... what did he say?'

'He told me he was here to bring my granddaughter to me,' Brigid said, her lips curving slightly in recollection. 'After Grey... he absorbed some of your grandfather's stories, Sysa,' Brigid said in explanation. 'He knew about me, and I knew about him… well, from that moment I began to, at least. Although my visions hadn't told me everything, I had my suspicions that he was part of the Trinity, part of you. But that story was his to tell, Sysa, and he's told it. When he spoke to me back there, he was just a boy who wanted to bring you to me. Not everything he says is a lie.' Brigid cast a thoughtful look over her shoulder. 'Whatever he's done, there's some truth in what he says. I see good in him.'

Brigid was rolling Sysa's hands in hers, as if she were warming them.

'But my parents… Elva… if they're sick, it's because of what he did.'

'I know that,' Brigid said, pursing her lips together and taking a deep inhale through her nostrils. 'But he has also done other things – like the times he helped you, against Rogart,' she murmured, her eyes searching the sand in consideration. 'I saw glimpses of some of that when I met him back there. There's more to this,' she concluded, nodding, as if convincing herself of her own thoughts. 'But right now, our family is in danger, and we need to go,' the old woman said in a voice that was both authoritative and gentle.

'I'm ready,' Sysa said, turning back towards the circle, wondering if she had ever truly felt ready for any of this.

Across the sand, Brodie and Lavellan waited, caught up in the wind like two scattered pieces of her heart.

★

Brigid raised her arms, the silk of her gown draping in smooth rings around her elbows. She lifted her head to the sky, her nose pointed upwards like an elegant arrow in the air. All around her, the wind boomed and swelled, once again emboldened by her actions. There was no direct portal to the fae lands here, Sysa thought, as she cracked one eye open, feeling shards of fine sand pressing against her eyelids. It was just Brigid and the force of her will, a will that seemed capable of bending tides and oceans. Sysa shivered, wondering what she herself might be capable of one day, if this Trinity of theirs hadn't imploded by then.

Around the beach, there was a strange sort of stillness that contrasted with the force of wind and sea, as if everything that lived had stepped away to make room for Brigid, this formidable force of nature. The birds were gone, the sea creatures dispersed to watery hideouts, leaving only rock, cliff, sky and sea for the old woman to contend with as she continued to pull the world apart.

Her hair whipped up in soaked threads, and she made a strange humming noise, the glass-rim noise, Sysa thought, that she was becoming more attuned to. Brigid's eyes were clamped shut and her tipped ears pointed to the cliffs behind her, while sand blew up around her legs in bursts of grey and silver, painting the beach in moving whorls. Out at sea, white-fringed waves danced and curled, peaking to V-shaped echoes of Brigid's movements. Above them, the sky seemed to be throbbing, and now bloomed with a myriad of colours, as if a rainbow had spilled itself on the air.

Sysa thought back to the times she had felt this pull before – when she had first left Grey, when Krystan had sent Peter back to Caithness and, more recently, with Lavellan.

Each time the sensation had been irresistible, yet painful, like a kind of longing was unravelling itself from the centre of her chest. There was no way to resist, no matter the direction or the destination. It was the same force that pulled her towards Brodie and Lavellan; something entirely separate to her but part of everything she was.

When she peeked at the two of them out of her half-open eye, they were both standing grim-faced and steadfast. Though their heads were bowed, she could see that Lavellan was also peeking one eye open, a blue glint that lit his face like the flash of a shining jewel. There was something in his half-a-look that made Sysa want to step out of the circle and go to him. Then she thought of her father, her mother and Elva, all sick and sleeping. Something hardened in her again, and she turned her face away.

As she did, the noise grew and the wind flared, forcing her to push her heels deep into the sand beneath her. Arno and Three-Wings began to shriek – strange, painful sounds that Sysa had never heard from birds before. Star-Steed rose up, circling his forelegs in the air, his hooves clamouring at some unseen boundary. Soon, there was a rushing feeling and then a sucking, as if the whole sky was gathering itself to burst.

In the next breath, the wind drew back, like a catapult firing itself inwards. Sysa felt herself swept up into a melee of limbs, wings, arms and hooves. The noise Brigid was making had lifted to a climax, and there was a sound like a glass bowl shattering.

Then, the world went completely still and quiet. Sysa took a deep breath, inhaling everything she could of Caithness. A moment later, she closed her eyes, knowing it was once again time to say goodbye.

PART THREE

THE COMING OF WINTER

CHAPTER TWELVE

Arriving was easier than leaving, Sysa thought vaguely, as her eyes drifted open and she looked out over the familiar contours of Fyrish. She blinked a few times, clearing the glassy haze that clouded her vision, before casting her eyes over her companions, who were all in similar states of readjustment following their passage across the realms. She was aware of a strange sort of sharpness in the air, a mist that shrouded their surroundings like freezing sea haar. It had the effect of colouring the environment – not in the way Rogart's darkness once had, but in a strange, altered sense of shade. Sysa looked up at the once pale blue sky, and saw it was now washed through with icicle-like lines that struck out in all directions. Where the meadow had once been carpeted in the lush greens of summer, the grass was now tipped with a white and wintry sheen.

And the air – it smelled foul and sickly. Sysa covered her mouth with her fingers, fighting down the instinctive urge to retch. When she looked around again, the others were fighting their own version of that reaction, as they stumbled to feet or hooves, or flapped wings unaccustomed to such insults.

All except Brodie and Arno, who looked resigned to it.

'The air. You'll get used to it shortly. It won't harm us,'

Brodie confirmed, with a glance at Lavellan that suggested he wouldn't have minded the third Trinity member being an exception to that rule.

'Your parents, Elva and the others aren't strong enough to withstand it,' he explained, directing his words at Sysa. 'When I saw that it hadn't affected me, that's when I began to put the pieces together about the Trinity. That, and knowing there was a reason behind him wanting you out of the fae realm.' Brodie jabbed a thumb over his shoulder at Lavellan before flashing a grateful look at Arno, who angled his head in response. 'And I'm guessing it won't affect you either, Brigid,' Brodie said, glancing with a degree of awkwardness towards the older woman, who nodded back mildly. If anyone had been unsure of her capabilities before, Brigid's performance on the beach would have answered them, Sysa thought.

'No, I'm sure I'll be just fine,' Brigid said, gulping down a few breaths of the pungent air in demonstration. After a slight pause, she shook her head, dispelling any further concern over her well-being. 'There,' she said, with the tiniest note of triumph. 'Old, but still alive.' She turned on her heel and began an inspection of the grass.

'I'm all right too,' Lavellan offered from nearby, although no one had asked after his condition.

'Then I think we're all safe from it, whatever it is,' Sysa said in a clipped tone, ignoring him. The air's assault against her nostrils seemed to have subsided, as if it had drifted off like quickly forgotten smoke. It still held that sharpness that pressed against her like a blade, but at least the smell was gone. Now that their surroundings were slightly more palatable, she looked around, realising that they had arrived at the same mound she'd first appeared at in Fyrish all that time ago.

'We're close to the castle,' she began, a surge of desperation in her voice. 'I have to go and see my family.' She pictured them then, stepping out from between the tall trees when they had first welcomed her to their kingdom. Now that space was empty, save for the cold shadows that fell in shafts across the ground. Sysa had the sense that beyond the trees, there was only more emptiness to be found, and she pulled her cloak around herself tighter. Behind her, Star-Steed snuffled around, dispersing motes of welcome brightness into the freezing morning, while Arno and Three-Wings jostled for position atop the mound.

Sysa began to walk, the others following behind, Lavellan still being pushed along like a criminal by Brodie.

'She'll see, she'll see what you've done to them,' Sysa heard him hiss from behind her.

Her feet felt like lead weights with every step on their passage through the trees.

*

When they arrived at Steel Castle, it looked different too, as though it had been cast in a strange, unfamiliar shadow. Sysa stood, craning her neck up towards the high peaks and turrets, noticing the streaks of grey that slithered towards every window, like the tracks of a hunter seeking out its prey. She shivered, knowing that those marks traced the passage of whatever sickness had been thrown towards her family – a sickness that had found its way in through any available opening. She inwardly cursed herself for the hundredth time for leaving them exposed to it. Another thought gnawed at her: whoever was responsible was more powerful than Rogart, whose powers had never managed to penetrate the defences of her home. She looked at the ground, willing the fae lines the castle was built on to spring to life, mount some sort of attack against this insidious intruder. But the ground just stared back in earthy silence. For now, it held no answers, and seemed as choked into submission as the lower windows, which were cloaked with a growth of ivy that had attempted to hold the sickness back.

'The castle tried,' Brigid said softly, placing a hand on the prickled ivy, which petered out in the space above her fingers. It had not got far, Sysa noted, surveying the grey marks which crept upwards above it, snaking the wall like a twisted, mocking smile. She could see that the armoury of Steel Castle had been wholly overcome by this attacker, like a small army against the cavalry of kingdoms. She sighed, looking out to the gardens where Grey's statue stood with an unusual air of dejection, a hopelessness bolstered by lichen that now crusted over its surface like a new, embittered skin.

'Let's go in,' Sysa said, turning to Brigid, who was gazing dreamily over the castle. 'I'm sorry, Brigid. Do you need a moment?' she followed up, remembering that her grandmother had once lived here – ruled here. These walls must have held a thousand memories, Sysa thought, feeling guilty about the need to rush her grandmother towards whatever lay inside.

'No, I'm all right, Sysa. Just remembering, that's all. The place looks so different now.' Brigid's eyes swept around in recollection.

'It looks different to me too, Brigid,' Sysa said, grabbing the older woman's hand and pulling her gently towards the large wooden doors, which creaked open in invitation. From the corner of her eye, Sysa saw Brigid look back towards the statue, where her attention rested for a moment, apparently reeling in her thoughts of Grey.

'Come inside,' Sysa gestured to Brodie, before shooting an apologetic glance between Star-Steed, Sirius and the birds, who were hovering nearby expectantly. 'You'd best stay here, I think. But you come,' she directed at Lavellan, who stumbled into the space behind her, having been prodded between the shoulder blades by Brodie, who seemed intent on maintaining his position at the shape-shifter's rear.

Lavellan made a hissing noise, before Sysa turned around to them both, eyes burning.

'You, be quiet.' She levelled a warning look at Lavellan, who stared back at her through strands of white hair that fell in snowy streaks across his cheekbones. 'And Brodie, let him go,' she said in a softer tone. 'What can he do that he hasn't already done?'

Brodie let out a disappointed breath, before giving Lavellan another final shove forward. Lavellan stopped, cracking his knuckles and then tilting his head back and forth like the hand of a clock swinging between ten and two.

Sysa pushed the doors fully open, amplifying the creaking against the tiled floor of the entranceway. The floor was grimy, filmed with a layer of dust that Ida would never have tolerated, leading Sysa to the uncomfortable conclusion that the servants were somehow indisposed. The air was thick with the tang of that sickly odour she had inhaled outside, before her senses had readjusted. In the time it took her to cover her nose with her hand, the smell had virtually disappeared, leaving just enough of a trace to convince her of two things: that this sickness was in the building, and that whatever it was, it had spread fast, like an unforgiving fire.

She gestured to the others to follow and moved silently towards the Great Hall, which seemed to exude a sense of unease along the marble. Sysa padded carefully, mindful that the perpetrator of the sickness could be within the castle walls. She edged along the corridors, tracing her fingers over stone to convince herself that this eerie place was still actually Steel Castle. The dimness that shrouded the place gave the effect of wandering through an indoor twilight. Everything felt heavy, as if the very air were weighted with a bitter sense of loss.

As they turned in to the doors that bounded the Great Hall, something dark flapped out at them from an alcove, jolting them all into a moment of dispersal. It was a rook, Sysa saw, as she lifted her head towards the ceiling, watching the dark-winged bird skitter and flail across the hall. About halfway to the exit, it fell, landing on the tiles like a heavy, feathered stone, with a thumping sound.

'Is it dead?' she asked of no one in particular, something in her stomach sinking with a dull sense of realisation.

Brodie nodded.

'Let's go in,' he said, pushing the doors of the Great Hall apart in a way that would normally signal the start of a ceilidh, or a dance.

As the doors fell open, Sysa saw that what greeted them was no cause for celebration.

Slumped across a table were the prone forms of her mother and father, Elise's arms stretched out around her head in an awful arrangement of clamouring for something that had not been reached.

Not far away lay Elva and William, curled into each other on the floor like a pair of sleeping kittens. Elva's hair fell across the tiles behind her in an echo of their mother's – the only golden lights in a room devoid of sun. At the rear of the hall, the remainder of a small fire crackled with Telon sprawled beside it. Even from this distance, Sysa could see that the hound did not radiate his usual air of warmth and languor; that his coat was matted, and his furred body lay rigid and cold against the stone.

'Mother, Father!' she gasped out involuntarily, darting across the hall to the table, where her parents lay, surrounded by vines that had wrapped their way around the table legs. The vines crept over the corners of the table, edging their way towards her parents' faces in peaks of folding green. As Sysa looked around the hall, she saw that the vines were everywhere, growing up walls and climbing onto surfaces that had once bloomed with cascading foliage. The vines threw an ugly hue over the stillness, but somewhere else in the castle Sysa could hear the pulse of an evil kind of growth.

'What have you done? How could you do this?' she hissed, wheeling towards Lavellan as her whole world seemed to suddenly converge around him. Now that she had seen her family, she finally believed it – he had done this. It was all because of him. And not only that, but she had also kissed him, felt something like love for him – still felt something like love, she thought, with a painful stab of guilt that choked her senses. He had tricked her, and now he stood staring at her with that awful, empty look on his face.

Something ripped through her, a rawness that lifted her arms and flew light-hewn daggers from her fingers.

When she looked at Lavellan again, he was pinned to the wall, held there by the force of the same hand she had so recently placed upon his back.

'Who are you working for? Why did you do this?' she shot out, as Lavellan stood with his mouth slightly open, a silent offering of nothing. Sysa twisted her hand, pinning him to the wall harder, but he didn't flinch, and his eyes remained fixed on her in pleading rounds of blue. She raised her arm up, pushing him higher up the wall, her eyes streaming with frustration and sadness. Her arm ached, as if she were betraying herself.

A sound emerged into the silence, a long low moan of absolute sorrow. Sysa dropped her arm to her side, wondering how she could have caused him so much pain.

But as he fell to the floor, Lavellan flicked his chin, signalling the direction of the table. He rubbed at a minor injury on his elbow and Sysa realised she hadn't hurt him – perhaps even wanted to – at all.

She turned in the direction of the sound, seeing that it came from Brigid, who was slumped, half-covering Bruan like a protective coat of armour.

Brigid's son, her child – Sysa had been so busy in her own anger she had forgotten that Brigid had been separated from Bruan, only to reunite in this place of sickness.

'Brigid, I'm so sorry. Can you help them? The stone, Brigid. Will the stone help?' The words tumbled out of

Sysa as she swivelled her eyes towards the pocket of Brigid's gown.

'Yes, the stone, the stone,' Brigid said, her own words emerging in an uncharacteristic fumble as she fished her hand around her pocket. She pulled the stone out, its bright gleam strangely at odds with the dimness of the room.

She stared at it for several seconds, as if that could imbue an understanding of the gravity of the current situation.

Behind them, Brodie hovered, content until now to let Sysa play out her distaste for Lavellan by herself. He placed a hand on her shoulder, and she lifted her fingers to meet it, glad of the familiar comfort and the contact. Further behind, Lavellan was edging towards them, craning his neck to peer over the gathering into the palm of Brigid's hand.

Sysa felt him approach, and turned her head infinitesimally to breathe 'No,' at which Lavellan halted, stilling the room around them. Brigid was still looking at the stone, murmuring words with the ebb and flow of a language Sysa didn't understand. Finally, Brigid clasped the stone between her hands and lifted it above her head, her voice rising with her prayer, like the breath of the sea and the wind in unison. As she spoke, something flashed across the room as if a star had burst into lightning.

The room went dark, and then returned to its previous, meagre dimness.

As Sysa's eyes readjusted, she saw that Brigid was leaning over Bruan, holding the stone against his body in the region of his heart.

Whatever power the stone possessed was filling the room now. Sysa felt a wind curl up around them, not the familiar wind of outside, but a force that belonged only to the stone. It fired light, too, a light that surrounded Brigid and Bruan in whorls, like shells of shelter. There was a noise too, a screaming kind of sound, a high-pitched echo of whatever prayer Brigid had recanted to the room.

As the screaming noise reached a peak, Brigid cupped the stone in her palms, threads of light bending between it and Bruan's heart-space. Sysa could sense a sort of lifting, as if the stone was pulling – or perhaps pushing – something out of her father's heart. Bruan's body was lifting too, his torso arced up in the tiniest curve of awakening as Brigid crouched beside him.

'He's waking up,' Sysa whispered to herself, squeezing the hand that Brodie had kept on her shoulder.

As Bruan's eyelids fluttered, another force entered the room, sending cold into the Great Hall, like the arrival of a sudden winter into spring.

CHAPTER THIRTEEN

t all happened so quickly that Sysa felt dizzy, both with the cold, and the shock of seeing the stone fly out of Brigid's hand towards the doorway.

More than that, she felt a dull sense of horror as her father's eyelids stilled, and his body slumped back down onto the wood.

She spun around in the direction of the doors, where a woman stood with one arm up, awaiting the arrival of the healing stone.

Sysa watched as the stone reached her hand with an awful thumping sound. The woman smiled, closing her fist around its power.

In that moment of realisation, Sysa stared back at the female, transfixed by both her smile and her appearance. The woman was beautiful, a sharp, crystalline sort of beauty Sysa knew from somewhere else. She had entered the room and brought cold, a cold that was echoed in the tight-fitting white gear that covered her limbs and clung to the honed curves of her body. Above the gear, she wore a steel-blue coat that tapered out behind her and fringed her wrists with hems of granulated ice.

The woman's hair was snow-white, shot through with silvered streaks that belied her ageless beauty. Her cheekbones were pointed, announcing themselves like summits beneath her skin. Above those cheeks, her cool blue eyes surveyed Sysa, taking the measure of her in a cold, lingering assessment. Then her face broke into a grin, displaying polished white teeth, hedged by an impressive set of fangs.

Sysa heard a moan that she thought at first came from the female, whose head was now tilted back in a grotesque, mocking laughter.

She realised quickly that the moan had come from Brigid's mouth.

After the moan, came a name, which Brigid, still crouched over beside Bruan's half-alive form, whispered up to the ceiling:

'Neven.'

Sysa stilled, thinking of another time when the doors of the Great Hall had been parted by an ice-cold visitor.

As the thought came to her, Lavellan stepped forward.

'Hello, Mother,' he said, his voice as cold as the woman's laughter, which lifted on the wings of winter up towards the roof.

CHAPTER FOURTEEN

Sysa stared at the fire, as outside, snow flurries danced in the air like white leaves of winter.

The fire warmed her, adding a soft glow to her cheeks as it crackled and spat against the hearth.

Nearby, Grey was bustling around, clearing the dinner things as he hummed to himself in soft melodies. The fire and the wind beyond the walls seemed to join in his tiny orchestra.

The weather outside was fierce, but here with Grey in the cottage, a warmth lived, like their own perpetual sun.

'Grandad, will you tell me a story?' Sysa asked, wriggling her toes under the woollen socks that supplemented her nighttime attire in winter.

'Of course,' Grey answered, throwing a cloth over his shoulder with a tiny slapping sound.

He smiled at her then, the look on his face full of pride, and apparent surprise that at thirteen, she was still so enamoured with his stories. He shook his head, as if he were reminding himself of something he had forgotten in the snow. Sysa wondered if it had anything to do with the feeling inside her chest, like a bud waiting to bloom in springtime. She still loved Grey's stories, and though she didn't understand why, she knew she needed them, like the earth needed the moon and stars.

'What story shall I tell?' Grey asked eventually as he glanced at the window where the glass was streaked in wet lines of snow and moonlight. He paused for a moment before turning back to Sysa, his green eyes lit with whatever he had conjured in his mind. 'A story of winter, and how it turns to spring, I think. What do you reckon, Sysa?' he asked, placing the cloth back down on the counter and venturing towards the rocking chair beside her.

Sysa had grown too big to climb onto his lap now, but she squeezed his hand as he made his way past. 'Sounds perfect, Grandad.'

Grey sat down, folding himself into the chair that now rocked gently with his weight.

Sysa turned her face, lit up both by the fire and the sense of her soul lighting up somewhere inside her. Whenever Grey told her stories, she experienced that same feeling, as if something was being switched on inside her – a feeling of rightness in the world. Grey nodded at her, encapsulating his understanding of the bond that existed between them in either silence or stories. He folded his hands over one another in his lap and eased himself back slowly. Sysa smiled at him, an old man in a rocking chair who was also her north star.

'What season is it, Sysa?' Grey asked eventually as he leaned forward in his chair, his features bright with the excitement of a story.

'Winter, Grandad,' Sysa said in a reproachful tone, though her lips were curving upwards. Though she was older now, Grey often started his stories with a question, as he had when she was small. Sysa suspected Grey just enjoyed applauding her answers, in the way he had when she was still learning about the world, so she went along with this small façade of theirs. Tonight, Grey replied by whipping his arm through the air in a downward gesture of triumph.

'Yes, winter!' he said, his eyes gleaming with pride at her. Sometimes Sysa thought Grey seemed most alive when he was praising her. 'And what comes after winter, Sysa?'

'Spring, Grandad.' She gave him a playful slap on the knee, and he responded by catching her fingers in his hand.

'I'm sorry, Sysa, yes, it's spring, of course,' Grey said, cowed into seriousness by the look of mock anger Sysa was shooting him from underneath furrowed eyebrows. 'And between winter and spring comes the time of Imbolc – which is a bit like Beltane. You know about Beltane, of course.'

Sysa nodded, thinking of the fire-lighting that heralded the turn towards springtime in Caithness.

She winced a little, remembering the Beltane when they had been accosted by that Lavellan creature down at the riverside. Grey seemed to recognise her discomfort, and resumed his story in a more subdued manner than before. They didn't talk much about Beltane these days, but Sysa knew the old incident had affected Grey in a way she didn't understand yet. She wished she could flip Grey back to his carefree mood of a few moments ago, and at the same time, grab on to him with all the strength she possessed and never let him go.

'Imbolc is the time when the land begins its turn towards growth and renewal, Sysa – a time of fertility and nature. Some believe that winter here is overseen by an old goddess – the Cailleach.' Grey said the name with a guttural sound that seemed to emanate from somewhere in his throat.

'The Cailleach rules the winter, Sysa, taking the form of an old woman at Samhain to control the months until Beltane. She commands the weather too, bringing in the storms and the snowfall.' Grey tilted his head towards the window, indicating the consequences of the Cailleach's influence outside. 'Her footsteps change the land too,' he continued, nodding at Sysa, who was staring back with a dreamy expression that often characterised her reaction to Grey's stories. 'She made all the Scottish mountains, you know, by dropping the rocks she carries in her basket, and the glens were formed where she drove her hammer into land.

'Not only that, but she can also freeze the earth just by touching it with the staff she carries,' Grey explained. 'Imagine that – being able to command the weather as you please.'

Sysa looked towards the window, wondering what sort of mood the Cailleach must have been in to unleash the weather outside tonight.

'So how does spring come, if the Cailleach exists, Grandad?' Sysa asked, wondering about this wintry architect.

'Well, a few things happen, Sysa, and the first is Imbolc. You can tell a lot then about winter, and how much longer the cold is going to last. If the Cailleach chooses bright, sunny weather for Imbolc, it means she's outside collecting firewood for a longer winter. If the weather's poor, that tells us the Cailleach is sleeping. That's good news, really – it means the harsh weather will be over soon.

'But the other way that spring comes is in the rising of another goddess, Sysa – a goddess called Brigid.'

Grey's eyes drifted over to the window, as though he saw something out beyond the wintered glass.

'Who's Brigid, Grandad?' Sysa asked, tugging on Grey's sleeve with a note of impatience.

'Mmm, Sysa?' Grey murmured, apparently absorbed in some sort of inward story of his own.

'Brigid, Grandad, who is she?' Sysa asked again, startling Grey back into the moment.

'Ah, yes, child, Brigid. Well, if the Cailleach is winter, Sysa, then the goddess Brigid – she relates to spring. Brigid rises at

Beltane, overseeing the world until Samhain. Brigid is associated with fertility, learning and healing. A very powerful goddess. A very beautiful one too.

'It's said that when Brigid rises, the Cailleach sleeps in stone, awaiting the coming of another winter,' Grey said, something in his voice catching every time he mentioned the goddess Brigid.

'Whatever happens to the Cailleach, it's the natural order of things – the receding of winter, and the coming forth of something new. From Samhain, the Cailleach dominates again – it's all part of the never-ending cycle of the seasons. Like day and night, the moon and sun, ice and fire – everything in nature needs its opposite. It's how this world of ours balances itself,' Grey said, lifting his arm in a sweep of demonstration.

'Winter in itself is nothing to be afraid of. Just like the dark, Sysa – it's natural. But an unbalance in these forces – that's what we have to be wary of.' Grey made a clicking noise with his tongue and shook his head in a tiny, cautious line.

'So, what would happen if one or the other didn't want to give up their power, Grandad?' Sysa asked, taking a few steps forward in her internal appraisal of Grey's story.

'Now, that's a very good question, Sysa,' Grey answered, shaking his index finger in the air in approval of his granddaughter's curious mind. 'If one of them decided they wanted to hang on to their power, that would cause a lot of trouble,' he said, his brows furrowing in the same way Sysa's had a few moments earlier. 'The world could be locked into a perpetual winter, or a perpetual spring,' he said, glancing over at the window, where rows of white were smashing against the pane.

Sysa followed his gaze, arriving at the assessment that a perpetual spring would be more welcome than a perpetual winter. As if reading her thoughts, Grey turned back to her.

'It sounds nice at first, doesn't it? Spring all year round.' Grey smiled in an evocation of healing and renewal. 'But the world doesn't work like that. We need the dark to bring the light, Sysa. It's the natural order,' he said, looking wistfully at the window again.

After a moment, his eyes cleared, as if he had remembered something, a memory transfused through the windows and the walls.

'You know, some say the Cailleach and Brigid are one and the same, a shared entity who transforms from the old woman in winter to a younger beauty in springtime.'

'Is that true, do you think, Grandad?' Sysa asked, her eyes gleaming in the dusky evening.

'No, I don't believe it is,' Grey said, folding his hands together, his long fingers connecting on his lap.

'I'm fairly sure—' Grey spoke with his usual unaffected air, leading Sysa to the conclusion that his belief was irrefutable— 'that they are two quite separate beings. And, more than that, I believe that in their lives in the otherworld, they may have gone on to have families of their own.'

'So, they're faeries?' Sysa asked, latching on to the first part of Grey's reasoning. The thought of faeries always sparked excitement in her, a surge of emotion that originated somewhere in her chest.

'In as much as faeries relate to those outside the veil of the human world, then you might say that, Sysa,' Grey said, smiling at Sysa's preoccupation with the fae folk. 'But they are different too, in a way that's more akin to gods. That's one reason their descendants are so powerful, Sysa – why they are also important in the order of things.'

'And you think the Cailleach and Brigid have children of their own, Grandad?' Sysa asked, leaning forward.

'I do. In fact, I'm certain of it. I'm fairly sure the Cailleach has a daughter, who has no doubt gone on to have children of her own.'

'Who is the Cailleach's daughter?' Sysa asked, the idea of this winter-born descendant swirling in her mind like the flurries outside the cottage window.

'There are a few possibilities, but I think the most likely is the Queen of the Unseelie.'

'Unseelie?' Sysa said, her voice altered by the mention of the malevolent fae.

'Yes, an Unseelie queen who does the Cailleach's bidding while she languishes in her sleep, Sysa. A powerful force, no doubt about it.' Grey's mouth tightened, and he shook his head.

'What's her name?' Sysa asked, wondering if she had ever heard of this menacing character.

'Neven, Sysa. I believe her name is Neven.'

Grey sighed, looking at the window again, as if another answer could be found out in the dark.

CHAPTER FIFTEEN

Sysa winced, surveying the welts that streaked the inside of her wrists in lines of red ensnarement. She rattled at the bonds which held her to the wall, but it was no good – she could see the chains were made of iron. Through clenched teeth, she roared, shaking her whole body in anger and frustration. She wanted to connect with that anger, to send it flying down her arms in the way she had trained herself not to. Nothing happened though, and she slumped against the wall, letting out another futile groan.

She looked around, taking the measure of her surroundings. She was in a cell, a dark-walled place that smelled of damp and cold. No doubt the dungeons of the Castle of Thunder, she thought, though her memory of getting here was patchy. One moment they had been in the Great Hall of Steel Castle, and the next she had woken up here, presumably having been kidnapped by the Unseelie queen. Sysa assumed that the shifting of the stone from Brigid to Neven had caused some sort of surge, which had rendered herself and the others unconscious just long enough for Neven to take advantage. However the Unseelie queen had managed it, the result was being chained to a wall in this godforsaken place. Sysa looked up to where a small, rectangular window allowed a sliver of light into the darkness. Outside, the sky hung in a grey-blue curtain, cut through with lines of white that tore at it like ice.

She rattled at her chains again, and then stopped. It was a waste of energy.

From somewhere in the distance, she heard a familiar voice threading through the dark, hardly more than a whisper.

'Sysa? Are you there?'

'Brodie? Is that you?' Sysa turned her head, trying to discern where the voice was coming from.

In the dim light, she saw bars lining the front wall of her prison. Across a corridor, there were more bars. She focused her eyes to get a better look.

'Yes, it's me. I'm in the cell opposite you. Are you all right?'

It was strange hearing Brodie's voice but not being able to see him.

'I'm fine. But my magic is drained. I can't even see you properly,' Sysa replied, annoyed that her fae eyesight wasn't adjusting, however much she squeezed her eyelids and willed them to ignite her powers.

'Same here,' Brodie said, and then paused, the silence magnifying all the things that lay between them. Sysa still needed to explain about her kiss with Lavellan, but now hardly seemed the time.

She batted the thought away – it would have to wait until later.

'Where's Brigid?' she asked, more immediate concerns over her grandmother's well-being taking precedence.

'I'm here,' a small voice said from somewhere in the dark.

'Brigid?' Sysa said, her voice coming out in a high-pitched squeak of worry. Brigid sounded fragile, as if she had been drained of more than just her power.

'I'm along the corridor from you, in another cell. I've just woken up too. Where are we?'

'We're in the Castle of Thunder, Brigid.' Even without having seen this place before, Sysa recognised the smell, the thick air and the cloying sense of menace that had accompanied her previous visit.

'She has the stone.' Brigid didn't need to say any more about the 'she' for Sysa to understand – Brigid meant Neven. While Sysa had been unconscious, something had come to her – an old story from Grey that had settled on her like the branches of a tree being coated with falling snow. Neven was the Queen of Faeries, the Queen of the Unseelie – and also, it appeared, Lavellan's mother. And more than that, they came from the line of the Cailleach – the cold one whose job it was to spin a web of winter around the world. And Brigid – Brigid was more than just a faerie too – she was a goddess of springtime.

Sysa furrowed her brow, wondering why she hadn't remembered that winter's night in the cottage and the story Grey had told her before now.

'What does it mean, if she has the stone, Brigid?' Sysa asked, a sense of foreboding rising within her like an insect crawling up a drainpipe.

'It means she has taken my magic, Sysa. The stone is more than a healer, it's the lifeblood of my power.'

'And will it transfer your power to her?' Sysa asked, imagining the consequences of the Unseelie holding not just a power over winter, but over springtime.

'Not necessarily. The stone may not fully yield to her initially. It's bonded to me and will remain so if it can. But, for now, Neven holds enough power to drain my magic while she tries to turn it.'

Sysa thought back to the time she had wielded her own magic to turn Krystan, albeit in an entirely different way.

'So, how much time do we have until she's able to do that?' Sysa asked, raising her voice to be heard in the heavy atmosphere.

'I'm not sure, Sysa. But I'd guess not long.' Brigid's voice sounded strained as it drifted between the dungeon bars.

'She was the one you were worried about when you were guarding the Northern Gate,' Sysa said, thinking back to her conversation with Brigid outside the cave at Dunnet Head.

'Yes, she was, Sysa, and it seems my fears were not unfounded. I believe Neven's plan is to hold these lands in eternal winter, and at the same time become all-powerful in the faerie realm.'

'And this person is Lavellan's mother?' Brodie interjected from across the corridor, evidently struggling to keep pace with these new developments.

'Yes, she is. And Neven is the daughter of the Cailleach, a force of winter – and my grandmother's opposite,' Sysa replied, remembering that Brodie had not been party to her dream.

'So, you, Lavellan and I need each other, and she needs us, and Brigid's stone, to achieve this eternal winter?' Brodie asked, his voice carrying an edge of growing understanding.

'It looks that way,' Sysa answered, rattling at her chains

again, still struggling to understand Neven's motivations for keeping them chained up to these walls.

The sound of sliding metal and footsteps was the only answer to Sysa's wonderings. She turned her head to see Luna appear at her cell bars, looking perfectly unharmed by their previous encounter in the higher reaches of this place. In human form and draped with the silken threads she had been wearing when Sysa last saw her, the mermaid flashed a triumphant smile through a gap in the bars, her teeth glinting against the light that fell in from the window.

'Well, well, if it isn't the mighty light-bringer,' she said, coiling a tanned leg around one of the bars and resting the ball of her foot on the dusty floor of Sysa's prison cell. She wrapped an arm inside too, the image reminding Sysa of the ribbons of sickness that had snaked their way up the walls of her family home.

'You,' Sysa said, pulling against her chains and spitting the word in Luna's direction. 'You were in on this.'

'Of course I was,' Luna replied with a brittle laugh. 'Did you really think you'd managed to hurt me? That was all down to Lavellan. He tricked you. You silly, silly girl.'

Sysa kept rattling at her chains.

'All of it was about getting you out of the fae lands, so Lavellan's mother could advance on Fyrish while you were away, while that family of yours were vulnerable.' Luna ran the ball of her foot up and down the bar and flicked her tongue out over her lips like a serpent. 'And it worked, didn't it? You went running off after him, just as we all knew you would.'

Sysa licked her lips, realising that Luna's tongue was loosening in response to her own displays of anger. She decided to play along, jarring at the chains again, making a wailing noise that filled the darkness of the cell.

'You didn't know this was all part of a bigger plan, did you?' Luna said, delighting in the chance to stretch out her sense of victory.

'No, I didn't,' Sysa said, looking down at the dusty stone floor of her prison, doing her best to further her own imaginary humiliation while gleaning as much information from Luna as she could.

'Neven sent Lavellan to Fyrish as a baby, under the care of an Unseelie family who were willing to sacrifice themselves for the cause of winter,' Luna said, wrapping a finger around a lock of her hair, where it coiled itself, snake-like. 'Neven knew Rogart was looking for the Trinity. At the same time, the giant was also in Neven's way. So Lavellan was planted in a Seelie court, with Unseelie parents who were happy to die for Neven when Rogart finally came to scorch the village.'

Sysa thought back to the story Krystan had told her about Rogart's *sacrifices*. She shuddered, thinking of the infant Lavellan, pushed away by his own mother, and then forced into darkness as Rogart's charge.

'Lavellan's job was to make sure you were safe, so that you'd get rid of Rogart before he grew powerful enough to challenge the Unseelie. At the same time, Lavellan had to convince Rogart that he was doing everything his master asked of him. And Rogart fell for it. Clever, *mmm*?' Luna's mouth lifted in an icy, callous smile. 'And, of course, Neven knew that both you and Lavellan were part of the Trinity,' the mermaid drawled, apparently unable to stop the words spilling out of her as she luxuriated in her victory. 'She's not the only seer around here.' Luna flicked her head in the direction of Brigid's cell. 'And now she knows who your other teammate is,' she said, turning to blow a kiss at Brodie, 'she's got the three of you right where she wants you.'

'And where's that?' Sysa asked, trying hard to keep as submissive a tone to her question as she could.

'Here, in the Castle of Thunder. Enslaved to her. Didn't you notice she's got you chained up, your powers in limbo, Sysa? The only way to get them back will be to submit to her, to kneel before her, to profess yourselves as her Winter Three. One, two, three.' Luna counted on her fingers and let out a hiss-like laugh that echoed around the dungeon.

From across the stony corridor, Sysa heard Brodie rattle on his own chains, releasing a futile roar.

'And what makes you think we'd do that, at least Brodie and I?' Sysa asked, surveying the mermaid intently. Sysa couldn't quite decipher Luna's role in all this, apart from as a hanger-on. Like Krystan and Lavellan, Luna had been captured by Rogart when he'd stormed their village, and Sysa assumed that, like Krystan at least, she'd been born of the Seelie. Unlike Krystan though, Luna had not turned from the darkness when Sysa had given her the opportunity, even knowing, as she must have by then, that she was not one of this chosen three.

It seemed to Sysa that Luna preferred to stick where she felt least vulnerable. There was the matter of William, of course, and the fact that Elva had, in Luna's eyes, stolen her beau away. Aside from that, though, Luna must have known that not being part of the Trinity put her at a disadvantage, and, to someone like Neven, made her effectively disposable. Luna was evidently clinging onto her place in Neven's court by any method possible.

The mermaid's attributes did not appear to extend to discretion, though, and she answered Sysa's question in a blink.

'Why will you kneel? Now let me see...' Luna said, placing her index finger in a line under her chin and offering an expression of exaggerated consideration. 'You'll kneel because she has your family under a sleeping spell, and because, on top of that, she now also has your old granny's stone. With that, she can choose to heal them, or, once the stone turns to her completely, to kill them. All except William,' Luna said, as an afterthought, as bile rose in Sysa's throat like a searing, soaring flame. 'He's my reward for my part in Lavellan's trickery.' Luna ran the inside of her foot up the bar again as Sysa felt the burning start to explode inside her ribcage. 'So, I suppose, in summary,' the mermaid concluded, drawing out her gloating for as long as possible, 'you'll kneel because you have to. You'll kneel, Sysa, because if you don't, your family will all die, and you'll lose everything you love. Well, just about everything,' she hissed, her eyes prowling the cavernous dark towards the cells that housed Brodie and Brigid. 'You'll kneel, Sysa, because you'll simply have no other choice.'

Luna let her words linger in the air for a moment, echoing from the walls like the drips that fell from the gaps in the stone like teardrops. Then she turned, swivelling on her barefoot heels and slipping down the corridor beyond. Sysa watched through burning eyes as a waft of silk fluttered against the bars of the cells, before sweeping away to follow Luna on her passage.

The welt of fabric mirrored the flame that burned in Sysa's eyes, her heart, her whole body.

As she heard an iron lock slide back into place with a screech of triumph, Sysa opened her mouth into the half-light.

This time, the scream that escaped from her was real.

CHAPTER SIXTEEN

The dungeon was dark and damp and very, very cold, Sysa reflected, hours later, as she wrapped her thoughts around Luna's story for the umpteenth time that evening. She went around and around it, circling back on herself and trying to retrace her ragged steps. All this time, Lavellan had been protecting her, but not for the reason she'd hoped, she thought, lifting her shoulders towards her neck in an attempt to generate some warmth for herself. No, he had been using her, keeping her safe to advance his mother's interests.

And yet, she remembered what he had said on the beach after she'd kissed him.

Somewhere along the line my feelings for you changed.

She sighed into the dark, wondering if Brigid and Brodie were still awake across the corridor. She tilted her head, straining to catch the rise and fall of Brodie's breath. But once again, her fae hearing eluded her and any sound from the others was masked by the splash of drips and the scuttling noise of insects. Sysa shook her head, trying to dislodge a tear that was tracking her cheek like the drops of moisture that fell from her prison's walls.

It had been hard to know what to say after Luna had left, or how to even begin broaching a plan of action. Sysa had forced her anger in on herself, full of shame at falling for Lavellan's tricks. She had felt more than just the distance of bars and iron between her and Brodie as they'd discussed Luna's words with Brigid, the three of them whispering into the half-light. They hadn't come up with anything substantial and the conversation had finally petered out, like the evening light that slipped away into the dark veil of the night.

And now, she thought with a sigh, the two of them were probably both sleeping. With their powers drained by the iron bars – and, in Brigid's case, the loss of her stone – fatigue had hit each of them like a wall. Only Sysa herself appeared to have any remaining strength left, and she'd been concerned by the weakened thread of words that had drifted their way across the dungeon as the three of them had spoken. Even Brodie had seemed to be losing his grip on things.

Or perhaps, Sysa thought with an uncomfortable feeling, he just wanted to lose his grip on her.

She shrugged off the thought, angling her head to nudge at an itch around her jawline. As she moved, she heard the slip of the lock again, making its passage with the tiniest of squeaks. *Luna back to gloat again*, she thought, puffing a miserable exhale into the darkness.

But when she turned, it wasn't Luna's face she saw staring back at her across the bars.

'Ida?' she shrieked, half-shocked, half-delighted to see the servant woman, who was standing behind the bars in all her round and aproned glory. 'What are you doing here?' she quickly followed up, noticing the tray Ida was holding like a shelf beneath her ample chest.

'*Shh!*' Ida whispered back, putting the tray down and lifting her index finger to her mouth, the action prompting Sysa to fall silent as she instinctively yielded to Ida's authority. The older woman looked around slowly before licking her lips, apparently satisfied that her entrance hadn't stirred anything in the dark.

'The others seem to be in a deep sleep,' Sysa whispered, as Ida's eyes darted about like flashing green buttons.

The maid lifted her finger to her lips again, the familiar gesture bringing a slight warmth to Sysa's chest.

'I managed to get past the guards with a believing spell, and the pretence of bringing you a little to sustain you,' Ida said, gesturing to the tray, which held a few scraps of fruit, some unappetising-looking cheese and a wedge of thinly buttered bread. 'Just enough to keep you going for the queen, I said, though I think one of those guards wasn't far from sleeping anyway.' Ida wittered on, apparently oblivious to her own suggestion that their conversation should be brief.

Sysa nodded in a way that she hoped was encouraging, while also imparting the need for a quick despatch of information.

'But how did you even get here? With the sleeping sickness, I mean,' she whispered into the darkness, watching Ida's green eyes flare with a vision of unwelcome memory as she spoke.

'That sickness, it caught your family off guard,' Ida said, pressing her lips together with a nervous look at the doorway. 'But not me, I held out against it. I was still half-conscious when that Neven one came to survey what she had done in the castle,' the servant said with a note of pride.

Something in Sysa's heart lifted at Ida's small victory against the Unseelie. It was hardly a surprise to her that this small powerhouse of a woman had found a way to be immune to Neven's wicked charm.

'And so, she took you? Back here, to work at this castle?' Sysa asked, making a quick assessment of the situation.

'Oh yes, and I had no choice in it,' Ida replied with a grimace. 'She knew I had the strength in me, and she wanted me working here, for her. But you know where my loyalties lie, Sysa,' Ida said, casting another glance at the entrance, before moving her mouth closer to the bars that lay between them. 'I may cook and clean for Neven, but she'll never have my spirit. My loyalties are with you, and your family – they've been good to me. And to think of your poor mother, lying there, her hair spread out across that table. For the love of fae, I said to myself as they pulled me out of there...' Ida's words tailed off, and she shifted her gaze down to the floor. 'Anyway.' She sighed and pushed one of her hands into a pocket under the waistband of her apron. 'I have information for you.' As Ida spoke, she fished out a key that shone in the half-light like the edge of a sharpened knife.

'Where did you get that?' Sysa asked, as Ida fumbled with the cell's lock, the tremble of her small hands betraying her nervousness.

'I got it from the guards, of course. With my believing spell.' Ida's eyes twinkled at her own ingenuity as the door of the cell creaked open. 'Neven's going to have a ceremony tomorrow night, a coronation where she plans to anoint you, Brodie and Lavellan as her Winter Three, so that she can keep this place in her icy fist forever.' Ida's words rang with a growing sense of urgency.

'I know about the Winter Three. Luna was here. The mermaid,' Sysa followed up in explanation, and Ida's eyes bloomed wide again.

'But I didn't know about the coronation. Thank you, Ida.' Sysa's eyes filled with tears as her maid stroked at the dark welts above her wrists.

'So, you know that she plans to enslave you, to threaten to kill your family unless you bow down to her?' Ida asked, turning Sysa's wrists this way and that to get a better look at her shackles.

'Yes. I know that. But how on earth am I supposed to get out of here to do anything about it?' Sysa tilted her head in the direction of her chains.

'That's where I come in,' Ida said, fishing about in her apron pocket again, before producing a bunch of herbs and plants, bell-shaped pink petals that fell from her palms in bursts of fragrant colour. 'All that time spent in and out of kitchens, I know a thing or two about reducing the power of iron, you know. And I've spoken with that bird of his,' Ida continued, flicking her head in Brodie's general direction.

'You mean Arno?' Sysa asked, her voice full of wonder at the older woman's nerve.

'Yes, I've sent him to gather help from your friends at Selkie Island. But you all need to help yourselves too,' Ida said in her usual authoritative tone.

'Thank you so much, Ida,' Sysa whispered, as the servant began rubbing at the iron chains with her flowery concoction, streaks of colour emerging in the spaces between her fingers.

'There we go. That should be just enough to start

weakening the iron's hold.' Ida nodded to herself and shoved the remnants of the magical bouquet back into her apron, leaving tendrils of green hanging over the fabric in petalled loops.

'I must go now, before the spell I set on the guards lifts,' she said after a pause, during which she had been chewing on her top lip nervously. 'Once that iron's power starts to loosen, you must do what you can to get out of here. And do it quickly, mind,' Ida suggested with a cautionary air.

'I will, and as soon as I get the three of us out of here, I'll come for you, I promise.' Sysa looked up at the servant through strands of hair that fell in damp streaks against her forehead.

Ida leaned forward, lifting the hair from Sysa's face in a long sweep before pulling in a sharp breath and turning quickly on her heel. When she reached the cell door, she swivelled, looking back at Sysa before stepping over the threshold. Then she bent down to remove the food items from the tray, carefully placing each morsel on the floor.

'In case you need them when you get out of there,' she said, her voice an odd squeak as she gestured towards the chains that bound Sysa to the walls of the Castle of Thunder.

Sysa mouthed the words 'thank you', but Ida was already leaving, her chin lifted high as she scurried her way along the stone.

As she departed, Sysa heard two circling clicks, the sound of Ida unlocking the doors to Brigid and Brodie's cells, which were left hanging ajar behind her.

A moment later, from outside, came the sound of raised voices, some sort of struggle, and then the clamour of receding footsteps quickly fading towards the shadow of the dark.

★

It was a waiting game, Sysa thought as she eyed her iron chains, looking for any sign of a developing weakness. The iron stared back, as if it too were waiting, coldly peeking through flecks of desiccated leaf and smudges of grass-green herbs. Sysa wondered if there would be a fracture, some sort of splinter that would rip through the chains quite suddenly, tearing her way to freedom.

In the end, the moment came as softly as a whisper, creeping up to her and filling her senses like a jug.

Her sight returned first, as she began to make out every mote that lingered in the air despite the darkness. Next came her hearing, her ears suddenly alert and pricked to every sigh of Brodie and Brigid's breath. Across the bars, she heard their hearts beating in their chests, and smelled their scents, the soft, salty tang of Brodie's skin wafting across the corridor. From somewhere far away, though, she could also hear dissenting voices, and a smell that curled against her nose like the food that was rotting in the corner – a smell she recognised as fear.

She squeezed her eyes shut, willing herself to unfurl her powers more quickly. She was worried about Ida, about what had happened to her after she had left this awful cell. She heard a noise like heels scraping along stone, a dragging sort of sound that made her shudder from the very centre of herself. She had to get out of these shackles, and she had to do it now.

As if in response to her thoughts, something burned

along her arms, the sensation of fire and lightning. It seemed to emanate from her ribcage, scorching its way up through her chest and across her limbs. As it reached her fingertips, the iron of her chains shifted, turning to something softer, something between a solid and a liquid.

In the next instant, the chains fell away from her, pooling on the floor in a spiral of grey and silken folds.

Sysa looked at her now-free hands, turning them in half-circles, marvelling as the dark welts around her wrists faded away into blush-pink echoes. She stood up, feeling her powers surge through her, pushing their way along the lengths of her body, pulsing through every pathway from the very marrow of her bones. She felt herself unfurl as she lifted her head towards the cell's ceiling, feeling as though the sun shone down on her in the darkness.

A noise escaped from her, a sound of triumph and awakening.

In the next breath, she was across the cell, next to the bars that held Brodie and Brigid, ready to tear the walls of the Castle of Thunder down.

The voice that responded in the dim was not Brodie's, or Brigid's, who both lay sleeping in the darkness. The voice that came to her carried its way along the corridor like ribbons, seeking out Sysa just as Ida's key had sought its lock. Sysa turned to the voice to hear her name, held in the air like a precious gemstone.

'Sysa.' Lavellan's eyes said a hundred words and sang a hundred songs to her.

They stood there looking at each other in the darkness, each one bound to the other like the chains Sysa had only just escaped.

'Why didn't you tell me that Neven was your mother, that this was what you planned?' Sysa said after a long moment, which had somehow conveyed everything and nothing about the impossibility of their situation.

'I did try, if you remember, before events somewhat overtook us,' Lavellan said, jerking his chin towards Brodie's cell and the hunched form that lay sleeping in the dim.

'So, all of it, everything, was about keeping me safe so that your mother could enslave us?' Sysa knew the answer to the question and also knew her voice was coated with a sheen of desperation. She wanted to hear him confirm it or deny it. She didn't know which she wanted.

Or *who* she wanted, she thought with a sinking feeling, as Lavellan stared back at her, his blue eyes boring into her like an ice-cold missile that somehow also burned with heat.

'Yes, it was all about keeping you safe. Yes, Sysa. I won't lie to you again,' he said with a pained expression that made her want to close the distance between them and crush her hands around his face, to protect him, or to hurt him.

'As I told you, though, somewhere along the line my feelings changed, or perhaps, I suppose, developed into exactly what they were always meant to be. You know there's no point in fighting her, Sysa, and what are you even going to do if you get away, the two of you, without me?' Lavellan pleaded. 'Like it or not, we need each other.'

Sysa sighed into the darkness and tipped her face towards the floor.

'So, you want me to just give up? To yield my powers to her? To surrender my family's kingdom?' she finally asked, lifting her eyes and making two hurried steps towards him.

'And what will she do to my people, the Seelie folk, will she just let them live out their lives in peace, do you think?' she asked. 'Something tells me your mother isn't the welcoming kind.'

'My mother isn't the maternal kind either,' Lavellan said, reaching out to take Sysa's wrist with a grip that held just enough pressure to act as a warning. 'You're hurt,' he said, looking down at the lingering welts on her skin as he turned her wrist towards him.

'That's nothing. They'll be gone in a minute. Anyway, what do you care?' She laughed bitterly. 'You let this happen, and then you left me here.' Sysa turned away, folding her arms across the stinging feeling of betrayal that surged across her chest.

'Left you here? You think I wanted to leave you here?' Lavellan eventually answered, his voice sounding strained, as if something was obstructing it. 'I came as quickly as I could.' His words floated towards her, thick with apology and regret.

'And what have you been doing all this time, *mmm*? Catching up with Mummy dearest in the parlour?' Sysa's question snagged with resentment.

In a second, Lavellan was in front of her again, taking both her hands towards him in the dark.

She tried to pull away, but as she did, she noticed his wrists, each pale round exposed under the hemline of his jacket. She lifted one of his arms towards her, seeing the dark lines that streaked his milky skin. He had been held prisoner, too, and the mere presence of his wounds told Sysa that his mother had not been lenient towards her offspring. Sysa knew that, like her scars, they would be in the process of fading. The fact that they were still so severe made her wonder what they had looked like when they were new.

'As I said, Mother's not maternal,' Lavellan finally repeated, after Sysa's assessment of his wrists was complete, and she looked up into his face, eyes pooled wide in understanding.

'How did you get away?' she asked, and he shrugged, pulling his hands back to his sides.

'That doesn't matter right now. The point is, I'm here, and I knew you would be on your way out of here. I'm here to tell you not to do it, Sysa, there's no point, and for everyone's sake, you need to do what my mother wants.' Lavellan's tone carried the sense that he knew his words would make no difference to Sysa's plans.

'Are you crazy? You think I'm just going to let her decide the fate of Fyrish? Of my people?' Sysa flew back at him.

Lavellan's returning sigh indicated this was just the kind of reaction he'd expected, and he rubbed at the skin between his eyebrows, looking tired.

'No, I didn't expect you'd let that happen without putting up a fight,' he said eventually, his eyes drifting over her head towards the back of the dungeon. 'But you also need to think about your chances in all of this, Sysa. She has your family. What's she going to do to them if you don't kneel tomorrow night?'

'She could be bluffing,' Sysa said, with a little more confidence than she was feeling.

Lavellan raised a dark eyebrow. 'My mother doesn't play games, Sysa. You're not dealing with Rogart any more.'

'I need to help Ida,' Sysa suddenly rushed out, her

thoughts sweeping back to the scuffle she had heard outside her prison. Lavellan's words had sent a chill through her, and she remembered that sound of raised voices, of heels scraping against stone.

'There's something I need to tell you… about your maid,' Lavellan said, glancing over his shoulder and pursing his lips in a way that made Sysa feel even more nervous.

She held a hand up in front of him. 'We don't have time for this, Lavellan. I need to get back to my family… to Ida.'

Something in his tone had made Sysa want to shut out any more of the words he planned to say. She paced around in small circles, trying to come up with a plan that involved getting them all out of there, making whatever he had been preparing to tell her not true, not possible.

'You have to give this up, Sysa, there's nothing you can do now.' Lavellan's voice drifted towards her, but when she looked up at him, his eyes were cast down at the cold stone floor. 'I'm here to convince you not to go any further down this path. The guards will be here soon.' Lavellan glanced over his shoulder again.

'And if I go down this path, as you put it, are you coming with me?' Sysa asked, wrapping her arms around herself again, protecting her heart from an answer she already understood.

'She's my mother,' Lavellan said, expelling a long breath that punctured the air around them. 'There's no way for me to get away from her. She'll hunt us down, and in the meantime, she'll have your family under her cursed sleeping spell. Now that she has the stone, it won't take long for her to gain enough power to kill them all. And she'll do it to punish us if we challenge her. I can't go along that path with you, knowing where it will lead and how much it will hurt you and those you love. In the end, it will all be pointless anyway. So just stay, kneel, give in to her, Sysa. I'm begging you.' He took her hand and stared down at it.

When he lifted his eyes, they were rimmed with circles of moisture.

'Please.'

He sighed, his breath dissolving in a wretched bloom into the air.

When she didn't answer, he took a step closer to her, stooping to come level with her eyeline. He placed his hands around her cheeks, so that his face was only inches from her own.

'It won't be as bad as you think. I'll protect you, and your family, and even *him* from the worst of it.' He darted his eyes in Brodie's direction and then back at her. 'I can temper the worst of her excesses. The Seelie folk won't have to suffer.' There was a growing sense of desperation in his words. 'Besides all of that,' he said with an awkward smile, 'it seems I find it very hard to live without you. All of a sudden, I can't bear the thought that you could be somewhere I am not.' He shook his head, closing his eyes briefly as if he couldn't quite believe what he was about to say. 'I know I'm not the only one with these feelings for you, but I need to tell you, just in case you hadn't realised it.' Lavellan breathed in a gulp of air, and the words that followed escaped him like a release valve. 'I love you, Sysa, and that's never going to change.'

'Then you have to let me go,' Sysa said after a long pause, during which she had lifted a hand up to her cheek so that it covered the hand Lavellan had placed there.

He searched her eyes for a moment, before dropping his hands, his palms slippery from the moisture on her face.

'I suppose I do,' he said, turning away so that Sysa couldn't see the pain he bored into the wall in front of him as he placed a hand against it, steadying himself. 'I'll let you go, I'll create a diversion while you get past the guards and get Brigid and Brodie out of here,' he began, speaking into the wall, his voice now clipped with an authoritative tone. 'But you don't have long, so I suggest you go now,' he said, holding the wall as if it were bearing the weight of his emotions.

'Thank you.' Sysa placed a hand on his back before letting the tips of her fingers drift like an echo down his spine.

She felt his body stiffen then, as if for a moment the world had been suspended around them. He closed his eyes and dropped his head towards the floor, his palm lifting from the wall like a steeple, the pads of his fingertips resting lightly on the stone.

'Promise me something,' he said, after a moment in which he had remained supported by the wall, his breath curling in ragged loops around them.

'Anything,' Sysa whispered, feeling his pain as if it were her own pain, understanding that in some unseen way, it was.

'Promise me that whatever happens, you'll find a way to keep me in your life always, however this turns out, and whoever you choose to love,' he said, turning towards her again, his eyes so huge and dark that Sysa felt he could almost swallow her into the blue depths of him.

'You're already in my life,' she answered, leaning

towards him. 'You always will be, and neither of us have any choice about that, it seems.'

'Then that will have to do,' he said, something in his eyes receding, like a blue sea falling away into himself.

He closed the gap between them and took her face in his hands for a second time.

'May I kiss you goodbye?' he asked, as Sysa's face tilted up towards him, the returning nod of her head echoing the tears that ran down her cheeks and pooled into his palms.

When he finally pressed his mouth on hers, Sysa felt something flood into her body, a cascading, surging thing that fell into her and through her, reaching out to fill every space in her like a watery blue lightning. When he pulled away, she stared at him with a questioning look that he returned with a small, indecipherable nod.

As he turned to walk away, he paused for a moment, his shoulders rising and falling once, as if he were righting himself before he stepped forward. He looked back only when he had reached the exit.

'Now go,' he said, opening the door, leaving it hanging so that he looked exposed, for a moment only half of himself.

Sysa dipped her head as he swept around the corner, surging into the darkness like the blue flood that trickled through her bones.

★

'Wake up, Brodie, we have to go,' Sysa hissed, leaning over to tug at the fabric of Brodie's jacket.

When he didn't answer, she crouched down, making the

skirt of her gown balloon with air around her. She placed a hand on his shoulder, surveying him with a concerned expression as she absorbed the familiar shape of him, his dark mop of hair, his long eyelashes, the pink bloom of the lips she had kissed so many times. She shivered, thinking of how she had betrayed him by kissing Lavellan again, a kiss that had felt so right, so true, so *necessary*. But here in front of her was Brodie, the man she loved, the man who might, if she had not totally ruined things, still love her with a love as wide and open as any sky. She didn't know who she was betraying, or how she felt any more. She only knew that the sounds of violence coming from outside the dungeon meant that Lavellan was fighting for them, and she didn't have much time to free them from this place.

She looked down at her hands, seeing the small veins that tracked her palm, strangely bluer and brighter than they had ever been before. And in that moment, she knew that when she'd kissed Lavellan again, something had been both given and received. The kiss *had* been necessary, and whatever had been given to her was going to help them escape from here.

She lifted her arms, clasping her hands together.

When she let them fall downwards, they slipped through the iron of Brodie's shackles, leaving the shards to fall to the floor like broken glass.

Brodie slumped away, mumbling to himself as he roused into a groggy awareness of his surroundings.

'Brodie, get up,' Sysa ordered, pulling him by the shoulder, willing him to move.

'*Mmm*?' he said, looking for all the world like he had just woken from the sleep of the dead, his eyes half-open, his dark lashes fluttering like the wings of a butterfly.

Sysa let out a long breath, realising she would need to do more to wake him. She leaned down, grasping his face in her hands the way Lavellan had held her own face just a few moments before. Then she kissed him, feeling the surge pass through her lips like sweet lightning, making his eyes bloom wide as, after a moment, he pulled away from her.

'What's going on?' he said, apparently now fully returned to himself.

'We're getting out of here, that's what,' Sysa replied, her eyes flashing with urgency as she pulled him to his feet.

'What happened?' Brodie said, looking around as Sysa dragged him into Brigid's cell, where she was already preparing to minister a similar treatment to her grandmother.

'No time to explain now,' Sysa said, glancing up at him from her crouched position next to Brigid as she swept her hands through the old woman's chains.

Without hesitating, she followed up with a kiss on Brigid's cheek, and Brigid woke up, her eyes shining like emeralds in the darkness.

'We need to go,' Sysa said, to which Brigid just nodded back, apparently unruffled by the immediacy in Sysa's voice, and being woken from her slumber. 'Lavellan's out there, holding back the guards for us.' Sysa was aware of Brodie stiffening beside her as she said Lavellan's name, as if the word conveyed a bad smell or a bitter taste, something rancid. She carried on, doing her best to avoid making any contact with Brodie's stare. 'We have to go – now,' she said, moving as she spoke, gesturing to encourage the others to follow. 'Come on!' She swept towards the exit, climbing the two steps to the door Lavellan had left ajar.

As they emerged out into the corridor, the noise of a scuffle drifted in from the right, prompting Sysa to turn her head in its direction. Where the corridor ended, Sysa could see into an open round, where she could make out slices of movement, the swipe of a cleaving arm, the flash of a sky-blue light. In between flashes, Lavellan – or some part of him – would appear, his body moving fluidly, striking, smiting, charging. His movements were accompanied by the percussive rhythm of groans, yelps and the thudding noise the guards made when they met with the stone floor below.

Sysa watched him move, half-frozen in the corridor's darkness. She was so entranced that, for a moment, she didn't see the figure that appeared between the flashes and the blows. And then, as Lavellan shifted to one side, she saw it, a body hanging on the wall like a piece of laundry, nailed by an icicle. Sysa gasped, her mouth opening in a silent scream as she absorbed the sight of her maidservant Ida, her head hanging limp, a nail of ice driven deep inside her chest.

CHAPTER SEVENTEEN

'Ida!' Sysa breathed, instinctively taking two steps along the corridor.

'Sysa, don't. It's too late,' Brodie whispered, grabbing her shoulder and pulling her towards him. 'She's gone. We have to leave now, or we'll lose our chance to get out of here.'

Sysa looked up at him, her eyes burning with guilt and a green-eyed rage that lit the murky walls.

'We can't just leave her there like that,' she cried, twisting her arm away from him, feeling her insides churn with an awful sense of wrenching. She thought back to what Lavellan had tried to tell her in the cell, the words she had forced him not to say. Somewhere inside herself she'd understood, though – that somehow Ida's spell had failed and the guards had figured out what she'd been up to. That the maid had been punished for it, and Lavellan had been too late to save her. Sysa thought of the way Lavellan had looked at her then, the way his eyes had misted over with something she recognised as shame. She turned to take another look at Ida's drooping body, the same Ida who had brushed her hair and cajoled her into silken dresses. To see her bowed like that, dripping with the blood that fell from her chest, the same Ida who had so recently been alive and strong and vital… it felt like someone had plunged an icicle into Sysa's chest too. She had a vision of Grey, dripping his blood onto Brodie as the unicorn. But where Grey's blood had been a life-force, Ida's was just a puddle, pooling on the floor, dispersing futility across the stone.

'Brodie's right, we have to go, Sysa, there's no time for this.' Brigid's voice punctured Sysa's thoughts, and the older woman placed her hand on top of Sysa's – the hand Sysa had laid flat to the wall, clinging on for support in the way Lavellan had a few moments earlier. Her hand was also there as an anchor, rooting her to the spot, keeping her close to Ida until Brigid gently prised her fingers from the wall. 'We have to go,' Brigid repeated, her look conveying the knowledge that without the strength of her powers and the healing stone, fleeing was, for now, their only option.

'I know,' Sysa breathed, glancing back as they careered along the corridor, leaving Lavellan to play out his part behind them, leaving Ida hanging pendulous in that cacophony of strife.

They tore along the corridor, zig-zagging this way and that, bouncing off walls as they rounded unexpected corners. Eventually, they came to some steps, lit by a cool blue flame that hung suspended, like a candle in mid-air. Vaulting the steps, Sysa flung open a door onto the same oval-shaped reception hall she had encountered on her previous visit. Across the hall lay the corridor through which she had entered. In the space between was the staircase, rising up like a steeple and converging towards the upper floors as if to remind her of her earlier mistake.

'This way, the main door is over there,' Sysa said, gesturing to the others and jutting her chin across the oval.

'If we just get to that corridor over there we're out,' she whispered, starting her passage across the flagstones, Brigid and Brodie following behind.

As she neared the entrance to the corridor that would provide their exit, an ice-cold voice curled its way down the stairs like a snake of winter.

'Going somewhere, light-bringer?' said the voice with a chilly timbre.

Sysa looked up to see Neven staring down at her from the staircase, one arm wrapped around the balustrade, with Luna clinging onto the opposite handrail, the air around the pair spun with iced motes that swirled in the freezing dim.

Sysa opened her mouth to speak but felt as frozen as the air that surrounded them. She whipped her head round to Brigid and Brodie, who seemed as immobilised as she was by the sudden frigid air.

'We're all leaving, yes,' she said finally, lifting her chin a notch, 'and there's nothing you can do to stop us.'

'Oh, there isn't, is there?' Neven replied, baring her white teeth in what might have been a grin, or a grimace – at first Sysa couldn't tell. The cackle that emanated from Neven's throat soon confirmed that it was meant to be the former, though, and Sysa planted her feet a little wider, bracing herself for whatever that cackle heralded.

The icicle that flew from Neven's hands didn't follow the path that Sysa expected.

Instead, it darted towards Luna, breaching her skin and plunging deep into her heart.

For a moment, the mermaid stood open-mouthed, her lips curving to an 'o' that remained a silent scream of shock and horror. In the next breath, she cupped her hands around the icicle before her eyes glazed over, their lustre fading like the turn of an autumn leaf. Sysa watched, frozen, as threads of blood dripped from Luna's chest, weaving a path down her legs like red veins tracking her flesh on the outside. Then the mermaid slumped, collapsing on one knee to the steps beneath her, her hands still wrapped around the ice. For a second, her face cleared of all expression, and she took one last deep breath in, as if inhaling everything she could of life. And then she fell, plunging forward down the steps in an awful contortion of tumbling before landing on the stone floor of the hallway, her eyes fixed in a frozen stare towards the roof.

'No,' Sysa gasped, running towards the mermaid and tugging uselessly at the ice which speared her.

'What have you done?' she said, lifting her eyes up to Neven, a sense of rage and futility leaking out from every pore across her skin. Brodie and Brigid gathered around too, completing a triangle of disbelief around the mermaid.

The tinkle of harsh laughter floated down the stairs towards them.

'Isn't it obvious what I've done, Sysa? I've killed her. That's what happens when you choose to challenge me. People die. Continue to defy me, and your family will be next.'

Sysa dropped her head, the tips of her hair grazing Luna's face as she crouched above her. She could smell the mermaid's salty skin, the tang of her blood, a mixture of metal and sea-spray that curled into the air.

When she lifted her face again, she met Neven's blue eyes with a glare as thunderous as the castle they stood in.

'Stay and kneel, tomorrow night, at the little party I've arranged for us,' Neven said, the ice that still fringed her fingers retracting into her painted blue fingernails. 'If you don't, I'll hunt you down, and I'll kill your family as punishment. For now, I've been lenient with just a little sleeping spell. Kneel for me, and I'll lift it, and they can live out their lives in peace – under my rule, of course.' The Unseelie queen spun her fingers in the air, a gesture that reminded Sysa of Lavellan. She winced at the thought, the idea he could be born of someone who wreaked violence and death with so little regard. No, Lavellan wasn't like Neven, Sysa told herself, scrambling through memories of the pain she'd witnessed Lavellan suffer after killing her grandfather. She blinked hard, trying to fend off the wave of grief and horror that threatened to hit her, a wave that had been rushing towards her since she'd seen Ida nailed to the castle's wall.

And beyond that, there was another wave that reared up in the far distance of her consciousness. It was the next wave of grief – the one that would break on her if she lost her parents, Elva, William too. Her thoughts flickered back to the months following Grey's death, months that had seen her wandering the halls of Steel Castle, stepping in and out of her grief like the arches and doorways she passed through. At times, her grief had felt so deep it was like being trapped in a house of endless walls. There had been no windows or doors in that house, not even a chink of light that fell through a slit or opening. That house of grief had been stifling, smothering. Sysa didn't know if she could bear to live in that house again.

She opened her mouth to speak, words of submission

forming on her tongue like the ashes of a fire that was going out in her. Neven raised her eyebrows. 'Well?' she said. 'Do you plan to kneel or not?'

'I...' The rest of Sysa's words were halted by a commotion coming from outside the castle doors, the sound of wings beating and swooping around the walls in an avalanche of challenge.

'Guards?' Neven said, her expression faltering for just a moment. 'What is that racket?'

'Arno.' Sysa heard Brodie whisper behind her. 'He's come for us.'

If Sysa needed a sign, it had come to her in a burst of feathers, beaks and wings.

'Let's go,' she said, scrambling with the others towards the corridor and the doors that lay beyond, doors that had been flung open as a flurry of guards had attempted to intercept whatever was out there. In the gaping space, though, Sysa could see exactly what had come for them, as huge dark wings criss-crossed the open doors. Arno was there, with some of the other eagles, the same ones, Sysa supposed, who had once helped them escape from Rogart. They had shifted to their larger incarnations, plunging and diving around the castle entrance, picking off guards with their huge claws and sending them flying in great sweeps towards the trees.

'Arno!' Brodie called out as he, Sysa and Brigid made a desperate clamour towards the creatures. In the background, Neven was screeching and shouting in a high-pitched voice that cleaved the icy air. From her hands, she threw icy darts in all directions, hopeful of securing her targets without fatally maiming them. Sysa allowed herself a tiny smile as she ran: Neven couldn't afford to kill them. Without the healing stone turned to her completely, she needed Brigid, and without Brodie and Sysa, the possibility of her precious Winter Three was gone.

Sysa hurtled to the exit, pushing Brodie and Brigid in front of her. Just as she did so, she felt a rushing and then a halting sensation, and looked down to see one of her arms pinioned to the wall by an icicle secured to the fabric of her cloak. Behind her, she heard Neven's triumphant laugh as Brodie and Brigid turned, scrambling back to help her.

'No!' she called, straining with the effort to free herself. 'Go, don't wait for me.'

The look in Brodie's eyes told her he had no intention of following this particular command.

Outside, the birds' wings lifted and fell in a feathered chorus of growing urgency. Behind her, Sysa could hear the click of Neven's advancing footsteps, and felt the cold jab of the shards of ice the Unseelie queen was discharging to the air. Somewhere in the distance, Sysa knew that Lavellan was still fighting for them, holding back guards that were advancing towards the hallway. Just as Brodie and Brigid reached her, she made a final, huge tug at the icicle, ripping it from the wall with a roar that came from deep inside her chest.

In a beat of an eagle's wing, they were out, over the threshold of the door and careering towards Arno and his two companions. Sysa threw herself onto Arno's back, feeling the familiar stiffness of his feathers as she pushed her fingers into the gaps between the quills. She glanced towards Brigid and Brodie who were clamouring onto their own birds with a similar urgency. As the eagles lifted,

Neven's cries came from beneath them, shattering shrieks that mirrored the ice-darts she flung into the sky.

The eagles swung this way and that, trying to evade the darts that flew towards them. Sysa felt the wind rush up into her face, as Arno plummeted towards the ground and then rose again, crying out warning notes to the eagles that followed at his rear.

'She's going to hit the birds,' Brigid called, her words laced with alarm, and the threatening wind that carried them. Out on the coast, Sysa could see the sea rise, and briefly thought back to Lavellan's words about the storms that raged whenever a mermaid died. She realised now that on the night they'd left Fyrish, the sea hadn't been angry with her, but with Lavellan – with the trick he had played on her. She remembered the way she had bumped into him on the hillock that night and felt an echo of the lightning that had run down her spine as a result.

Her memories were pierced by an ice dart that plunged the air at her side, ominously close to Arno's feathers. The eagle tilted, trying to evade it, and Sysa clung on, knowing there could only be moments before a bird was felled. She squeezed her eyes shut, trying to connect with some sort of magic that might restrain the path of Neven's anger.

When she opened them again it was as if the sky had answered, and she lifted her head to see starry motes drifting down and tumbling onto Arno's wings like the rain of falling stars.

'Sysa, look, it's Star-Steed,' Brodie called out from behind, his head lifted to the scene above them. Up among the clouds was Sysa's star-steed, pounding gracefully through the sky in the space above their heads. As they watched, the creature fell away, dispersing into starry lines that fell around them like ribbons from a maypole. Sysa's eyes widened when she realised what was happening – her steed was multiplying, changing into six new horses that fell towards them like the spawn of stars and sky. As she watched, each starry line halted to a full stop, which then bloomed into a whole new creature. Sysa turned her head as buds of light traced hooves and wings and swept manes into the air. The sky sparkled and shone as the new horses were born, each taking up a space around the flying eagles like armour. Sysa smiled to herself, dipping her head with a new sense of determination. They had their way out – the horses would protect them against the darts. Arno levelled a beady eye back at her and Sysa nodded, digging her fingers a little deeper into his feathers in understanding. Behind her, she felt that same sense of understanding from Brodie and Brigid. They were going to escape, flying away from the Castle of Thunder with their own personal shield of stars.

On the ground below, it was evident that Neven had also reached the same conclusion. She spat wayward darts from her fingers, shrieking as they fell away from the horses like gentle rain. As Sysa looked down for a final time, she saw Lavellan burst out of the castle doors, gaping up into the air as his blue gaze sought her. When he finally found her in the sky, Sysa thought she saw a small smile on his face, and she smiled back, her eyes blooming with reflected stars.

Tearing her attention away, she turned again, and called out to the horse leading her starry cavalry.

'To Selkie Island!' she commanded, her voice carried by the winds that chased the starlight through the sky.

CHAPTER EIGHTEEN

Arno drifted down, planting long claws on the shingled shore of Selkie Island. Sysa breathed in, enjoying the salt-stung air that fell around her head. Behind her, Brigid and Brodie were disembarking, gratefully clapping their eagles' wings and ruffling feathers. Nearby, Star-Steed was shifting back into himself, the other versions of him reforming into one like a pack of cards folding inwards in starry lines. Once the transformation was complete, the steed shook out his mane, sending silvered specks flying into the air around him. Finally, he settled himself on the shoreline, thrumming his hooves and mingling stardust with grains of sand.

'Thank goodness that's over,' Sysa said into Arno's face as she nuzzled him in appreciation. Their journey towards the island had been turbulent, and they had spent most of it pressed against sharp winds and howling rain. As they'd passed above the sea, it had spat out with the foaming, frothing fury of a cauldron. The world seemed to be laced with a knife-cold sharpness, and Sysa pulled at her cloak, watching her breath plume in the air in front of her like a cloud.

'Are you both all right?' she asked, making the few steps to meet Brodie and Brigid on the shoreline. Brodie opened his mouth to answer, and then grinned, lifting his eyes level with something above Sysa's head. When Sysa turned, she saw Frode and Krystan coming down from the ruined castle that sat atop the island, Roman, Dursten and some of the other seal-folk following behind them. In the distance, Modan stood, still in the horse form he had evidently maintained since their battle with Rogart. Sysa grinned too, rushing to meet her old friends with outstretched arms, her cloak flapping in the wind.

'But how… you're all okay? You weren't affected by the sleeping sickness?' Sysa said after a few moments in which they had made their renewed acquaintance.

'No,' Frode answered, slapping Brodie on the shoulder. 'It still seems that Selkie Island isn't touched by these awful, awful things. You'll remember Rogart's darkness didn't spread here?'

Sysa nodded, remembering that this seal-place didn't belong to anyone.

'Well, it seems this magic of Neven's doesn't penetrate us either.' Frode looked at her with dark eyes that seemed as deep as whatever barrier protected Selkie Island from the world.

'But you've heard… about what's been happening… about what happened to my parents?' Sysa felt the events of the last few days falling out of her in a tangle.

'Yes, Arno told us,' Krystan said, flicking a look towards the assembled eagles on the sand.

'And I see you've brought new friends again?' Frode's voice lifted as his eyes drifted over the starry horse and then across towards Brigid.

'Yes, how rude of me, let me introduce you to my

grandmother, Brigid.' Sysa wrapped her arm around the older woman, who smiled and stuck out a hand.

'I see the resemblance,' Frode said, after a brief pause in which his raised eyebrows suggested he had adjusted his understanding of the composition of Sysa's family. 'It's a pleasure to meet you, Brigid,' he continued, dropping his lips to the back of Brigid's hand.

'And for me too,' Krystan said, dipping into an awkward curtsey, apparently unsure of the latest protocol on meeting yet another member of Steel royalty.

'Please,' Brigid implored, making an upward gesture with her hands, her palms lifted skywards.

'Come on,' Sysa instructed. 'We have a lot to catch up on. Let's go to the castle and I'll explain everything, okay?'

★

'We were expecting you, of course, after your maid sent word with Arno,' Frode said later, making Sysa wince at the memory of Ida. 'If you hadn't made it here to us, we were going to come up with a plan to get you out of there. But from what you've told us, I'm rather glad it didn't come to that,' he murmured, his eyes flickering at Sysa's reaction to Ida's name.

'So, the Young Trinity, *hmm*?' he continued, apparently trying to divert the conversation elsewhere. He nudged Brodie with his shoulder and followed up with a ruffle of the dark mop that crowned his nephew's head.

'It looks that way,' Brodie said, shrugging off his uncle's playful gesture.

'Who'd have thought it when you were running around

here as a youngling?' Frode laughed, his eyes glazing over in remembrance of Brodie's childhood. 'And Lavellan, too,' he mused, his expression shifting as he rubbed at his skin, his middle finger tracing a line of contemplation across his brow. 'So, your parents and Elva, they're still at Steel Castle?' he asked Sysa eventually.

'We're not sure. After Neven took the stone, the next thing the three of us remember is waking up in the Castle of Thunder,' Sysa explained. 'It's possible she took my family back there too, imprisoned them in another room, perhaps. I honestly don't know,' she said, looking around as if the walls of the ruin could invoke some sort of memory. She thought back to the time she had spent here before, sitting around in a circle, making plans to retrieve Elva. The space where her parents had sat now lay empty, its barrenness goading her to come up with a way out of this awful mess.

'So, we need to find a way to get the stone back, heal your family and overcome Neven,' Frode said, puncturing Sysa's thoughts with his own assessment of the situation.

'If only it were that easy,' Brigid interrupted. 'Neven knows we will be trying to do those things, and she also has Lavellan, meaning the power of the Young Trinity is scattered once again. The longer Neven has the stone, the more chance she also has of turning it. I can only assume she hopes to do that by tomorrow night, in time for this coronation. If we don't defeat her by then, I fear we'll have a choice between losing everything and asking Sysa and Brodie to kneel for her.'

Brigid flicked an apologetic look at Sysa. She didn't have to explain what she meant by *losing everything*. Losing everything was right in front of them, in the empty space that stared back across the sand.

'Well, we won't let either of those things happen,' Krystan said, grabbing Sysa's hand and squeezing it. 'We'll think of something.' The faerie offered Sysa an encouraging look.

'I just don't know what that something is,' Sysa sighed, lifting herself up off the shingle. Above her head, Arno and the other eagles were climbing skywards, regaining their normal size as they soared into the swathe of frigid blue. 'Where are they going?' she asked the group in general, her hand lifted to her forehead.

'I'm not sure,' Brodie answered, following the direction of her eyes in a line across the sky. 'They'll be back soon, no doubt,' he said, brushing flecks of sand from his trousers. 'Perhaps we should take a walk; might help us come up with something,' he suggested, the look on his face giving Sysa the impression he wanted to talk about more than just their plans.

'That might be a good idea,' she said, instinctively pulling her cloak a little tighter, as if that might offer some sort of shield from the looming conversation. 'Brigid, do you mind if we…?' Sysa's voice trailed off, and she made a curling gesture with her hand across the air.

'Not at all. Sounds like a good idea. I'll stay here with the others and see what we can come up with,' Brigid said, returning her attention to Frode and Krystan.

Sysa gestured in the direction of the rocks and Brodie followed her. She felt his footsteps behind her, silenced by the sand yet thumping in her head like a beating heart. When they had reached a safe distance from the group, she turned and looked into his eyes, which were bright with a stinging betrayal.

He had obviously waited long enough for an explanation about her and Lavellan.

'Brodie, I...' she stammered, looking into the shingle, her shoe scratching a line of guilt across the sand.

'I understand,' he said finally, expelling a long breath that softened the air around them.

'You do?' Sysa snapped her head back up and saw the loosening in his eyes.

'I do,' he said, rubbing his jaw as if he couldn't quite believe what he was saying. 'It makes sense – he's part of you, part of the Trinity. I understand that means you have certain – *feelings* – towards him.' Brodie bristled, as if shaking the thought away. 'It's the same thing that gave you those feelings for me, Sysa, I get it. Would you have even felt that way about me if it weren't for this?' He swept his hand around, as if tracing the bizarre triangle they were in.

'And would you still have felt those things for me?' Sysa snapped, the words springing from her with an unexpected edge of bitterness.

'Of course I would,' Brodie said, his expression hardening. 'Nothing could ever change how I feel about you. But this isn't really about how I feel, is it?' He looked back at her, a strange sort of emptiness creeping across his face.

'There's more you should know. About what happened back at the Castle of Thunder,' Sysa said, turning her body away from him so that her heart faced towards the shoreline. 'When Lavellan came to help me in the dungeon, we...' Sysa stopped, her words halted by Brodie lifting one hand into the air.

'Don't, please, I don't want to know. I don't *need* to know,' he said, the words emerging in a stiff rhythm, as if they had been caught up in their passage out of him. 'Whatever's happened, I don't want to hear about that. I only want to know about how you feel now, and who you plan to choose.'

'It's not about choosing, Brodie, it's always going to be you, you should know that,' Sysa said, flopping on a nearby rock, defeated by her own emotions. 'But with Lavellan, it's different, it's this other kind of pull... I can't explain it.' She turned her head to look at him. 'And I can't promise you that's ever going to go away.'

Brodie sighed, sitting down beside her, both now facing out to the horizon. Sysa leaned her head onto his shoulder, thinking back to the hours after the battle with Rogart, when they had sat on another rock and tried to untangle their feelings from a complicated web. Now, there was someone else involved and his shadow hung over them like the clouds that gathered out at sea, restless and undecided. The sun peeked in and out in the vast palm of the skyline, peppering rays like jewels across the etched surface of bobbing waves. For now, the storm had stilled, and the world was quiet, as if reflecting this time of contemplation.

Sysa sucked in a deep breath and then released the question she had been keeping curled up inside herself. 'Do you still want to marry me?'

Brodie took her hand, pulling it over to rest on the hard mound of his thigh.

'I'll always want to marry you. For me, there's no question. And if I have to, I'll accept that the feelings in your heart have to be shared with him, as much as I hate it.

And I do,' he said, offering her a sideways glance. 'There's no other way for me than to be with you. We both know that.' As Brodie spoke, his eyes drifted out to the horizon. 'But the question is, do you really want to marry me now, knowing how you feel, and that it may not ever go away?' He turned to her, his eyes blooming into hopeful, desperate rounds.

'I don't know,' Sysa said, finally allowing herself to release the answer that had been hiding inside her. 'It seems wrong, expecting you to go along with this, while I try to understand my feelings and what they mean.'

'Then we wait. It's not as if we don't have other things to keep us occupied,' Brodie said with a lopsided smile that broke the surface of Sysa's heart like the ripples that were breaking across the water. 'We do this, we win this, and then we decide – then *you* decide – what our future's going to be. But I haven't forgotten the promise we made to each other – that whatever came for us, it was you and me always.' Brodie lifted her hand to his mouth and pressed a kiss on her skin before searching her eyes with a question. 'Do I still get to kiss you?' he said finally, rubbing his thumb over a tear that stained Sysa's cheek.

'Yes,' Sysa said, leaning into the soft warmth of him.

She swallowed the knowledge she would never now disclose to him.

That when she had kissed Lavellan in the Castle of Thunder, she'd known it would be for the final time.

CHAPTER NINETEEN

'It's been a lot, everything that's happened lately,' Brodie said, some time later, when his eyes were back on the horizon, and his mouth was no longer on Sysa's.

His gaze drifted over the shore while Sysa nestled in beside him, enjoying the temporary comfort of his arm around her waist.

'I still can't believe Ida's gone. And Luna… it's all so horrible,' she said, knowing they had to move, but wanting to hold onto this moment for just a little longer.

'Neither of them deserved that,' Brodie replied, his mouth a hard line of resolution.

Sysa watched as the streaked ripples of the water reflected like tiny waves on the surface of his eyes.

'They remind me of jewels,' she said finally, diverting the train of her thoughts as she focused on the shards of light that were fluttering on the ocean. The sun had reappeared, sending flickering rays towards them, yet devoid of the familiar warmth that normally accompanied its presence in the sky. Sysa shivered, wondering what that meant about Neven and her progress with the stone, as well as the matter of her own family.

'*Mmm?*' Brodie said, turning to her.

As he did, a thought occurred to Sysa, arriving like the

dark-winged creature that was now making its way towards them across the sky.

'Arno?' Sysa blinked into the air, recognising the looming form of their companion. He was carrying something that was hanging from his claws like some sort of garment, or perhaps a piece of cloth. The thing flapped underneath him, rippling against the winds that eddied around him.

'What's that he's got?' Brodie asked, just as Arno answered by dropping the thing with a thump onto the sand.

'It looks like some sort of skin,' Sysa said, peering down at the oiled garment, and then up again at Arno. The bird responded by dipping his beak a notch, before descending to the rocks in a graceful downward turn. 'You brought this here for us?' she asked, directing her question at the bird, who cocked his head in a half-impatient gesture. 'What is it?' Brodie and Sysa huddled around the thing, scanning it in a questioning, sweeping line.

'I think I know what it is,' Brodie said finally, casting a look at Arno, whose returning nod seemed to confirm Brodie's suspicions. 'It's the sealskin your mother found me wrapped in when I first arrived in Fyrish. Remember, when Frode and the others left me.'

Sysa nodded, thinking back to the story her mother had conveyed about Brodie's arrival. *We kept the seal skin we found him in, but it held no power to transform him to a seal.*

'So, this sealskin must be capable of something,' Sysa said, trying to decipher what power it held, if not of transformation.

'It seems that way,' Brodie agreed, looking down at the skin, his brow furrowed in thought.

'Let's see what Frode thinks,' he suggested eventually. 'He was the one who found it back in the human world – it was my mother's, remember?' Brodie said, recalling Frode's discovery of the skin when he'd visited the human world to find out what had happened to his sister. Brodie's eyes clouded over briefly at the memory, before snapping back into the present moment. 'He might have an idea of what it can do to help us now.'

'Let's go and speak to him, then,' Sysa replied, stooping to gather up the dark garment. As she made contact with it, she felt a familiar sparking in her hands. Like the lighting up of a fire, a streak of something flew through her, flooding her limbs, her chest, her senses. She shivered, realising quickly the feeling was less like a fire, and more like the gathering of a wave. It seemed to rush through her body, cool blue and clear, sending trickles right to her toes, as if the sea had hurried in past the sand and delved inside her. She glanced over at Brodie, who was grasping the other end of the skin, his curled fingers pinching its corners.

'Did you feel that?'

Brodie looked up from his inspection of the sealskin. 'Did I feel what?'

Sysa shook her head, dismissing the moment as if she were shaking the skin loose of its connection to her soul.

'I just felt something, as if the skin were having some sort of effect on me,' she said finally, accepting she would never find another good reason for keeping anything else from Brodie. Whatever the power of this skin was, it related to her, and though Brodie had been born of it, its power was obviously hers alone. Brodie nodded, the gesture conveying acceptance of both Sysa's rank in the Trinity and the loss of any hope that the sealskin might be linked to his own powers.

'That might make sense,' he said, eyeing the skin with blue-eyed wariness.

'Does it?' Sysa asked, a hint of desperation in the words she threw back at him. 'Nothing makes much sense to me right now.'

'You were going to say something, before Arno arrived, about the sea,' Brodie said, apparently sensing a need to divert Sysa from the sealskin.

'Was I? Oh yes,' Sysa replied, still feeling disorientated by her recent experience. 'It was about the jewels... the way the sun landed on the water. It made me think of the jewels in Luna's cave, you remember, the ones that were piled high when we found William chained up there. And the ones Modan and the kelpies kept in their home beneath the sea.'

'And you think we might have some use for them now?' Brodie asked, glancing in the direction of the coast that edged Luna's old hideaway.

'I don't know. But something tells me they could play a part in all this.'

'What have you got there?' Frode's voice interrupted the conversation as he made his way across the sand.

'Oh, Frode, we were just coming to talk to you,' Brodie said, turning to his uncle, who was now hunched over the skin, cradling one elbow as he drummed his fingers on his mouth in contemplation.

'It's my mother's seal skin. Arno brought it – he must have gone back to Steel Castle for it. It's had some sort of effect on Sysa. Uncle, what do you think it all means?'

'*Mmm*,' Frode murmured, lingering over the skin and rubbing his fingers lightly along its surface. He closed his eyes and breathed in, as if inhaling the scent of the sister he had lost. Eventually, he lifted his head, turned to Sysa and Brodie, and gestured towards the rocks they had been sitting on a few moments earlier.

'Come over here, I need to talk to you.'

Sysa and Brodie sat down beside him, watching the seal-man rub his palms up and down his thighs, garnering some sort of friction that seemed to build like static in the air.

'My parents – your mother's parents too, Brodie – were once the leaders of the seal-folk. That skin belonged to my mother, and when she died in childbirth, the skin passed on to the baby, my sister. Did you know my sister's name was Senga?' Frode's face lit up briefly in memory as he spoke. 'My parents believed that the skin had a special purpose and possessed a certain magic. There were tales told in the seal realms that the skin would one day weave into a bigger story. But all it brought to my family, and your mother, Brodie, was tragedy. Both my mother and my sister died in childbirth – both of them, can you imagine?' Frode's expression twisted into something hard. 'And the skin killed my father too. After my mother died, it sent him crazed with grief until he eventually killed himself. And so, it was just my sister and me, and I disavowed my place as the folk's leader. Until, of course, that day with the hunter in Never Night. When I went to look for my sister, and found that she was dead, I took the sealskin back to Fyrish, not sure what to do with it. And then you arrived,' Frode said, glancing at Brodie, his dark eyes flashing in recollection.

'And you gave it to me? But why, after all the trouble it had caused?' Brodie replied, a flicker of anger creeping across his face.

'I know, I know,' Frode said, lifting his hands so that his palms faced outwards towards his nephew. 'But there was a reason.' Frode fastened Brodie with a cautionary look.

'When the hunter drove that dagger into me that day, I saw something – you might call it a vision.' Frode carried on, lifting his eyes skywards. 'I saw, or rather felt, that the sealskin was needed. In that moment when I was close to death myself, I knew that the skin could somehow foster life. I can't explain what I felt, other than to say that the knowledge was driven into me in the same way that knife was. And so, when you arrived, a new life, Brodie, it felt like the right thing to do to wrap you in that skin. Ever since, I've wondered if I made the right choice that day. After that, of course, I took up my role as leader of the seal-folk – another consequence of the experience with the hunter.' As Frode spoke, the pinching creep of anger fell from Brodie's face. 'And things went on – you'd been accepted by the Steel family and the skin appeared to hold no further influence. So, I tried to put it to the back of my mind, but here it is, and from what you say, it seems to have some sort of link to Sysa.' Frode glanced in Sysa's direction.

'So, hang on, you think—' Brodie began, standing to face his uncle— 'you think it might be dangerous for Sysa, in the same way it was for my grandmother and my mother, Frode? If that's the case, we need to get rid of it.' Brodie lifted his arm, instinctively shielding Sysa from whatever threat the skin might present.

'Come on, help me, Frode, let's throw it in the sea,' Brodie called, bending to pick up the skin as Brigid and Krystan appeared in the background, watching him grasp at it with urgency.

'Brodie, stop.' Sysa's voice was clear as she lifted his fingers, pulling him away to look into her eyes. 'If there's a reason for the skin connecting with me, then it's a good one, Brodie. I'm not frightened, look at me. It's going to be okay.'

Brodie swiped a hand through his hair and then glanced around the group, his eyes darting from Brigid to Krystan to Frode, apparently hoping someone might agree with him.

'Sysa's right,' Brigid said eventually, prompting Brodie to let out a long sigh and spin on his heel, his chin tilted to the sky as he drilled his frustration into sand. 'If the skin can do something, you have to let her try,' Brigid said, offering Sysa a nod of encouragement.

'So, what should I do?' Sysa asked, her eyes reaching over the expectant half-circle who were all looking down at the skin that fringed their feet.

'You wear it,' Frode replied. 'You claim it. You own it.'

Sysa hesitated for the briefest of moments, before reaching out to the ebony veil that had already lifted from the shingle, ready to fall across her shoulders like a blanket drifting above the sea.

PART FOUR

PIECES OF
SKY AND STONE

CHAPTER TWENTY

As the skin fell towards her, Sysa felt a crackling across the blades of her shoulders. Every part of her came alive in the skin's presence, as if a meadow of buds were opening underneath her flesh. They reached up, like a swarm of tiny hands, trying to forge some sort of union with the garment. When the skin finally settled on her body, she felt complete, the new mantle flowing around her like the first breath after a scorched inhale.

She looked around, seeing motes of gold and silver flutter around her new cloak like stardust. Not far away, Star-Steed watched, casting long looks at the flecks that danced around like sun-kissed seas. Modan, too, observed from afar, drawn to the glistening motes that whirled like echoes of the jewels he had once collected. Sysa stared back at him, a silent understanding passing between them, forged in the folds and creases of the garment that had now become her second skin.

As she stood there in the centre of the circle, Sysa knew that she had been given a gift again. Just like the stories Grey had told her, the skin had come exactly when she needed it, another guide along a path of destiny and fate. Lavellan's last kiss had given her something too, more than she could know, perhaps. And then there was Brodie, who had been giving her whatever she needed from the first day they had met.

Alongside these thoughts, Sysa knew what she needed to do now. It came to her in a whisper, in a raft of words that floated from the sea. The words belonged to the skin, the skin belonged to the words, and the sea knew all of it. Sysa lifted her arms, raising her palms above her head as if she were lifting the sonnet of the sea to kiss the fingers of the sky.

But when the two met, it was not words and kisses that collided. Instead, Sysa's arms pulled like a magnet until the sky was alive with jewels that floated from the waves like upward rain. The jewels rose and curled, drawn first from the kelpies' land beneath the water, and then across the sea from Luna's hideaway. Sysa watched, mesmerised, as they drifted above the ocean, scattering the world with pieces of sky and stone.

She flicked her palms inward in suggestion. First, the jewels stilled, suspended like tiny dragonflies in a sudden ambered air. Then, all at once, they turned, sensing, as the kelpies once had, that they'd found a new master. In unison, they raced towards Sysa, like a flock of geese flying arrow-like through the sky.

When they came close, Sysa pushed her palms out again to face them. The jewels halted, hanging in the air in a wall of precious stone. Sysa surveyed them one by one, sweeping her gaze slowly from left to right before speaking.

'Where are you?' she called out to them.

The jewels stirred and buzzed like bees around their queen.

In the next breath, the sky stilled, the harbinger of an

agreement. All across its blue, the jewels shattered, cracking like shards of breaking ice. They fell away into the sea, each one leaving vertical, coloured streaks across the skyline. All around there was the sound of smashing and the smell of mingling salt and ice.

When it was done, there were two stones left hanging in the skyline. Two stones, positioned like two vertices of a triangle, with the apex at the crown of Sysa's head. Sysa stretched her arms out to her sides, reaching to them.

'There you are.'

As she pulled her hands back together, the stones flew to her, each resting in one palm, as if they had finally made it home.

CHAPTER TWENTY-ONE

'What are they? What does it all mean?' Brigid asked, stepping in front of her granddaughter and looking down at the stones Sysa held in each palm like upturned sunbeams.

'They're two parts of another kind of Trinity,' Sysa said, lifting her gaze up to meet the older woman's. 'Three stones altogether. The other one is yours.'

'But how… how did you come to know this?' Brigid said, glancing over her shoulder as if Sysa was watching a vision that was unfolding somewhere in the distance.

'I felt it through the skin. From the moment Arno was flying through the air with it, it sent me the beginning of a story. And then when I touched the sealskin, when I wore it, I just knew.'

'Knew what?' Brodie asked, looking at Sysa with a slightly less anxious expression than the one he'd worn earlier.

'I knew that amongst the jewels in Luna's cave, there was a stone I needed, and somewhere in the kelpies' treasure, there was another one,' Sysa said. 'All I needed to do was pull them out of the sea, and the cave, and ask them to come to me. And here they are,' she said, offering the group a smile before returning her attention to the stones.

'And you think these form some part of another Trinity

– a Trinity of Stones?' Brigid asked, her eyes narrowing as she tried to keep pace with the revelations she hadn't been party to.

'I know they do, Brigid. I can feel it in my bones, and everything I've done since I've arrived in Fyrish has been part of it. I was meant to meet Modan, I was meant to go to Luna's cave.' Sysa's voice bristled with excitement as she spoke. 'It's all been part of this bigger story, and everything's connected,' she said, 'just the way Grey told me it was. The whole world, the sea, the sky, the stones, us...' Sysa whipped her hand around, emboldened by the skin that flapped in the wind like a salty sail.

'That's true,' Brigid said, her eyes warm with pride and understanding. Behind her, clouds stirred in the sky like blossoms, before galloping like horses through the freezing blue expanse.

'And like me, Brodie and Lavellan, the stones will be drawn to each other,' Sysa explained, her words joining with the rhythm of the sky above them. 'Your stone will be seeking its partners, and now that we've found them, these stones will be seeking it out too. Feel them – they're warm,' Sysa said, thrusting her hands out towards Brigid, who lay her palms face-down on the stones, her features blooming with recognition. 'See?' Sysa said, jutting her hands towards the rest of the group, who in turn repeated Brigid's action, each murmuring whispered agreements about the warmth that flooded Sysa's hands.

'And you think if we get the stones back together, we'll be able to win this?' Brodie said, blowing into his hands as he readjusted to the cold that now permeated everything away from Sysa's contours.

213

'I think so,' Sysa said, curling her fingers around the stones. 'We need to get back to the Castle of Thunder, reunite the stones and then save my family and my people.'

'Then let's do it,' Frode said, stepping in front of Sysa, the scar the hunter had left upon his chest shining like the blade that had once sung its way across his heart.

★

'Thank you for the stone, Modan.' Back on the other side of the island, Sysa rubbed her face into the stallion's silky mane, prompting the horse to emit a loud snuffle. 'And thank you, Luna, too,' she whispered into the bed of Modan's tresses, as she thought about the mermaid who had unknowingly given her something amongst the piles of jewels she had amassed. Sysa remembered Grey's stories, about caves laden with the treasures of boats wrecked on the rocks or destroyed by waves gathered from the depths of the ocean. She knew that the sea had sent the stones to her, just as it had sent the skin that now wrapped around her body as a cloak. She thought of Ida too, as she trawled her fingers through Modan's mane, the same way Ida had once pulled a comb through the folds of her own hair. Inwardly, she vowed that all these losses would not be for nothing. She turned back towards the others, surveying, for the second time, a battalion that belonged to her on Selkie Island, a fellowship forged in magic, destiny and stone.

At the shore, Star-Steed thrummed his hooves on sand, dispersing grains in dancing sparkles. In the air, Arno soared, joining his companions who had returned with dark wings tilted to the sky. Sysa glanced over to where

Brigid stood and thought of the conversation she had just had with her grandmother, when Brigid had told her that the sight was one of the gifts the sealskin had given her.

'I can see it in you, my dear,' Brigid had said, cradling Sysa's hand like it was one of the precious stones her granddaughter still clutched in the pink softness of her palm. 'Your understanding of the stones, the sense that you knew what was needed when you put the skin on. That's how it starts, that's how the visions come to you. It will take time for you to see them all clearly, to use that second sight as part of the magic that is yours.'

'Then part of that also came from you,' Sysa had replied, understanding that some of Brigid's powers had also flowed to her, in the same way she had received Grey's magic in his stories, in the same way power and magic had fallen into her heart in Lavellan's kiss, in everything that had crossed her path since she had arrived in Fyrish. She thought of Three-Wings, and the vision he had given her, and she wondered what the raven and the wolf were doing now. And then she thought back to Lavellan and the power that was hers to bequeath on those she loved, even when love existed before she even knew it. She felt the stab of something in her throat as she thought of Lavellan's blue-inked body, the way he had transformed, the way power and magic floated like a river between hearts and souls and minds. And then she looked at Brodie, knowing she still held his power in her hand like the two stones she clung to. She felt them weighted in each palm, each one filled with those feelings, both exerting a singular pressure on her skin.

'It's time to go,' she said eventually, returning to the

present moment and the expectant faces that now looked to her across the shingle. 'Come,' she directed, beckoning the others to mount a steed of star or sky, a fizz of sparkle circling the air above. Still holding onto Modan's mane, she watched as Brodie mounted Arno, while nearby, Brigid climbed onto Star-Steed. At the shore, Frode and Krystan climbed atop another eagle, now swollen to its dragon-like size as the two of them pressed together on its back. It had been agreed that the remaining seal-folk would stay to guard Selkie Island, and Sysa nodded at them, her lips curved in a smile of gratitude.

'Looks like it's you and me again, then,' Sysa said, returning her attention to rubbing Modan's mane. She thought of the last time she had crossed this water on the stallion, when her parents had ridden straight-backed beside her, all eyes focused on the task ahead of them. This time, her parents were back at the Castle of Thunder, a piece of information Brodie had managed to secure from Arno after his excursion to fetch the skin. Sysa bristled, thinking of her family being dragged there in their current state of half-life. A spark flew from her fingers, casting a bright ripple along the cords of Modan's dark mane.

She climbed on his back, steering him towards the shoreline as the skin flew out from her shoulders, blanketing the air behind her. The stallion entered the shallows, water rounding his hooves in blue-white wheels. They moved out into the waves, the beating of Sysa's seal-cloak the only cry towards battle.

Behind them, the others followed, taking their place on the sea's surface, or lifting great wings to the vastness of the sky.

Sysa tilted her head up to the air, enjoying the sight of Brodie and Arno in the sky above her. Further back, Frode and Krystan's eagle soared in sweeping, climbing arcs. Not far away, Brigid and Star-Steed thrummed the sky, the steed's hooves trailing lines of stardust through the air like breadcrumbs. Sysa and Modan rode the waves, hurtling into spray, which rose in salty beads and torrents around their heads. Sysa could see the line of the coast now, the land tinged blue with the slashes of an icy hem that fringed its edges. She dipped her chin low, willing Modan to move faster through the waves.

When she lifted her eyes again, she saw something come into focus on the headland. Or rather *someone*, she thought with a dull sense of realisation, as she made out a sharp-edged figure on the cliffs. Neven was there, flinging long arms to the sky as she swept up shards of air, which soon transformed to ice-cold daggers. *She knew we were coming*, Sysa thought, wondering how far Neven had got with turning the stone to her, and remembering Luna's words about the Unseelie queen's powers including sight.

Before Sysa had the chance to consider this further, Neven's arms shot out, sending her daggers flying across the ocean. The blades reached up and over, firing towards Sysa's group like a wave of steel that hurtled through the sky. One dark blade flew ahead of the others, careering towards Sysa like a bullet. Before she could even cry out, it had brushed against her face and landed on her shoulder, searing her skin with a crooked claw.

Instinctively, she touched her hand to her cheek,

expecting to see blood dripping from her fingers. It took her a moment to realise her skin was as unmarked as a new page. When she turned her head, daggers still falling like rain from the sky above her, it was not a blade she saw pricking into her shoulder, but Three-Wings. He nodded a beady look at her before lifting away from the pelt of her sealskin. As he soared skywards, Sysa called out in gratitude.

He had offered her a vision, and now it raced before her eyes.

'Something's coming in from the Swelkie,' Sysa called out, lifting her voice to the group above her. As she called, she kept her eyes closed, watching a vision of the storm-bringers Fenja and Menja turning their grindstone in the sea. Neven must have enlisted them somehow, Sysa thought, remembering her conversation with Lavellan on the scrap of beach back at Dunnet. Aware of her thoughts layered over the scene behind her eyelids, she watched the two giantesses turn the grinder, their hair flying skywards in matching streaks of white and grey.

The ice-daggers continued falling into the sea around her. Through the dark veil of her eyelids, Sysa sensed them dropping to the waves in a cloud of knife-edged rain. From the horizon, came a swell, the surge of a wave that curled towards them with a rolling fury.

'Sysa, the wave!' Brodie's voice fell from the sky, hurtling Sysa back into the world.

As her eyes snapped open, Sysa lifted her arms from Modan's back, feeling the stones burn hot against her skin where she had tucked them into the neckline of her dress before departing Selkie Island. She cast her eyes downwards, summoning something she needed from the sea. The power of the wave advanced, lifting the ocean beneath her like a mountain rising underwater. Just as it was about to overcome them, she felt her summons answered, and heard the beat of a hundred hooves on water, battering down the swell and flattening the peak with the force of their kelpie hooves.

The kelpie army charged, a sea of stallions and intention. Sysa watched them, silently conveying her will across the patchwork of rippling blue. She stood on Modan's back then, realising with a perfect kind of clarity that although she was no mermaid, she was of the sky and the sea and the land – she was of all of it.

She lifted from Modan's back, her sealskin thrumming the air like the nearby hooves that raced across the sea.

In the next breath, she was moving across the sea's surface, the salty peaks of the ocean licking the soles of her feet in tongues that whispered from the water. When she looked to her side, the kelpies were curving around her, joining Modan to follow in a half-circle at her rear. She tilted her body forward, feeling salt and sea air mingle against her cheeks, her eyes, her senses. She inhaled all of it, her sealskin flowing in the wind behind her like the exhale of the wave that was now passing in ever-decreasing sweeps.

And when she looked to where it had arrived from, the sea lay still and empty, staring back at her as if in disbelief of her transformation. She looked up to the sky, where the same sense was conveyed in the open-mouthed expressions of Brodie, Brigid and her friends. In amongst the coming of the wave they had managed to dodge Neven's icy spears in twists and loops, plunging this way and that to avoid them.

But now, Neven's latest batch rose from the land above the cliffs, arcing into ribbons of ice that fell in looming curls.

Sysa lifted her eyes, feeling the stones burn hot inside the cavity of fabric next to her heart-space. She blinked, wondering for a moment if this was a vision or real life. But the eyes she saw through were her own, and she splayed the fingers of each hand, feeling the crackle of her powers gathering inside them.

When she lifted her arms higher, her body climbed through the sky as the warmth in her hands took hold.

It took her a moment to realise that Neven's threaded ice had halted in mid-air, suspended above her head like the captured moment of a painting. Sysa pushed her palms upwards, holding the icicles back as if she were holding up the sky. She squeezed her eyes shut, summoning another sort of power as she pushed up with a strength that came from somewhere deep inside her bones, from somewhere deeper than the ocean. And then she pushed again, forcing the daggers to pedal back along the arc they had just traversed.

Sysa watched as the icy spears flew back and splintered into the ocean. They fell in floods and torrents, hitting the sea like sheeted veils of rain. Somewhere in the distance, Neven cried out on the cliff, her shrieks as pointed as the spears she had set flying. The Unseelie queen readied herself to release more of them, apparently unaware that they would meet with the same fate.

And so it continued, with Sysa pushing back on Neven's ice like she was rolling a rock across the ocean. Sysa dipped her chin, full of the strength she had now accepted as her own. Somewhere inside herself, she also knew there was more to come, more to be unlocked inside her. The stones tucked inside her dress glowed white-hot at the realisation, as if confirming the passage of her thoughts across the sea.

In the air, Brodie and the others watched on as Sysa harnessed the power of the sealskin. She knew it was more than just the skin, though, it was the stones, the visions and the call of something else. Somewhere out there on the cliffs, the third stone glowed back, immersed in Neven's world of cold ambition. In between it all was Lavellan, who Sysa knew had sent Three-Wings to warn her with his vision of the wave.

As Sysa rolled away the falling ice, she saw Neven fling her arms up on the headland. After a few moments she swivelled on her heel, pulling along some companion, possibly Sirius, in her wake. She appeared to be returning to her lair, to formulate some other plan of action.

As the sea stilled, Sysa forged on, ready to make her passage home.

CHAPTER TWENTY-TWO

'I need to get back to Steel Castle,' Sysa said without preamble as they arrived on a craggy outcrop of shingle a few moments later.

'Sysa… you were… floating… over the sea back there,' Brodie said, gently pulling her by the shoulder so that she turned to face him.

'I was,' Sysa replied matter-of-factly, evidently feeling less surprised than the group who looked back at her across the rocks. 'It's the skin, I think, and the stones – it feels like everything's falling into place, like something that's been sleeping inside me is being awoken.'

'*Mmm*,' Brigid said from somewhere in the background, her eyes tracing the curves of a rock in the distance. Sysa glanced over at her grandmother, who was beginning to look increasingly unwell, and strangely older than she'd been when they'd departed Selkie Island just a few short hours before.

'Brigid? Are you all right?' Sysa asked, noting the way Brigid was resting a long hand on a rock, the way her back was hunched over, the slight pinch of the skin around her cheekbones.

'I'm fine,' Brigid said, waving away the concern with her free hand, her breath coming in ragged curls that seemed to enter the air with more effort than her answer had implied.

'She's fading,' Sysa said in a whisper to Brodie, who glanced in Brigid's direction, his eyes still lit with the surprise of encountering Sysa's new abilities. 'It's because Neven still has the stone, and it's turning to her. Every minute lost is a loss of Brigid's strength, Brodie.' Sysa aimed a quick jab at his forearm, jolting him back into the present and the matter of Brigid's dwindling powers. 'I need to get to Steel Castle,' she repeated, as Brodie returned his focus to her, his head tilted to one side in query. 'I have an idea,' she said, before he'd had a chance to open his mouth again. 'It's about the fae lines – the lines the castle are built on, the tracks that can be used to harness the light-power.'

'Go on,' Brodie answered, his accompanying nod confirming his understanding of the invisible markers that lay underneath the castle floors.

'We know that the sleeping sickness Neven unleashed came from the fae lines of the Castle of Thunder, right?' Sysa said, fixing him with a stare of explanation.

'We do,' Brodie replied, reflecting her look with understanding eyes.

'So, in order to fight back, we need Steel Castle to unleash something to challenge it, to fight the sickness. We lift the sickness, we leave Neven exposed to us.'

'Sounds good so far,' Brodie said, 'but just one problem. Won't Neven have already thought of that? I mean, would she really have left Steel Castle just sitting empty and waiting? Won't she already know the potential of the lines?'

'You're right,' Sysa said, after loosing a long sigh of disappointment. 'Of course she will, and she'll have the

place armed to the teeth with her blasted guards. But...'
she offered, her features brightening with an idea, 'what if
I don't plan to enter by the front door?'

'What do you mean?' Brodie asked, his eyes narrowing
to blue triangles. 'How else are you going to harness the
fae lines?'

'From above,' Sysa said, her face breaking into a wide
white grin.

'You plan to fly...?' Brodie asked, taking one step
towards her, his arms instinctively curling out, as if he
planned to wrap her in them, to tame these sudden wings
he now imagined.

'Not quite,' she answered, brushing him off with a quick
eye-roll. 'I'll get Arno to take me. But when I get there, I
can ignite the powers of the castle's peaks. Remember the
starlights my mother took from the peaks of Steel Castle,
the ones I used to make Star-Steed?'

Brodie nodded in the affirmative.

'Well, they were gathered at the peaks of Steel Castle,
which means the fae lines must project upwards through
those peaks. So, I get to one of the turrets and ignite the
lines and, hopefully, none of the guards will even notice
me,' Sysa said, bristling with so much energy that the air
felt charged around her.

'Okay, let's give it a try then,' Brodie said, calibrating
his plans for their new endeavour. 'Let me just get Arno
and one of the other eagles. I'll be right back.' Sysa stood
still, the charged air hanging around her like a veil atop one
of Steel Castle's starry peaks. 'Ah. Let me guess,' Brodie
said with a raised eyebrow. 'This is something else you plan
to do without me.'

'I'm sorry,' Sysa said, 'but yes, I'm doing this alone, Brodie. We need to attract as little attention as possible. And I need you to stay here and look after Brigid for me, to keep her safe while I'm away. Once I've harnessed the lines, I'll be straight back to you, I promise.' Sysa stepped forward, placing a reassuring hand on his shoulder. 'I'll be fine, honestly,' she followed up when Brodie's only answer was a sigh.

'As usual, I doubt there's anything I can say to change your mind,' he said eventually. 'But if you don't come back, I'm coming after you.'

'I wouldn't expect anything less,' Sysa replied, pivoting on her heel to seek out Arno, her hair flying in a sudden wind that had curled up like a cold draught sneaking underneath a door.

★

'So, you'll stay here with Brodie and Brigid,' Sysa instructed Krystan and Frode shortly afterwards, as she prepared to mount Arno on the shingle.

'We'll keep watch from over there,' Frode said, gesturing at a piece of rock that jutted out of the headland. 'Any sign of trouble, and we'll be with you, straight away.'

'Sysa knows what she's doing,' Brigid interjected with a weak smile, maintaining her position as the only member of the group who didn't seem concerned about what Sysa was planning.

'I do, Brigid, thank you,' Sysa said, flashing a returning smile at her grandmother, while trying to swallow down the sense of concern she was feeling over Brigid's failing health.

'Good luck,' Brodie murmured, rubbing at one of Arno's sheet-like wings as he watched Sysa climb atop the eagle.

'Fly well, boy,' he uttered in a hushed voice, offering the bird a friendly slap as he bid them both farewell. As Arno lifted from the shingle, Sysa looked down at the faces staring up at her. She saw Brodie lift a hand to his lips before raising his palm to her, the remnants of his kiss drifting in salute across the sky.

★

Sysa felt the wind press against her like a cold, closed door as she and Arno soared up and over the headland. In the distance, she could see the starred peaks of Steel Castle and somewhere beyond, a clutch of forest and the turrets of the Castle of Thunder emanating streaks of sharp blue that cascaded like ribbons from its walls. *The sleeping sickness*, Sysa thought, noting the way the streaks curled and flashed, seeping their way around the kingdom. She could see it all so much more clearly from up here, with Fyrish laid out beneath her like a carpet. She grimaced against the onslaught of cold fingers as Neven's tendrils wound their way around the meadows and homesteads, dissolving into something murky as they embraced the walls they met.

At last, Arno arrived at Steel Castle's peaks, where pointed spires angled towards them as if in invitation. The great eagle hovered for a while, allowing Sysa to survey the scene below. Down at the castle's feet, guards spilled out like dark beads, wandering in ant-like formations around the castle's periphery. Sysa heard the crash and clang of swords and armour as they swept about in a chorus of latent energy, so consumed in their bundling that it appeared none of them had thought to turn their faces to the sky.

She gestured for Arno to move closer to a silvery-steel peak that extended from the highest spire of the castle. Arno obliged, angling his wings downwards until Sysa grabbed air, trying to reach the pinnacle that sprouted from the peak.

'It's no good,' she sighed, straining with the effort of reaching. 'I'll have to get off and do it myself, Arno.'

The eagle offered her a look of understanding.

In a heartbeat, Sysa had climbed from the eagle, and stood on a patch of air, as solid as if it were the first step of a staircase. She stepped down, finding her way level with the spire, the flap of her sealskin announcing her powers like a standard flying from the castle's peak.

Sysa placed her hands on the spire, wrapping her fingers around it like a goblet. All at once, she heard the sound of echoing and chiming, a sound that had now become as familiar to her as the hands she clasped around the steel. She breathed in through her nose, smelling the tang of fire-song and magic that crackled underneath her palms as they met with the power of the fae lines. She heard a rumble coming from somewhere deep within the castle. Her hands shook with the force of it and her body rattled with a vibration that surged through her like a flood.

Soon, the sky was lit with a lightning of colour. This was not like the lightning that had once cracked from the Castle of Thunder, Sysa thought to herself as she watched it, this was more like the lightning of a rainbow in the sky. It blazed blue and pink, then yellow and green and orange as it bled from the spire she was holding. She felt something reaching up the spire towards her, the rush of a kind of gathering.

If the guards hadn't noticed her at first, they certainly did now.

From below, came the shuffling sound of recognition, wafting across the swarm of guards like the cold breeze that stung the sky around them. Sysa could hear raised voices, a cacophony of alert that swum up the castle walls. From the ground, there were also sounds of a gathering that blended with the thrum that pushed its way upwards through the castle. Sysa saw a sea of faces turned up towards her, then heard the shifting of booted feet as the guards spread out like antlers racing towards the castle doors.

She clung on tighter to the peak, willing whatever energy lay in the fae lines to hurry. She tilted her head, hearing the thud of boots on stairs as she strained against the pull. The thudding got louder, until she let out a sound, a sort of roar as she clenched her teeth against the forces that surged against her palms now. Her roar was mingled with something else though – something that swept into the grounds of Steel Castle in a pack of fur and fangs and entered with a blood-hot growl.

'Sirius,' Sysa breathed as she looked down to the castle grounds, where the wolf was hurtling towards the entrance. And not just Sirius – he had brought a pack of wolves who circled at his rear. They followed him into the castle, disappearing like tendrils of smoke into the hallway. A second later, Sysa heard the shriek of guards as they came face to face with Sirius and his companions. She could visualise the wolves rounding on them, holding them back like a shield of grey fur and amber-coloured eyes.

'Thank you,' she whispered, as she dropped her chin, trying to block out the sounds of howls and toppling soldiers. As she closed her eyes, she heard the retreating of footsteps, the surge of a hundred feet on stone. She felt a rushing then, the sense of something pulling away from her. On the ground, the wolves were scattering the guards like pebbles, driving them out of the castle and into the canopy of the surrounding trees.

Free to concentrate again, Sysa gripped harder on the spire, willing the surge that was lifting towards her fingers. It thrummed with a strange metallic voice, spilling its multi-coloured rays out into the sky. She felt the ballooning of its power as it sped up the spire towards her like a train hurtling towards a destination. As it made its final passage, Sysa's legs flew out behind her, so that she was perpendicular to its life-force, her fingers curled around it like a stake being driven into the sky's own heart.

Her palms burned hot with the sensation of covered lightning. She felt her skin tingle, coming alive with the powers that seeped into her like water passing over stones. She took a deep breath in, knowing she couldn't hold on for much longer, and knowing that she had to. Just as she felt her fingers slipping from the spire, a final burst of rainbowed lightning escaped from underneath them, blasting into the sky like a volcano, erupting into the air in sweeps of colour and a thousand streams of light.

Sysa felt herself lift from the spire then, pushed up by a force that exploded against her fingers. She remained hovering for a moment, surveying the sky that now wheeled in threads of brightly coloured light. In the distance, the ribbons of Neven's magic stilled, understanding they now faced a different challenge. Sysa heard the sharp whisper of their awareness, and watched as they curved outwards, like a wind trying to bend its way around a rock.

The sky weaved with a thousand rays of colour. At Sysa's side, Arno's wings lit up in streaks of green and blue. Sysa saw herself reflected in his eyes, her body hanging in the reflected fire of amber. They moved together then, each reaching for the other, and as Arno waited underneath her, she dropped onto him, grateful for the familiar solidness of him as she curled her legs around his back.

'Let's get back to the others,' she said, leaning into him so that she felt the brush of feather against her jawline. The eagle dipped, following the lines of colour like he was writing a song across the sky. Then he swung, turning back on himself and sweeping into the path they'd followed to reach the castle. Sysa felt a shelf of cold air press against her face, tasted salt on her lips, and smelled the sharp tang of awakening. It felt like every part of Fyrish was coming alive, like the hills and trees and ocean were each throwing their support to her like spring beads that flew into the sky.

Behind them, the colours bloomed and stretched, drawing away towards the threads that emanated from the Castle of Thunder. Sysa allowed herself one final glance over her shoulder before she turned back in the direction of the faces awaiting her on the rocks. What she'd seen looked like an army of warmth advancing towards a battalion of coldness.

The threads moved ever closer.

She had lit the spark, and now it was time to fan the flame.

PART FIVE

THE TRINITY

CHAPTER TWENTY-THREE

'You did it.'

Brodie's words floated across the shingle as he advanced towards Sysa and Arno, his arms spread as wide as the grin that broke across his features.

'Of course she did,' Brigid said from where she was sitting on a rocky corner. Sysa threw her grandmother a nervous smile, wondering how much more she'd have to do to make this situation right.

'It's up to the fae lines to do what they can now,' Sysa followed up as she stared out at the sky, where a battle was unfolding in twisting rays and twining fingers. 'Now we have to get to Neven and the Castle of Thunder,' she confirmed, pulling her sealskin tight against her collar.

'And what then?' Frode asked, his brow tightening like the seal-cloak Sysa had just pulled against her neck.

'Then we face her, we get the stone, and we give it back, where it belongs – with Brigid. Then we hope the fae lines do their work and my family wake up from this awful sleeping ill. Then we... then... I don't know,' Sysa said, closing her eyes and rubbing at the skin on her forehead, feeling suddenly, inexplicably weary.

'Come, sit a moment,' Krystan said, stretching out an arm to her. 'You've just pulled the roots out of Steel Castle's fae lines. I think you deserve to rest a while.'

Krystan glanced round at the others, her eyes bright with affection and concern.

'Krystan's right, sit down,' Brodie said, offering Sysa a drink from the water canteen he had produced from inside his jacket.

For once, Sysa did as she was ordered, easing herself onto a rock, her fingers splayed over barnacles and stuck-on shells. She took a deep breath in, then sipped at the water, feeling it drip into her body like a cool, reviving waterfall. Something stirred in her stomach then, something that was gathering like the gathering of the power she had harnessed a few moments earlier. 'Come on, let's go,' she said, standing up and brushing a piece of sea-bark from her gown.

'You're sure?' Brigid said from beside her, something in the old woman's eyes making Sysa wonder if there was more to her question than concern over the present moment. What did she see, Sysa wondered, through that misty-blue gaze of hers? Did Brigid know something that Sysa herself still couldn't tell?

'I'm sure,' Sysa answered, covering her grandmother's veined hand with her fingers. 'It's time to get my family back.'

As Sysa spoke, an image of the blue-inked Lavellan crept into her mind and then faded into the distance. His features waned until Sysa stretched out a hand to him, only to find him melt away like the milky blue horizon that marked the boundary between the heart of the sea and sky.

★

Sysa dipped her head against the wind, feeling the heat of the two stones drum next to her heart in percussive rhythm. She was aloft again, flying through the air on Arno's back, plunging through streaks of colour that fought their way around the sky. The rest of the group followed at her rear with Brodie, Frode and Krystan riding eagles and Brigid atop a soaring Star-Steed. Down below, Modan led the herd of kelpies, guiding them back to their home across the sea.

They were on their way to the Castle of Thunder, a route mapped out in icy curls that wafted in the air like pathways. Arno flew over and above, dipping and curving like a leaping salmon in the sky. As they cleaved through air, Neven's cords met the flares of coloured light that struck out from Steel Castle. The cords entwined like tentacles, each trying to obliterate the other, each desperate to snuff out the power that its opposite strand held deep within its length.

'Look, Brodie, it's working,' Sysa cried out as she gestured to an icy cord that had been overcome by one of Steel Castle's light-rays. Brodie nodded, watching as the cold smear dissolved into blue shadow before disappearing into sky. All around them, the power of the Castle of Thunder's lines were being obliterated by surges of light that spun in cartwheels around the blue arena. Sysa smelled an odd sort of burning, as if the sky were alive with the remnants of a strange, retreating smoke.

They hurtled on, to where the Castle of Thunder rose up from the land like a summons. As they'd flown, Sysa had seen lines of guardsmen peppering the trees and paths that bled out from the castle grounds. Some guards were already felled; the ones Sirius and his companions had chased out of Steel Castle. Others were closer to the Castle of Thunder, unaware of the wolves that were prowling their way through the forests, mowing down soldiers like blades of grass.

'Look, it's Sirius,' Brodie called, looking down at the pack who were threading their way through far-off trees and hedgerows. Sysa smiled, grateful for Brodie's sudden acceptance of Lavellan's wolfish charge. Far below, rows of wolves now marched on the landscape in grey-furred formation. Sysa's army advanced, a cavalry that seemed to burst from the world like words from a poet's throat.

They were close to the castle now, and the turrets that flew up in blocky rectangles. Sysa angled her body, aiming Arno past the highest peak and down towards the castle grounds.

'Down below!' Frode's voice pitched into the air in warning. 'It's Neven!'

Sysa looked down to see the Unseelie queen scrambling from the castle entrance, her face contorted in fury as she flung streams of ice-darts up the castle walls.

Sysa and the others dipped, trying to evade the spiked lengths of cold that shot out from the castle's turrets. Arno swung this way and that; narrowly avoiding the jagged streaks that skimmed the edges of his wings. Sysa felt the air fly up towards her, pressing against her face in sheeted protest. Behind her, Brodie and the others were also diving and twirling, their mounts racing through air like the gulls who rounded the coast in arcs.

When something flashed against her face, Sysa thought she had been spurred by one of Neven's weapons. It took her a moment to realise that the flash was actually flapping, a familiar dark creature that possessed an extra wing. 'Three-Wings,' she breathed, grateful of the raven's presence amid the cacophony of cold and clatter. But when she looked into the raven's eyes, she saw something that sent that cacophony inwards, an image that charged down her consciousness and wrapped its fist around her heart.

It was a vision of Lavellan, pinioned to a wooden display built along three lines of a triangle and peppered with enough iron studs to limit fae powers. The shape-shifter's arms were bound to either side of the structure, pinned on with ice-ropes that wrapped around his wrists in spiralled rounds. He was similarly bound at the ankles, where his feet were joined at the downward apex of the triangle. Despite the cold, his chest was streaked with rivulets of moisture, and his head hung low, casting his hair around his face where white streaks grazed against his chin.

Sysa's mind raced, rushing like the darts that flew all around her. She was caught between the external world and the crashing and hurtling of her thoughts. While Arno rode the sky like a storm-battered boat, Sysa scanned her vision, trying to work out what she could do to help Lavellan. *Neven won't hurt him, she needs the three of us together*, she thought, pushing down the sick feeling that swirled inside her stomach.

As if in answer, the Lavellan in her vision lifted his head, conveying that same sense to her through steel-blue eyes that ravaged their way inside her soul.

'Thank you, Three-Wings, now go, go help Sirius,' Sysa said, focusing her attention back on the raven. The image she had of Lavellan stilled, replacing itself with the dark-webbed creature that flew around her head. She could smell Lavellan's scent on the air around her, the cool clearness of him still clinging to the feathered form of the raven. Sysa wanted to hold it closer to her, to keep it with her like the stones that were still tucked against her heart-space. Instead, she released it, signalling for Three-Wings to leave her with a reassuring nod.

Sysa watched the raven fly towards the wolf pack in a cascade of shining ebony. When he reached them, he took his place at Sirius's shoulder, leading the pack as both an outlier and a friend. Sysa knew that he was her friend too now – that they all were. Lavellan had sent them to help her, and his mother had punished him in the only way she knew possible. She was keeping him away and hoping Sysa would believe her capable of the unthinkable.

Unless… Sysa thought to herself, an uncomfortable thought prickling underneath her skin like crawling insects. Unless Neven had seen something, something that would mean her own son could be dispensable.

Something that meant Lavellan wasn't safe.

Sysa's eyes bloomed with another vision, of three stones hanging in the air like pegless laundry. Next, the three stones moved and cavorted, rearranging themselves into a triangle, the same shape Lavellan had been pinned to as she watched. The stones shone brightly, flickering in the sky like starry dancers, announcing their own ambition. *Or rather Neven's*, Sysa thought as a swirling tang rose up in her throat and she fought down the urge to vomit. Were the three stones as much of a Trinity as she, Brodie and Lavellan? And if so, what did that mean for the shape-shifter and her family?

Lavellan's words rushed back to her like the winds that flew against her body.

My mother isn't the maternal kind.

CHAPTER TWENTY-FOUR

Sysa's mind buzzed as she tried to make sense of her visions, while Arno continued to avoid the ice darts Neven was unleashing. The winds were getting fiercer, blowing the eagles and Star-Steed around like leaves as Neven's spiked fury swept its way across the sky.

Behind them, the coloured lines of Steel Castle were looming, pushing a path towards the Castle of Thunder. Sysa wondered how much longer it would take to overcome their opposites, and then, for a fleeting moment, wondered if they might actually prevail at all.

She looked down to where Neven stood and saw something moving in the space behind her. Sysa narrowed her eyes to ignite her fae eyesight and felt her stomach lurch as she saw a terrible repetition of the scene she'd just devoured. Lavellan was being wheeled out by a group of guards, his body pinned to Neven's triangular contraption like a sideshow. He lifted his head, offering her a look that made her feel like she was falling into the bluest, deepest ocean. But the meaning in his eyes was lost to her.

She blinked back tears, wanting to hurtle into the depths with him and carry him gently back to shore.

Neven laughed, looking over her shoulder at her son and then back up at Sysa. The sound crackled in the air, severing the connection that ran between Sysa and Lavellan like a cord. Sysa squeezed her eyes shut, and then opened them again, clearing her vision of emotion. At her side, she felt Brodie rear up and then stiffen. Like Neven's laugh, his body crackled with a sense of energy, and he looked down at Lavellan and swallowed, as if forcing his feelings into an ocean of his own.

Sysa offered him a weak smile, grateful both for his understanding, and for the brief respite from Neven's ice darts. The Unseelie queen was so busy in her gloating she had momentarily ceased her assaults into the sky. Throughout it all, Krystan, Brodie and Frode had been fighting back with their own light powers, while Brigid's involvement had been limited to evasion. Sysa's concerns bounced between her grandmother, Lavellan and her family, who were no doubt still asleep somewhere in the Castle of Thunder. The threat to them all formed its own sort of triangle, careering around Sysa's consciousness like a ball bouncing off the corners of a room.

'Do you think she's going to hurt him?' Brodie asked eventually, his eyes tracking the line of Sysa's concern as he hovered in the air atop his eagle.

'I don't know,' Sysa shouted back over the wind gusts.

'But I think she knows something, Brodie. That the three stones alone might be enough.'

Brodie stared back at her, his eyes rounding into pools of realisation as he absorbed Sysa's words over the throng of noise and colour. If Lavellan's gaze was the ocean, Brodie's was the one that lifted Sysa's heart into the sky. Over his shoulder, she watched as Frode and the others reared up in the air, sweeping their way into the fringes of the conversation. The looks on their faces were enough to tell Sysa they had heard everything.

And the look on Brigid's face was enough to tell Sysa that her fears about the stones were more than just a possibility.

The look on Brigid's face told her they were real.

'So, she's going to try to get the other two stones,' Brigid said, her voice flat with a weak sense of alarm that bled into the air around them.

'Not if I get your stone back first,' Sysa answered, lifting her chin a notch as Arno tossed his head, making Sysa slide on his back before she placed a palm to his wing to steady him, his movement stilling underneath her legs.

'There, there, boy,' Sysa whispered, rubbing at the bird's stiff feathers and offering him another murmured reassurance. The group's uncertainty smarted like the bite of a wound that had torn the surface of the sky.

Behind them, the rayed lines of Steel Castle sped through the air like racing currents, searing into their sickness-inducing opposites. Sysa exhaled, feeling her breath whistle through her teeth like a final prompt to charge. She called out to the lines then, willing them to make a collective surge against the sickness.

Down below, Neven had resumed her attack, flanked by guards who shot leaping arrows into the cathedral of the sky.

Sysa's group split and veered, turning and twisting to avoid the attack while lashing out light rays against the onslaught.

'Get behind me!' she called out to her grandmother, and Star-Steed moved into the space at Arno's rear. Arno flew on, tailed by the steed who nosed his back, leaving a trail of starry motes to follow. A ray from Steel Castle nudged at Sysa's back, as if in question.

She felt her own body answer, and as her back arched, the ray flew through her, searing into her heart-space and emerging out into the sky in an explosion of colour and never-ending light.

'Sysa!' Brodie cried out, as she held her position, lifting her arms to each side as the rays struck through her insides like bladeless knives entering her back in formation. Again and again they came, each one drawing to a point at the base of her spine, then slipping through her body in waves of coloured light. They painted her sealskin in bright rainbow swirls, until the mottled skin shone in a paintbox of colours. Sysa threw her head back, her hair flying out behind her in streaks above the sealskin, painting the sky like the waves that were exploding from her chest.

And the feeling, Sysa thought, as she surrendered herself to the moment, was a revelation. She felt no pain, no tearing, only the cool blue pass of something, like the cold that had ensnared her when she'd entered the water at Dunnet Head. Each pass seared in and then out of her body, leaving the kind of clarity that only came from the sky and the ocean. These rays belonged to her, they were part of her, and now she was giving something of herself to them.

She was giving them something that could not be *taken*, just like the stories and the power Grey had given her. Just like every single thing she had been given, every act of love that had led her here to this.

The others watched, enthralled by the rays spilling

into the world around them. Down below, Neven was throwing shrieks of scissored pain into the air. Through her closed eyes, Sysa knew that Lavellan was also looking up at her, she could almost see the twitch of his lips behind the red gauze of her eyelids. The thing that had pulled for so long at her ribcage was unravelling. She was letting go and sending her own heart into the world.

And when she opened her eyes, she saw the fruit of that unravelling. A thousand spirals of colour danced in the air like painted rain. The rays surged, ensnaring Neven's wisps and dissolving them into nothing. The lines of sickness crept away like injured warriors. They fell into themselves, slowly faded and then died.

As they died, something else was awoken. Sysa felt that rumble of awakening, a sound that came from inside the Castle of Thunder and beat its way to her like a drum. Her family and the others who were sleeping were waking up, she could feel it. The sickness was falling away from them, shrugging itself off like a cloak slipping softly to the floor.

In the next moment, Sysa heard voices, footsteps, movement. Her family were moving out of the castle, racing to the place where Neven and Lavellan were. Sysa looked down, seeing the faces of Bruan, Elise, Elva and William upturned towards her. From the trees, Three-Wings, Sirius and the wolf army swarmed in, clawing their way towards the castle where they surrounded Neven and the guards like the curled fingers of a hand.

'You did it, you stopped the sleeping sickness,' Brigid whispered from where Star-Steed had shifted to Arno's side during the light-war. Sysa turned her head, watching Brigid's gaze drift to where Bruan stood, his eyes anchoring his mother's in a moment of recognition, followed by twin understanding nods. Brigid's eyes flickered with light and moisture, reflecting the colours that had flagged the sky just seconds earlier. But there was an ashen look to her expression, Sysa saw as she watched the old lady reunite with her son across the momentary silence. Brigid was half-slumped over Star-Steed.

'It's not going to be enough,' Sysa said, trying to convey her own message to her family over the distance. 'We need to get the other stone.'

She felt the heat of the stones that were cradled at her breast, thrumming and protesting like two heartbeats. She knew that they needed to be with their other, and felt them pull away, railing against the fabric that still held them to her heart. She remembered the way her own heart had felt pulled to the Castle of Thunder, to Lavellan, at the start of all this, and the way she had also felt pulled towards Brodie. Somewhere inside herself, she understood the stones' longing, and her own heartbeat chimed alongside them, as if trying to bridge the separation, to forge some way across.

On the ground, her parents and Elva were throwing out light rays at Neven and the guards in a melee of battle. William had huddled into a corner, tucking himself into one of the castle's walls like an upright human brick. Elsewhere, the wolves were swarming around guards, sending them tumbling into the air with lashing paws and fangs that flashed bright white and hungry. Krystan, Frode and Brodie were now swooping down low, picking off guards with the clawed feet of their eagles and scattering them into the trees like curled-up swords.

Arno hovered in the air, allowing Sysa's thoughts

to guide him. She waited, knowing that their bond had now shifted, that the sky seer could now sense the inner workings of her mind. The sealskin had brought her close to the sky and ocean, and all the things that belonged there. Arno knew what Sysa was thinking: that if she joined the others in battle, she would be taking the stones closer to Neven and the possibility of capture. Neven, too, seemed to understand the dilemma, and she stretched her arms to the sky, willing the stones towards her, imploring Sysa to come close to her proffered hands.

'What do I do?' Sysa said eventually, both to the air and to Brigid. 'I don't know if I can hold them.'

Brigid turned, her hoarse voice scraping the space between their eyes.

'You know what you have to do,' she said, her gaze liquid, understanding.

The stones pressed against Sysa's gown, as if the sky was sucking in a deep, long breath in the distance.

The only thing holding them to her was the beating of her heart.

CHAPTER TWENTY-FIVE

There was no other option, Sysa knew, than to plummet the depths of the sky and join the others near the ground in battle. She could tell, even from this distance, that her parents and Elva had been weakened by their time under Neven's sleeping spell. They were jabbing out darts that sprung into the air before falling to the earth like limp arrows. Although a few were meeting with the odd leg or body part of some or other guard, they were only doing enough to stun them, hold them off. Brodie and the others were having more success, but Sysa could see that it was only a matter of time until the guards regrouped, putting her family in danger. And there was still the matter of Lavellan, who remained tethered to his wooden prison, the sight of him making Sysa's throat constrict like a fire burning inwards on itself. She watched him, wondering what her parents might be thinking about his presence – if they'd made any link between his imprisonment and Sysa, it wasn't evident in the frenetic charge that was happening below.

'I have to go, Brigid,' she said eventually, sucking in her breath as if that might keep the stones close to her. Beneath them, Neven was reaching her arms outwards, sending out ice streams that fell to the ground and then swept upwards, hardening in the air like glass. The ice formed a dome around the Unseelie queen, offering the appearance that someone had tipped a glass bowl upside down around her. As Sysa watched, Neven shot spiked darts through the domed roof, twirling her index fingers to sear away at a section that fell to the ground and then shattered, leaving a perfect open round behind.

Neven's face turned upwards in the round, giving her angular form a strangely circular echo. She lifted her hands, channelling her powers like the seeking branches of a tree. Her fingers were fringed with a frost that Sysa felt pricking the air around her, plummeting the sky into colder and colder temperatures. Neven had made herself impenetrable, and the light rays that were being aimed at her now bounced off her icy shield in a hopeless rhythm, as if even they knew how fruitless their efforts were.

Despite the blistering cold, Sysa felt the stones burn hot against her. They made a sound that was almost like singing, the same chorus of echoing and chiming that Sysa had heard so many times before.

'Stay here,' she ordered Brigid, offering her grandmother what she hoped was a reassuring look as she gestured for Arno to fly downwards.

'I will,' Brigid said, leaning further into the shining mane of Star-Steed. As Arno's beak dipped, the steed thrummed its wings and hooves against air, doing something akin to treading water in the sky.

The wind rushed up to Sysa's face, sending her hair and her sealskin flying out behind her. Arno was by now positioned vertically, like a winged arrow that had been dropped from a high cloud. Sysa saw Neven's hands and face loom larger and larger, and watched her cool blue eyes bulge with concentration. Sysa could even see her eyelashes, the tips of them coated with ice crystals. The sugary granules topped Neven's brows and darted silver-white flecks across her features, while around her body snow-white wisps climbed the air and seeped out of the opening, entering the world in dazzling lines.

Sysa blinked, blinded by the light, and felt Arno flailing underneath her as the wispy streaks climbed against his passage. The eagle flung his head about, sending Sysa skidding around his back until she clasped her hands tight to his feathers, calming him with a steady, gentle touch. The eagle reared up again, before forcing his way down into another piece of sky so far undisturbed by Neven's meddling. Below, the Unseelie queen bared her teeth, the white of them almost as blinding as her light rays. She continued sending her ice strands out in all directions. All the while, Sysa felt the thrumming of the stones next to her and felt their sense of longing, a feeling she had become accustomed to, and could recognise like a friend.

Arno maintained his carousel of diving and rearing while Sysa held on, trying to connect with an energy that might bring the other stone to her. Neven struck out in the language of *taking*, trying to pull Sysa's stones to her in the same way she had pulled the other from Brigid; that magnetic force that had sucked it through the air of Steel Castle's hall. Her face was contorted in effort, her pained expression suggesting to Sysa that Brigid's stone was also trying to reunite with its counterparts. A realisation settled on Sysa in a shroud of understanding.

The stones would not be reunited by *taking*. Like the

powers she had been bequeathed in stories, the stones could only be reunited by *giving*. As the thought occurred to her, the stones at her chest seared her skin in hot unison.

The stones had given themselves to her back in that space above the water.

The only way through this was for the other stone to be given to her. The three stones would not be joined by the forcing of either her or Neven's will.

Sysa stilled, feeling numb about her realisation and how she could find a way out of this stalemate. She glanced over her shoulder and saw Brigid slumped even further over her starry steed. Her grandmother, she knew, was weakening, fading away as her stone's powers remained far away from her. As if to confirm that suspicion, Brigid and Star-Steed started to literally fade, parts of them falling away as if they were images being rubbed out of a scene. It started with Brigid's feet and the steed's hooves, which were dissolving into air as Sysa watched on in horror. Brigid remained silent, her acceptance of whatever fate was being doled out to her kindling the beginnings of a fire in Sysa's throat. All around them, the stars that belonged to the steed were bursting and popping, dying in the sky's blue blanket. Sysa turned her face back to Neven, only to be met with a snarling grin of victory.

'You can't win this. Kneel for me, Sysa, just as I planned you would. Lavellan is ready and waiting for you. Can't you see?' Neven jerked her head towards where her son was still hanging like a piece of meat on his wooden frame.

Sysa breathed in, calculating the line that ran from Brigid, through Neven and on towards Lavellan. Along that line she felt the presence of others, the souls who had lost their lives in the pursuit of this Trinity, this thing of power that had become nothing but a curse. She saw an echo of Ida, swirling around the air as she fussed with silverware and sharp corners. She saw Luna, combing her hair on a rock made of a cloud. At the end of that line, she saw Lavellan, whose head was lifted towards her, his face lined with rivulets of sweat, his blue eyes narrowed into painful triangles. And then along the length of that imagined line she saw something white, something of hooves and mane and magic, something headed with a horn. It was the unicorn, the one Grey had once been, or at least some vision of it. Sysa couldn't tell if she was dreaming or seeing, but she watched as it ran from Brigid, past her memories and Neven, and along towards Lavellan, opening like a white cloud in front of his face before dissolving into sky.

As the unicorn dissolved, so did Sysa's images of Luna and Ida. She blinked herself back into reality, where Neven's expression indicated she had not shared the vision Sysa had just watched. Behind Sysa, Brigid was still fading slowly into nothingness. The battle being played out by her family below had stilled, and a row of upturned faces now awaited her response.

All but one – Brodie, who had, in that moment of quiet, moved towards Lavellan. Sysa watched as Brodie stood in front of him, each eyeing the other as if they were the only two beings in the world. Brodie said something, but in the high-pitched quiet, Sysa couldn't hear it. All she heard was the chiming sound, and the beating of her heart.

Neven was so busy in her gloating that she didn't turn to see what was happening. Instead, she kept her eyes narrowed on Sysa while Brodie swept his arms silently

251

through the air. With each swipe, the bonds that kept Lavellan prisoner fell away from him. He stepped out of the wooden contraption, clicking his neck to each side, uncurling his fists like opening stars.

'I'll kneel,' Sysa said eventually, feeling as she said it that there suddenly wasn't enough air in the world for her. Neven's face lit up in a twisted glimmer, and she turned her head to where Lavellan was now standing, her victory eclipsing any concern that he was free.

'Well, well, well,' she said, drawing out a long breath. 'All friends together.'

Sysa looked down at her parents and Elva, not sure if the thing she saw reflected in their eyes was pride or something else.

'Down, boy,' Sysa directed to Arno, who hesitated for a moment before dropping towards the ground, his claws scarring the earth in jagged patterns. Nearby, Krystan and Frode had also alighted, and stood next to Sysa's family in a line. As soon as her feet touched the ground, Sysa ran to them, thumping into her father's chest to be enveloped in the arms that were so familiar to her.

'Mother, Father... I'm so sorry, about all of this,' Sysa said, shaking her head while Elise murmured gentle words into her hair, her lips grazing the salty tears that were running down Sysa's cheeks.

Bruan caught her face in his hands as Elva rushed into the huddle.

'None of this is your fault, Sysa. But are you sure about this?' Bruan's eyes drifted up to where Brigid was slowly dissolving into air.

'It's her, Father, it's Brigid – your mother,' Sysa said,

trying to convey everything she needed to tell him in this space where time seemed to be squeezing in on itself.

Bruan nodded, and Sysa saw him swallow down his emotion, feeling an indescribable pain at the tiny bobbing of his throat.

'And yes, I'm sure, because she doesn't have much time, and Neven has something I need, something I can't just take,' Sysa said after a moment in which a change had come over her father's face, a new veil of understanding.

'You will do what you must,' Elise said, her words clipping the air, at once soft and resolute.

'Then I'm ready,' Sysa said, turning back into the world, emboldened by her family's blessing.

She felt like she was about to leap from a cliff face, hoping to be caught in a net of her own instincts.

She took a breath, hoping the net was cast.

CHAPTER TWENTY-SIX

rodie and Lavellan stood waiting, two points of the triangle Sysa now joined in an echo of the wooden structure that lay discarded behind them.

Sysa met each of their eyes in turn, sensing agreement in the stares that were returned to her in lines of blue. Around them, her family and the others moved in, compressing the air in a small, defeated circle. At the fringes, Sirius and the wolves hovered, their advance to the castle now layered with a scent of submission that nosed its way into the gaps.

From the trees, the guards stunned by Sysa's family were rising in haphazard wobbles of confusion. Some stumbled their way towards the castle, while others remained groaning amongst the leaves. Those who had been struck by Brodie, or Frode and Krystan's rays, were destined to remain floored for longer, and lay balled around earthy lumps or splayed out over the roots of tree trunks. From his vantage point on the castle wall, Arno cast Sysa a beady look that was matched by the one Three-Wings offered from nearby.

Not far away, Neven was searing away at the ice dome she had created around herself, which she now scissored with knife-sharp nails, her arms tracing the arc of her surroundings in the shape of a sun sinking into the horizon. Her domed shield fell away, shattering to the ground in lines of sheeted ice like rain falling from a roof. As the air around her cleared, Neven stepped out of her previous enclosure, her advance pushing out a front of cold that travelled alongside her. The sky was draped with a clear, crisp mantle, and Sysa felt the assault of an ice-sharp clarity waft up to settle underneath her nose.

As Neven advanced with long strides, Sysa allowed herself one final glance over her shoulder. She looked up, watching as Brigid continued to melt into the sky. There was little left of her grandmother and Star-Steed now; everything beneath Brigid's chest was gone, replaced by the blue rub of the skyline. Above and around, the flurry of colour that had filled the sky just moments previously was also fading like the final seconds of a sunset. Sysa wondered what kind of sun would rise to follow it, and bit her lip, hoping her gamble would pay off.

She turned back and watched Neven come closer. The Unseelie queen's lips lifted in a triumphant smirk as she cast her eyes over the three of them, offered up in front of her like food.

'I see you managed to release yourself, or did your new friend here help you?' Neven said, sweeping a disgusted look at Lavellan, and then at Brodie.

Brodie made to take a step forward, but Lavellan halted him, holding a hand out just in front of Brodie's arm.

'Mother...' Lavellan began, his voice strange and docile.

'It doesn't matter.' Neven waved the word away with a flick of her wrist, her long fingers flashing in the air. 'You've done your bit, and she's here, ready, isn't she? Saved me untying you myself, and now we're ready to move on to my winter ceremony, just as planned.'

Sysa narrowed her eyes at Lavellan and Brodie, trying to convey a million questions.

The only answer was the line of blue eyes that stared back, like arrows pointing to her heart.

'It's not quite the setting I'd hoped for,' Neven said in a sterile tone, turning her head this way and that, as she made a show of appraising the surrounding environment. 'I'd imagined one of the castle's throne rooms, the three of you resplendent atop a dais. But given that your grandmother doesn't appear to have much time left,' she gloated, her voice searing the air like her ice darts, 'I suggest we get on with things. Such a shame, really, you're all so untidy looking, standing out here in the dirt.'

'Before we begin, I want an assurance that you're going to keep up your end of the bargain,' Sysa said, her clipped voice interrupting Neven's drawn-out performance. Sysa had felt an uncomfortable prickle run up and down her spine as she'd recognised the similarities between Neven and her son. Lavellan's grand gestures and drama were all emulated in the female in front of them. As that thought arrived, she sensed Lavellan's gaze bear down on her.

He's nothing like her, she thought, repeating the words inwardly in affirmation, as if her faith in him could make her feelings true.

'I said if you kneeled, your family would be safe, and so will old Granny,' Brigid replied, jolting Sysa back into reality. 'And, as I'm feeling generous, I'll allow your little insubordination back there to go unpunished.' Neven made a clicking sound through her teeth, as if dismissing the events of the last day as something of little consequence to her. 'But your family's powers, and dear Brigid's, of course, will remain diminished. I mean, my three darlings, we can't have anyone upsetting the natural balance of things now, can we? You'll be mine, just as you're meant to be, and things will settle into the order that they should. It's all this unbalance, all this vying for power that's been causing this trouble since Rogart. After this, we'll all live in a perfect winter harmony, and perhaps my own mother, the Cailleach, can join us too. It all sounds so much better for everyone, don't you think, Sysa?' Neven's expression was smooth, glass-like. Sysa took a deep breath in through her nostrils, trying to contain the fury that was building behind her eyes.

She wanted to say that she had never seen any *vying for power* from her family, from Fyrish. That she had never seen anything except a defence against actions – actions like Rogart's and Neven's – that were wrong. But she bit down on her words, feeling the scratch of a new anger fizz inside her fingertips. She pressed her nails into her palms, knowing she was leaving behind indent marks, like moons.

She dipped her chin, trying to display some sort of deference without answering Neven's question. If her eyes seared with the fury she was feeling, it wasn't acknowledged in Neven's returning stare. The Unseelie queen seemed to have grown bored with her own announcements, and whipped her cloak through the air, as if signalling the start of a new act in her performance.

'Now that we're all in agreement, let's get on with this. Get down,' she ordered, pointing her finger to indicate that it was time for them to kneel.

'Are you sure about this?' Brodie asked from Sysa's side, his head tipped low to keep his voice between them.

'As sure as I can be,' Sysa whispered from the corner of her mouth.

Brodie nodded, the tiniest of gestures that encompassed everything he had always promised her.

From now on, it's you and me, always.

His words from another time drifted back to her. Said or unsaid, she knew that the words still belonged between them. They hung briefly in the air before disappearing back into their hidden, silent world.

At Sysa's other side, Lavellan kept his eyes forward. She shot him a glance, but his gaze was penetrating something else. He looked like he was staring at something distant, something of another place or time, like the words Sysa had just heard inside herself. He looked like he was *preparing* himself, Sysa thought with an uncomfortable sensation. She knew Lavellan was aware of every tiny movement she was making, that he was waiting for her to drop to the ground, so he could follow. But something in his expression – or lack of it – made Sysa feel that he was also waiting for some other thing, as if he had already made a decision, as if he had already stepped away from where she was.

She felt a hand on her shoulder and turned her head, seeing a guard looming behind her. Evidently, some of the guards had reassembled and, assuming insurgence, had decided to help get her and the other two to the ground. A pair stood behind Brodie and Lavellan, pressing on them with meaty hands and pushing them downwards.

Sysa watched flurries of dirt and stone fly into the air like shrapnel as the males' knees landed on the mud-strewn earth.

She lifted her hands, her palms facing out, to indicate

that the guard should unhand her. Another heat grew in her fingers – she knew she could best the man with ease. Thinking of Brigid, though, she breathed in, clearing her emotions. For now, she had to be obedient, docile.

She dropped her knees to the ground slowly, never taking her eyes from Neven, who stared back, her expression bright with a growing thrill.

'What a lovely sight this is, *mmm*?' Neven said, lifting her chin to the assembled audience as she surveyed the line of submission in front of her. 'All three of them together.'

Sysa felt the sound of a rushed shifting from somewhere in the background and lifted her head to see Frode being held back by a guard.

'Don't,' she whispered, giving Frode a look that she hoped would do enough to appease him. In response, Frode shook his head, shrugging off the guard and hissing at the man in a way that made him jolt.

Sysa scanned her eyes over the rest of the watching group, lingering on her parents and Elva, who were huddled together in a line, which William now completed. Something tugged at her heart as she saw the expressions on their faces, the layers of pain and fear that covered them like masks. Elva was crying now, and stood with her face pressed into William's shoulder.

Sysa turned up the corners of her mouth, a curve that wasn't quite a smile but conveyed enough to let them know she wasn't frightened.

When she turned back towards Neven, something was leaping from the Unseelie queen's hands.

Sysa squeezed her eyes shut, snapping them open again to find that the thing was growing in an arrowed line that

259

pointed upwards. Neven gazed at it, her blue eyes lit in a reflection of its power.

The thing flashed like white steel, severing the air in a stroke of lightning.

Neven grinned, holding out her sword of ice.

CHAPTER TWENTY-SEVEN

Neven made a cackling sound as she wielded her new toy, her expression triumphant. She stood with both hands around the stem, pointing the icy arrow towards the sky, her feet planted wide, her cloak flapping behind her in the wind. The sword made a sound, like an echo of cold, Sysa thought, as she surveyed this new agent of humiliation. The sound was not dissimilar to the chiming she had become so used to hearing. It hurt her ears, and she had to stop herself from drawing her hands up against her head.

The sword was lit from inside, giving the appearance of a snowy arrow wrapped in ice and crystal. Neven held it away from her body, so that from where Sysa kneeled, Neven's top half appeared to be split into two perfect, icy halves. She looked adoringly at the sword, tilting her head this way and that to get a better impression of her own amazement. She rolled it through her palms so that it cast out a frosty rim around their surroundings, as if she had set a snow globe atop the world.

When she was done with her self-congratulation, she finally lifted the sword upwards, recanting words in a language Sysa didn't recognise. Sysa watched the movement of the queen's lips, remembering the words Brigid had offered up when she'd tried to revive Bruan

261

back at the Castle of Steel. There was something different about Neven's utterings, though, something cold and bitter in her incantations. Her prayer was pointed, as sharp as the arrow she was holding.

Sysa darted a look at Lavellan and Brodie, noticed the way their heads hung, the way strands of hair grazed their cheekbones. She wanted to memorise it all.

Finally, Neven stepped towards Brodie, lowering her sword against his shoulder.

'Will you submit? Will you become one of the Winter Three?'

'I will.' Brodie's words sounded blunt and cold, too small to convey the magnitude of what was happening.

'Then I anoint you Brodie of Winter,' Neven announced, lifting the sword over Brodie's head and resting it on his other shoulder. Brodie kept his head low, his face searing with inner rage.

Neven pressed her lips together, turning her attention to Lavellan as she bypassed Sysa in the line-up. The queen's mouth twitched in anticipation – it was clear she was leaving Sysa as the final prize. As Neven surveyed her son, she sighed and tilted her head, a disappointed look on her face.

'So, it wasn't really worth it, was it dear, this scurrying around behind my back to try to help her? In the end, she's finished up here, right where I always wanted her. But never mind, Lavellan, because now you can *be together*, just as you wanted to.' Neven said the words in a childish tone, spinning one hand in the air as the other wafted her sword around. 'But this time, of course, you'll be working for me – all of you will. But don't worry, sweetheart, you can still protect her, be the kind of man you want to be.' Neven rolled her eyes, shaking her head towards the sky.

'Sysa doesn't need my protection,' Lavellan said, a muscle in his jaw twitching.

Sysa glanced sideways, noticing him opening his mouth to say something else, before pursing his lips, thinking better of it. In front of him, his mother had grown bored, and whipped her sword downwards against his shoulder, impatient to move on.

'Do you submit?' she said, pressing the point of her sword between bones, pushing it deeper than she needed to. Sysa saw a bloom of red appear on Lavellan's shirt and wondered what other punishments would be doled out to him once this little ceremony was complete.

'I do,' Lavellan said, his eyes bright and clear as he looked up at his mother.

'Well, there we have it then,' Neven smirked to herself. 'My boy, my beautiful. I now anoint you Lavellan of Winter.' She lowered the sword towards his other shoulder more gently. Lavellan made a snorting sound, and his mother dug the point deeper, making him jerk as another circle of red appeared around his arm.

Sysa's fingertips crackled again, thinking back to his earlier words, the brief flash of pain that had appeared in his eyes as he'd said them.

My mother isn't maternal.

Something flickered inside Sysa's stomach, and she thought of the blue butterfly, like a caged creature fluttering underneath her ribs. Neven took a step back, her lips curling upwards in anticipation, and she held her sword aloft, making another show of the power she was about to wield. Sysa's eyes burned, and she clamped her fists tight, wishing Neven would just get on with it. As if hearing her thoughts, Neven flung her words out into the air like a cold, sharp blade of winter.

'Will you submit? Sysa, will you become one of my new Three?'

A million thoughts raced in Sysa's mind, and images swept across her eyes like the clouds in the sky above them. She thought of Ida, Luna, Rogart – she thought of everything that had led her here to this. She thought of Grey and wondered what he would say if he were here now with her. There were so many things she wanted to ask him. What sort of lives would her family live if she agreed to this? What sort of chance would they have if she said no?

She squeezed her eyes shut, trying to discern some sort of meaning from the vision she'd had moments previously. All around her, time seemed to slow down, as if the fae lands were already calibrating to a new version of the world. She took a deep breath, thinking of the way the unicorn had run towards Lavellan in her image, the way it had dissolved around him. Inside her head, she stretched out a hand to that image, trying to grasp whatever meaning it seemed to offer, wanting to understand something that lay just outside the reaches of her mind.

She was running out of time, though, and she knew it. Brigid needed her, and so did her family, so did all the people of Fyrish. But, she wondered desperately, did that make what she was doing right? Just a few moments before, she had felt so sure of her instincts, so sure of her own pathway. She had believed the answer would come to her, just like all the other answers. But right now, she could see no story, could discern no answer.

Just as that realisation dawned on her, she heard words that chimed in the air, words that only she could hear in that glass-rim language that had been following her since she'd left that night for the Castle of Thunder.

The voice was Grey's: *It's time to write your own story.*

The world in front of Sysa's eyes shook, and something thrust itself next to her face, landing on her shoulder and then searing off into the distance.

Three-Wings.

As the bird lifted from her body, Sysa saw part of that story reflected in the raven's eye.

*

Neven stumbled backwards, startled by the raven's appearance. Three-Wings was now flying for the trees again, with several guards following him, shouting out curses to the sky. Neven looked rattled and cast a sharp look at the departing figures.

'Get that ridiculous bird out of here.'

Lavellan looked up, his eyes narrowed into bright blue lines.

Finally, Neven turned back, and silence fell over the circle, the only sound the flap of Sysa's sealskin.

'Now, where were we...? Will you submit?' Neven said, trying to regain her previous composure as she lifted her chin a notch. This time, Sysa didn't pause, and she raised her own chin to meet the Unseelie queen's glare, seeing a slight flicker cross her eyeballs. Three-Wings had unnerved her.

'I will.' Sysa answered without blinking.

Neven breathed in through her nose, and a tiny smile appeared at the corner of her lips.

'Then you will no longer be known as the light-bringer, but Sysa of Winter,' Neven said eventually, raising her sword up and lowering it to Sysa's shoulder. From the corner of her eye, Sysa saw the blade's light reflect on Brodie's cheek.

Neven lifted the sword again, holding it above her head like an icy beacon as she revelled in her victory. While she was occupied, Sysa stole a look over her other shoulder. Brigid was almost gone, and Star-Steed had completely disappeared.

Sysa turned back and squeezed her eyes shut, waiting for the sword to fall on her other side, next to Lavellan. Beside her, she felt him stiffen, and felt the stones burn hot, like they were branding her, shouting out to her with their fiery heat. She saw a flash of cold, sensed the downward swipe of Neven's sword through air and felt every muscle in her body tense in anticipation.

As the sword made contact with her shoulder, she felt something strike out to the side of her.

Lavellan had reached out his hand to her.

She took it, feeling the white-hot heat of the final stone against her palm.

CHAPTER TWENTY-EIGHT

'What? You betray me?' Neven cried out, as the sword sprung back from Sysa's shoulder, as if recoiling.

The Unseelie queen looked down at Lavellan and Sysa's joined hands, seeing the faint light of the stone that lit their flesh.

Lavellan stared back, his eyes as hard as the stone they were still holding.

'The stone belongs with Sysa, Mother. Everything belongs with her.' He cast Sysa a sideways glance, the hardness in his eyes cracking, infusing the blue with darts of gold.

'But, how…?' Sysa whispered, echoing the words that Neven was now spitting into the air like shards of lightning. Lavellan shook his head no – there wasn't time to explain it all right now. Sysa could only assume that, somehow, he had managed to glean the stone from Neven's clutches, perhaps without her knowing what was happening. While Neven rained curses on Lavellan, the stone continued to glow between their hands.

At her other side, Brodie caught Sysa's free hand, so that the three of them were lined up, bound together in a seal of their agreement. Brodie flicked his head forward, offering Lavellan a quick nod along the line. Lavellan dipped his chin back, the gesture seeming to signify a new understanding between them. Then he squeezed Sysa's hand, pressing the stone deeper into her palm, like it belonged there.

Sysa squeezed back.

She knew he was trying to tell her to let go.

All around, her parents and the others were watching, their bodies angled forward in rapt attention. To Sysa, it seemed that the world had ceased to breathe in the moment between the sword falling and the touch of Lavellan's skin. She looked around, realising with a start that the world *was* actually frozen, holding its breath, waiting for her. Her family stared back like open-mouthed statues, while above, Brigid's face – all that now remained of her – hung suspended like a mask of ice.

Sysa's palms itched, not just with the heat of the stone but with the fizz of anger. Neven had tricked her. She'd had no intention of letting her family or Brigid live out their lives in peace. She had frozen the world with her prayers and her incantations, leaving only Brodie, Lavellan and Sysa – and herself, of course – any agency. Sysa didn't need the seeing stone to tell her the rest of that future. When that sword had fallen, her family would have been shattered, toppled like the icy statues they now were.

Sysa squeezed her eyes shut as hot tears slid over her cheekbones. For a moment, she was frozen in her own world, the only things that existed the images that raced inside her head. She saw the eye Three-Wings had just offered her, that polished black round that had reflected not her own image, but a picture of Lavellan. She saw Hugh and his father back at the cottage in Caithness, heard the echo of Geordie's voice… *'catch him one day and kill him… all-healing…'*

She squeezed her eyes tighter. She didn't want to see or hear the rest.

But still the images came, flickering across her mind, tracking the back of her eyelids like a dream or a nightmare. Her lips curved into a sad smile, remembering how Lavellan had interrupted her dreams back at the Castle of Steel. And now, in the space behind her eyes, she saw an image of Neven, placing Brigid's stone in Lavellan's pocket, ordering her son with a silent command as she patted at the fabric. Lavellan watching as she flung an arm into the air, instructing her guards to shackle him to the contraption he had been wheeled out on like part of some warped fair. Lavellan had hissed then, shrugging his shoulders as the guards had grabbed him, but his attempts were half-hearted. He was being obedient, being what his mother expected of him.

What Neven had expected was for him to dangle himself out in the courtyard like bait.

Neven had known, Sysa now realised, that Lavellan would draw her in, call to her like a magnet. With the stone in his possession, Sysa would be pulled in a way the Unseelie queen could never have managed by herself. Even with Brigid's stone, Neven's power over Sysa was limited, so she had used her own son as a pawn in it all.

Sysa had not been the only one gambling on her instincts, she thought to herself, a sickening feeling growing inside her stomach like a creature clawing its way out of a pit.

But in Neven's case, Sysa now knew, her instincts had misplaced Lavellan's loyalties. Tears streamed down her face as she thought of the child Lavellan, abandoned to this supposed destiny by his own parent, the one who was meant to love him most.

Lavellan's words grated on her, grinding her down so that she felt hollow and shapeless.

My mother isn't the maternal kind.

Sysa squeezed his hand again, not ever wanting to let go.

★

Sysa opened her eyes then, finding the world right where she had left it. Neven was still screaming out fury, while Brodie and Lavellan still clung on to Sysa's hands. She looked at Brodie, who nodded back at her before releasing his fingers so that she felt unhinged, unbalanced. She offered the same look to Lavellan and saw the same encouragement in his eyes. This time it would be up to her to pull away, though, and she tilted her head, her eyes streaming, pleading. Lavellan smiled back at her, his face stripped of all the layers he had used to conceal himself from his mother and the world. Only a second had passed since the sword had bounced away from her but to Sysa, it felt like an eternity.

Lavellan was the blue-inked boy he had been on the beach again. Sysa knew that she had done this, that she had made him into who he was meant to be. She dropped his hand slowly, pressing her own hand to her thigh, needing something to hold onto. Her heart was breaking, but in her most broken moment she knew she was also braver than she had ever been before.

She lifted her eyes to Neven, awaiting the onslaught of ice-light and fury. The Unseelie queen had lost everything, she now had nothing more to lose. Neven shot a dart out from her finger, a final cold spear that held all her fury and anger, and sent it straight towards Sysa.

She was bargaining on the last chip she could gamble with. That in order to beat the Trinity, her only option left was to break it. To separate the three of them, to separate the stones.

As the spear flew towards Sysa, she took a deep breath in, and waited for her heart to shatter. When Lavellan stepped in front of her, the spear landed, driving into his heart, the heart that had now become her shield.

As he fell to the ground, Sysa's own heart seemed to recede, folding in on itself with a pain that was worse than any dagger. She dropped to her knees, padding at the blood that was pooling around Lavellan's body like an awful, sticky shroud.

Above them, Neven's face had contorted into a horrified mask, her mouth hanging open in a silent scream of bewilderment. Sysa took Lavellan's hand again, rocking herself as she pressed his knuckles to her lips.

'It's okay,' he said, his voice raspy and thick, 'it's how it's meant to be. You showed me what love means. You showed me who I am, Sysa.'

'No, you can't go, I can't be without you,' Sysa cried, rolling his hand against her cheek, covering his skin in tears and desperation.

'You'll never be without me.'

Sysa kept her eyes on his, until his smile faded, and his hand slipped gently from her grasp.

★

Sysa wanted to scream, but what came from her open mouth was a void, silence. Her eyes streamed, burning tears across her cheeks in red-hot welts that licked her face like flames. The frozen-hard world spun around her, as unbalanced as her own body, which suddenly felt incomplete, lopsided. She thought of the word *grief*, how minute and how incomplete it was, how such a word could not convey the shattering she felt inside her head, her heart, her soul. Grief was an explosion, hitting her like a wall, an avalanche. Someday in the future it might become a flowing river or a wave that lapped the shore, but it would always be there, moving and changing, restless or rising like the wind. Sysa knew all of this as she looked into Lavellan's empty face, studying the features that weren't quite his anymore. She looked around, searching for whatever had flowed out of him, wondering where the thing that made him Lavellan had gone, how it could leave the world, just disappear into the air. How could the living hand she had squeezed so recently now be lifeless, the eyes she had looked into now be glazed, the lips she had kissed be parted without the passage of breath between them? She couldn't understand, and she swiped at her eyes, finding her voice again.

'Where have you gone? Lavellan, where did you go?'

She turned towards Neven, whose face was contorted into an expression of horror that blunted the coldness of her beauty. The Unseelie queen's eyes flickered with confusion, and she stood frozen, momentarily paralysed like the world she had set to ice. Her mouth hung open, rounded to the same void that Sysa had been trapped in, a circle of silent desperation.

Sysa knew she only had a moment until Neven

unfroze, until she adjusted herself to the nightmare of this new reality.

She felt Brodie's hand touch her shoulder, his fingers grazing the pelt of his mother's sealskin.

That skin... all-healing...

Sysa remembered Geordie's words back at the cottage. She suddenly knew, with a cold, sharp clarity.

It wasn't Lavellan's own skin that would heal this. It was the skin she would give him, the same skin that came from Brodie's blood.

Sysa reached her hand back, pulling the skin that had been her cloak from her shoulder. It swept through the air, and she placed it over Lavellan's body so that it floated over him, rippling like the nighttime surface of a silver sea. It came to rest on his body just as Neven regained her voice and screamed, just as she reached out an arm, which might have been reaching for her son, or reaching to begin another onslaught. Sysa would never find out, as the world now filled with coloured lights that were born on the surface of the sealskin. It blazed like a covering of stars atop Lavellan's body. It shimmered and shone, sparkling like a stone that had caught the blaze of a midday sun.

The lights from the skin rose, lifting into the air in columns that charted every colour of the rainbow. The columns were framed with blue, the same colour as the inked lines Sysa had seen track Lavellan's skin. They fanned out, lighting every corner of the world, until they lifted Lavellan and the skin from the earth, and began to rotate, so that Lavellan's shrouded body spun, sending beams of light careering around the huge bowl of the sky around them.

Sysa watched as Lavellan turned like a jewelled dreamcatcher, this male of her dreams and nightmares, this boy who was suddenly lighting up the world.

She opened her mouth to cry out, but the sound was swallowed by a flash, a crashing. The lights that had been grazing the edges of the sky had fanned, pressing its wall to penetrate whatever lay beyond. There was the sound of breaking glass, a sound like starlight exploding.

The lights fell, splintering like dry rain, resetting the world from its frozen aspect. In the same instant, Lavellan's sealskin-covered body lifted, then shattered, joining the raining world in an explosion of the brightest blue.

Sysa turned to face Neven, whose eyes were now frozen in an icy reflection of horror. She reached a hand out, but the Unseelie queen shattered, her body falling to the earth in a thousand pieces of cold, hard ice.

In the next breath, the rest of the world stirred, bringing Sysa's family and friends blinking back into the light as the kingdom around them settled into its new awakening. Above them, Brigid had returned, the last fragments of Star-Steed's hooves reappearing against the blue as if the sky was wielding its own paintbrush.

Sysa took Brodie's hand, lifting her chin to the new world.

PART SIX

THE BRINGER
OF THE LIGHT

CHAPTER TWENTY-NINE

It would take time, Sysa knew, to recover, to retrieve that part of herself that felt scraped out, empty. She ran her fingers over the glass that now housed the two stones, the cage she had magicked to shield them after she had returned the other to Brigid on their arrival back at the Castle of Steel. Her eyes rounded the surface of the stones on the velvet bed that cloaked them, and she watched as they nestled, content that their other was now close. Sysa's attention drifted to the open window, where outside, her family were assembled on the grass, eating and laughing in the sun. Brigid was talking animatedly to Bruan, her palm resting on his hand, both rapt in a routine of rediscovery. Not far away, the statue of the unicorn stood, watching over the family as Star-Steed thrummed behind it, nudging his starry hooves into the lawn. The steed nosed grass, sending Elva racing around the green to catch the motes he pitched into the air, her hands splayed out like the stars she was pursuing. Nearby, William watched from his place at the table beside Elise as they discussed wedding plans for the umpteenth time that week.

Sysa took a long breath in, enjoying the scene, yet feeling pain at the missing spaces. Since Frode and Krystan had left, the castle had quietened and there was more time for her to listen to her thoughts. Waving them away from the castle doors, she had known it would be coming, this creeping sadness that sneaked into her heart and wound its way through the gaps between her bones like unseen threading. She thought of Ida, who should have been scurrying around the castle, worrying over dinner and reprimanding anyone who dared step over the boundaries of freshly mopped halls. Instead, Ida was gone, and so was Luna, and the world carried on, absorbing all the things it had lost, starting anew, turning.

Sysa had absorbed what had been lost too, and the pain lived in her, in a place buried deep inside her heart.

She placed her hands against the wood of the windowsill, trying not to think of the other loss, that twinned pain that would never quite escape her. Grey and Lavellan, whose very names stabbed at her. When she thought of them, that pit in her stomach ached, as if someone was scraping away at it with a knife. The pain of losing Lavellan had crystallised the pain of Grey somehow, until Sysa felt she was living on a seesaw of grief on which she never quite came level. She touched a finger to the window, tracing the places where, below, they should both have been sitting. Sysa vowed that for as long as she lived, there would always be two extra chairs at her tables. There would always be two spaces that belonged to the two of them, both in her heart and in her home.

As if responding to that thought, Three-Wings alighted on the window ledge, flashing a dark eye at her. Down below in the garden, Sirius peered up, awaiting his companion on the grass.

Wolves and ravens. Sysa remembered Lavellan's words

and smiled in spite of herself. These two new additions to her family were a constant reminder of Lavellan, and, she realised, a comfort – even if Arno didn't always agree. Out beyond the trees, the eagle soared, reminding everyone of his presence while keeping a disgruntled distance. He'd come round eventually, Sysa knew, and as her gaze drifted, Three-Wings followed it, flapping off to annoy the eagle. Sirius bounded in their wake, keen to join in with the nuisance. Not far away, Telon, who the family had been surprised to find awake when they returned to Steel Castle, lifted his head from the grass before flopping it down again, apparently bemused by these new arrivals. Sysa wondered if the dog possessed more magic than she had previously given him credit for, and shook her head.

'Poor Arno,' Sysa said to herself, knowing how much Lavellan would have relished the departing scene.

'It's going to take a bit of getting used to, this new family of ours.'

Sysa turned her head and felt the slip of Brodie's arms around her waistline. He perched his chin on her shoulder, grazing a quick kiss against her cheek.

'It is… do you think you'll be able to?' she asked, feeling a pinch of anxiety. Since Lavellan's death, they hadn't had much chance to discuss everything that had happened, and the bustle of departures from Steel Castle had been almost a welcome distraction from it all.

'Of course I will. You and me, always, remember?' Brodie said, turning her around to face him.

'I'm sorry… about everything,' Sysa said, looking into the blue eyes that were her reset, her return to what levelled that seesaw she was on. 'It was never about choosing between you,' she explained, knowing that the thing between Brodie and Lavellan had never been a *choice*, that the word *choice* didn't even begin to encompass it.

'I know that. Things happened as they were meant to. All of it. The sealskin from my mother, the fae lines, the stones, Lavellan... it was all part of how things were meant to be. All part of the journey.' Brodie wiped a stray strand of hair from Sysa's face. 'And now we're on a new journey, one that's just us, and everyone out there.' He scanned the scene outside, looking thoughtful.

'Do you think we were wrong about the Trinity?' Sysa asked after a moment in which his eyes had locked back on hers again. 'That it was the stones all along, I mean?'

Brodie crouched down to come level with her and trailed a finger over her cheekbone. Sysa felt the wet warmth of the tear he was rubbing with his thumb.

'I think it was both, like Brigid said,' Brodie replied after he had stared into her face for a little longer. Sysa nodded, thinking back to a conversation with Brigid after the battle, when the two of them had tried to piece together the parts of the old prophecy their gifts of sight had not allowed them access to before.

'The stones are the real Trinity, but the three of us, we were needed to bring them together and to protect them. Rogart and Neven weren't wrong, at least not completely. Those stones wouldn't have come together if not for us, well, if not for you, Sysa.' Brodie offered her a faint, small smile.

'And Lavellan paid the price for that,' Sysa said, turning away to the window and wrapping her arms around her stomach. Something fluttered under her ribcage, like a butterfly answering the tune of Lavellan's name.

'That was his choice. He did what he wanted to do, for you, for all of this.' Brodie waved his hand around, and caught up to her, looking hesitant. Sysa remembered the time he had said something similar about Grey's death, and the reaction she had fumed at him. This time she just nodded, thinking about that word *choice*, how it meant so much more, how it couldn't really apply when there were no other options left.

'He chose you,' Brodie said, placing both hands on Sysa's shoulders. 'And I know you miss him, that you'll always miss him. And you need to know that it will always be okay.'

'Thank you,' Sysa whispered, her voice hoarse, her throat bobbing.

'Brodie… what did you say to him? When you released him, I mean, that day with Neven?' Now Sysa's eyes were hesitant, and she looked away, not sure if she had asked too much.

'I said thank you,' Brodie said. 'There wasn't much time to say everything I wanted to say, but in the end 'thank you' seemed to cover it. I think, somewhere inside myself, I knew what he was planning.'

'I think somewhere inside myself, I knew too,' Sysa said, thinking of her last kiss with Lavellan, of all the knowledge that had brimmed up in her as she'd been in front of Neven on her knees.

'And now, that part of the Trinity that was the three of us, the part that protected the stones, it's broken,' Sysa said, her voice cracking again.

Something inside Sysa's stomach fluttered for a second time, and she thought of the blue butterfly, the one she had released from her palm a long time ago, as she'd said goodbye to Grey.

'We'll see,' Brodie said, his eyes drifting to the hand Sysa had unconsciously placed on her stomach.

They wrapped themselves around each other, like a shield that bounded the stones in their box of glass.

CHAPTER THIRTY

Now that Brigid was back in control of her stone, spring came quickly to Fyrish, which now existed in a perpetual season of beginning. Back in the human world, Brigid's rise had tempered the worst excesses of winter, keeping the change of seasons even-handed as the Cailleach remained asleep. At Steel Castle, the ivy that had cloaked the walls with sickness receded and the statue of the unicorn on the lawn stood bright and fearless.

Sysa surveyed it all as she stood in the flowered archway, her father's hand looped over her forearm. On his other side stood Elva, who popped her head out, flashing Sysa an excited smile.

'We're both getting married!' she squealed, squeezing Bruan's hand as she hopped about on her feet, making scrunching noises on the stony walkway. Behind her, Telon mimicked her action, swishing his tail in hairy arcs. Sysa smiled, dropping her free hand to where Sirius stood behind her. She rubbed at his fur, remembering to cast an appreciative glance between Arno, Three-Wings, Modan and Star-Steed, who made up the procession that tailed her and her sister's gowns. At the last, Elise arrived, taking her place between Sysa and Bruan.

'We're so proud of both of you – aren't we, Bruan?' she

said, turning her head in the line of their family.

'We are,' Bruan replied, his voice catching. It was a lot, Sysa knew, this day where both of his daughters began a new chapter, another part of the journey of their lives.

'Thank you, Mother and Father, for agreeing to this,' Elva said, referring to her parents' permission to accelerate her and William's wedding plans to marry in this joint celebration with Sysa and Brodie.

'We just want you to be happy,' Elise said, when it became clear that Bruan's emotions had got the better of him. He managed to rub at Elva's knuckle, then pursed his lips in a protective line and smiled.

'I think it's time to walk,' Elise said eventually, tilting her head towards the rows of guests that had now turned towards them. At the end of the makeshift aisle, Brigid, who was to perform the joint ceremony, stood atop a dais. Somewhere, Sysa heard the low drone of the pipes, the hum of a tune that spoke of the sea, the land, the cliffs, a sound that transported her back to Caithness, to the Never Night world of her first homeland. She knew she would always belong there, be part of the field and the moor, like the motes Star-Steed dispersed to settle on the world. Blinking back into the moment, she fixed her eyes on Brodie, who had not yet turned, and she watched his broad back, noticed the slight tension across his shoulders. She could see he was as nervous as she was, as she swayed on her feet for a moment, hoping to find something to settle her like those stardust pieces of her soul.

And then she saw them, standing at the top of the aisle, two figures smiling out at her. First Grey, the Grey she had known back in her childhood in Caithness, the Grey of green eyes and stories and summer days. He was staring at her in that way of his, that precise curve of his mouth that said he was proud of her, that he loved her, that he was part of everything she was in life. Then he glanced down the aisle, his attention fixed on Brigid, and a moment passed between them, something as quiet as a whisper, and as loud as a giant's roar. When Grey turned back, he nodded, his eyes drifting to Sysa's stomach, and Sysa understood that he knew, of course he did. Under the newly rounded curve of her belly was a new story, a story that had begun the night she had left Steel Castle to find Lavellan, a story of her and Brodie and a new Trinity; a new protection for the three stones they had rejoined. And in the future, she knew, there would be other Trinities, other protectors born of her child, her children. She knew it would never end, this cycle, this thing that had begun with Brodie, her, Lavellan – all three of them. Stories, she now realised, were never-ending. Stories were the things of memory and future. Stories were the things that told her who she was.

Still rooted to the spot, Sysa tracked a line towards her image of Lavellan, who stood next to Grey, shoulder-to-shoulder. Beneath the rolled-up sleeves of the shirt he wore, Sysa saw the blue markings of the tattooed lines across his arms. He, too, was smiling at her, a smile that came from his lips, his eyes, and from every part of his body. He nodded, like an echo of Grey's earlier movement that rippled out in plated rounds across a river. His eyes cast out a line between them, the same line that Sysa had once felt pulling against her very bones. But now, the line was not taut, it was soft, and it hung in the air like a draped thread of morning. She knew that Lavellan was exactly himself, exactly who he needed to be. Her story had given him that, and she smiled at him, her eyes as glassy as the river, her heart as powerful as the stones.

Over Lavellan's shoulder, two more figures were waiting in the background. Ida and Luna were standing at the trees, framed by a canopy of leaves. Ida's hands were clasped together, her face brimming, overflowing. Sysa mouthed the words 'thank you,' and put a hand to her hair, wondering if Ida approved of the dark waves that rivered along her back. Then she glanced at Luna, whose own ribbonned plaits suggested Ida had found someone new to take care of. The mermaid glistened as if she had been immersed in an unknown ocean, and Sysa felt grateful, knowing that Luna had also found a kind of home.

As soon as Sysa felt those thoughts arrive, the two figures faded. Ida and Luna disappeared, retracting into the world they'd come from, a world that lay beyond the forest and the sea. Sysa took a step forward and then panicked, looking around for Grey and Lavellan.

She wasn't ready to let them go.

But they were fading too, falling away into that place Sysa couldn't reach yet. She knew she wouldn't reach it for years, until she had climbed the many summits and stairways of her life. In the meantime, she understood that now and again she would meet the pieces of her broken heart, that they would arrive to her unexpectedly. They would thump into her as she rounded corners, taking her breath away. They would nestle into all the parts of her, existing quietly and loudly. They would grow with her, another part of the tapestry of her soul.

She reached out a hand, but Grey and Lavellan were

still fading, leaving an imprint as if the place they'd stood in would cling to a sense of fullness. The last thing Sysa saw before they disappeared was both of them smiling at her, and Lavellan making a small sweeping gesture with his arm. He was turning his head down the aisle, to where Brodie stood, his eyes following the path of Sysa's future. Grey turned his head too, tracking the line of the new story Sysa was beginning, letting her know that her path now led another way.

'I'll always love you both,' Sysa whispered, before they disappeared completely, returning to that place beyond, a place beyond Fyrish and Caithness, a place beyond everywhere. Sysa wiped away the tears that were pricking at her.

Elise turned, looking into Sysa's face, her eyes round pools.

'Sysa?'

As her mother said her name, Brodie turned around, casting the net of Sysa's future along the aisle towards them.

'I'm ready,' Sysa said, realising that for the first time in her life, she meant it.

She lifted the hem of her gown and walked.

THREE YEARS LATER

Sysa sat on the lawn of her home, watching the children play, their faces lit with curiosity and sunlight. Brodie was showing them something, pointing to some creature in the grasses, and a circle of small faces looked up and down again, before they swarmed on some other adventure, their attention diverted to tumbling and toddling somewhere else. Brodie laughed, throwing his head back in his easy way as he called out cautionary advice about flowered displays and borders. Elva and William raced behind their small twins, catching one each, swinging them around in small circles of delight. Brodie glanced at Sysa, raising his eyebrows as their son darted around, firing out rudimentary light darts while Sirius skirted away, then came close again, enjoying the game of back and forth with his young companion. Nearby, Arno and Three-Wings hovered, while Star-Steed hooved the ground, bright motes of excitement drifting from his mane and over the lawn, which was now permanently flecked with dusty stars. Under the trees, Bruan, Elise and Brigid sat, enjoying the celebrations with amused expressions.

Frode, Krystan and Modan were there too, their first visit to the castle since Brodie and Sysa's wedding. Krystan cradled her new baby and wandered over to Sysa, while

Frode stood watching the others, his arms hooked in triangles against his waist.

'I can't believe how big he's getting,' Krystan said, flicking her head towards Sysa and Brodie's toddler, who was now bent over a sunflower, his gently pointed ears pricking up as he listened to the stories of the garden.

'I know, another birthday already,' Sysa replied, referring to the reason for the day's gathering, and her decision to observe the human tradition of marking birthdates. They meant little here in Fyrish, but she found them a comfort, a way of hanging on to part of the life she had once led.

'And what you've done with this place... really, it's perfect, Sysa,' Krystan continued, casting a look around the peaks of the Castle of Thunder, and the tower which was topped with the blue flag that had flown during Lavellan's tenure. Sysa smiled, following Krystan's sweep of the place she and her young family now called home. With a little hard work and magic, Sysa had been able to soften corners, shed light on the once-gloomy façade of the castle. Inside, she had swept away the living artwork, replacing it with paintings of Grey and Lavellan, and a likeness of the glen she had lived in in Caithness. With the powers she still held from the sealskin, she had harnessed the fae lines beneath the castle, sending starry light into the sky, in the place where thunder and lightning had once cracked and boomed, where darkness had once seeped and flourished. Over at Steel Castle, the lines joined, meeting in the air like threads of protection around the kingdom, allowing the people of Fyrish to live peacefully under the alliance of the forces of Thunder and Steel.

Sysa smiled, thinking back to her coronation, the one

that had been so different to the almost-event she had been party to with Neven. She remembered the way the golden circlet had drifted from Brigid's hands onto her head, crowning her as she had been anointed Sysa of all of those forces – Sysa Lightbringer, of Thunder and Steel. Next to her, Brodie had stood, taking his place as her consort, filling whatever space she asked of him. She remembered running her hands over the fabric of her gown, lacing her fingers under her rounded belly.

'Yes, it's perfect,' she said in answer to Krystan's appraisal, thinking of more than just the castle as she closed her eyes briefly against the sun.

Her eyelids twitched as images unfurled behind the dark gauze that screened them, as unexpected as a bolt of lightning. She felt a buzz at her fingertips, the bright fizzing of alarm she was now in control of, albeit after a lot of training and hard work. Still, the sensation unsettled her, and she tried to focus in on the images, felt herself fly over them, was aware of herself watching as muddy fragments lifted upwards from the earth of a distant mountain. She was above a crimson-heathered slope, one she recognised somewhere deep inside her bones as the place Rogart had been sent to by Brodie long ago. She heard a small sound of awakening, the slight shift in the air that signalled lifting, the smell of something rising, the sense of a giant no longer sleeping. And then she found herself over another scene, a place of cold, a place where another sleeping force was rousing. Behind a branch-covered den, the Cailleach was moving, her small scratching noises echoing around the sky in angry blades.

She's awake, and she knows about Neven, Sysa thought,

not fully understanding the rest of what her vision was telling her. She knew she was in some unknown future, but the ribbon of its place in time was lost to her. Would this happen regardless of her actions? Could the story unfurl another way? She remembered what Brigid had told her about the visions, about the hazy sense of what occurred around the pictures. Sysa was looking at the future through her own tunnel of perception, but as she tried to widen the vision it was lost to her, its meaning as fragile as blossom on the wind.

Her eyes snapped back open to the light to find Krystan gone, and Brodie walking towards her. He filled the space in front of her, replacing her scattering vision with a sense of wholeness. She jumped up to meet him, wrapping her arms around him tight.

'Hey, what's happened?' he said, frowning into her face as he pulled away just enough to survey her strained expression. Sysa shook her head, unable to hide herself from him; never wanting to again.

'I'm just thinking about today, about the future, wondering what will happen if we ever have to fight again,' she said finally, deciding that she wanted to hold onto this moment, let the ribbons of time and destiny stretch out ahead of them as they had to.

'Today, tomorrow, the future, we'll fight if we must,' Brodie said, taking her hand in his, the beat of his pulse melting against her wrist, a rhythm that meant Sysa didn't have to explain, that their two bound hearts would be enough.

'You and me, always,' he said, gazing over at their child, who stood upright, the new apex of their triangle.

'Our family, always,' Sysa answered, throwing the boy's name, like a song, across the grass.

As the boy turned his face, Sysa remembered a promise she had once made in answer to ten words – *find a way to keep me in your life always*.

A shaft of sunlight fell on the boy's head, binding that promise to the morning.

He ran into the arms his mother reached out to him.

The child's name was Lavellan Grey.

AUTHOR'S NOTE

Many of the names, places and legends in this book, and its predecessor *Castles of Steel and Thunder*, are real (and remember that to my Highland forebears, folk tales were as real as the sky above us). I've previously written about the debt I owe Donald Omand's *Caithness: Lore and Legend*, a collection of folk tales I had the opportunity to illustrate during my high school days. Here is a summary of some of the names, places and information from *Castles of Steel and Thunder* and *Pieces of Sky and Stone* which may inspire you to find out more about the far north, its legends and its stories.

Stories are everywhere if you know where to look for them. I hope these books have inspired you to connect with the stories of my home.

Sysa – The name of the female lead in both books is taken from Sysa, the name of a grassy hillock in the Caithness parish of Olrig, and the site of a well mentioned in the local *Piper of Windy Ha'* legend. According to that legend, the Piper of Windy Ha' – a young man called Peter Waters – was enjoying a drink from the well when he encountered a faerie offering him a choice between becoming a preacher or being the best-known piper in the land. Inevitably, Peter chose the latter, leading him to a life of merrymaking that culminated in him being carted away to the fae lands when he returned to meet with the faerie seven years later. In *Castles of Steel and Thunder*, Grey tells Sysa a legend based on this story (you can read much more about it in the book).

Numbers are also important in folklore and the numbers three, seven and nine are often associated with folk tales. I tried to pick this up in both novels – for example, the story in *Castles of Steel and Thunder* skips nine years in the early part of the novel, and in *Pieces of Sky and Stone* the story skips three years at the end. The Trinity is a force of three, and Peter returns to meet with the faerie Krystan after his seven years of revelry. Each book is divided into six parts (three by two), and there are three important stones in *Pieces of Sky and Stone*.

The Mermaid's Cave – Another legend recounted in *Castles of Steel and Thunder* tells of an ill-fated love affair between a Caithness man and a mermaid – retold as the story of Luna and William. In the original legend, the mermaid imprisons her lover in a jewel-filled cave at Dwarwick Head after she discovers him lavishing the gifts she had given him on human girls. Luna and William were names I made up to fit with my story – which also veered off from the original folk tale for the purposes of the plotline (in the original legend, William's character remains tied to a rock by a chain of gold in a cave at Dwarwick to this day.)

The Cave of Gold – The story of the cave at Dwarwick also weaves with a tale of a 'Cave of Gold' on the west side of Dunnet Head, which, according to legend, contains riches from every ship lost to the unforgiving jaws of the Pentland Firth and around Dunnet. In *Pieces of Sky and Stone*, I imagined this cave (which is not accessible by land) as the place where Lavellan and Sysa find Brigid early on in the book. The Cave of Gold story shows how folk tales intersect, and some of the legends I've described in this section will be subject to a degree of variation. The tradition of oral storytelling in the north Highlands has evolved through centuries, reforming in response to cultural, societal and religious change – and also, of course, to who is doing the telling of the tale.

Grey Steel – The name of Sysa's grandfather in the novel is derived from Grey Steil, an alleged robber, ruffian and freebooter who gave his name to a ruined castle in Caithness at Loch Rangag. Grey Steel and Grey Steil could not be more different (in *Caithness: Lore and Legend*, Donald devotes a section to Grey Steil and one of his murderous campaigns). In contrast, the Grey of *Castles of Steel and Thunder* is a kind and loving parent figure, and his relationship with Sysa is one of my favourite elements of the story. I liked the name Grey, and also wanted to use the Steel surname (which would later come in handy in the naming of both Steel Castle, and in the title of book one).

Bruan and Krystan, Frode and Modan – Sysa's father Bruan is named after a ruined broch at Bruan, near Clyth, the site of another faerie abduction mentioned in *Caithness: Lore and Legend*. Krystan the faerie was named after another person of note in *Lore and Legend*, Cristan McPhail, a supposed witch harboured by two men near Spittal in the early 1700s (apparently these men were punished by being forced to sit in sackcloth 'at the minister's pleasure' in front of the local church congregation. At around that time in Caithness, frequent reference was made in Presbytery records to the existence of witches and their powers). The name Frode was also mentioned in *Caithness: Lore and Legend* and appears in the tale of the Swelkie (see following paragraph). Modan was a follower of Saint Drostan, who was associated with many places in the north-east and was known as Trostan in Caithness. The story Grey tells Sysa of the water kelpies and their jewelled home under the sea in *Castles of Steel and Thunder* is based on a tale in *Lore and Legend* about a family of water kelpies who were once believed to live in one of Thurso River's deep pools.

The Swelkie – The Swelkie is a notorious tidal whirlpool off the north end of Stroma, an uninhabited island belonging to Caithness. According to legend, **Frode**, King of Denmark (and great-grandson of the Norse god Odin) once engaged two giantesses, Fenja and Menja, to work a millstone he had acquired called Grotte. Eventually, the two overworked females rebelled against Frode and conjured another king to kill him. En route to Caithness, the new king ordered Fenja and Menja to mill salt, which they did until there was so much salt on board their ship it sank into the Swelkie, leaving Fenja and Menja grinding to keep the sea salty forevermore. The story of the Swelkie illustrates the influence of Norse storytelling tradition on the far north of Scotland, where our culture is threaded with the interesting duality of both Celtic and Norse heritage. For more information on the history of Caithness, its people and its landscape, I recommend George Gunn's excellent 2015 publication *The Province of the Cat: A Journey to the Radical Heart of the Far North.*

The Selkie Grave – The selkie grave story Grey recounts in *Castles of Steel and Thunder* relates to a grave in a cemetery at Olrig thought to be the resting place of a seal person, or selkie. Local legend asserts that the mossy cavity in the grave does not go dry. The cemetery in which the grave is found also housed a chapel dedicated to Saint Drostan (Trostan). You can find out more on this subject by doing some research on 'The Northern Saints' Trails'.

Healing/Seeing Stones – In folklore, objects are often imbued with magical powers, and stones can be associated with 'second sight' and healing. In *Pieces of Sky and Stone*, Brigid's stone blends both these capabilities – a stone with a hole to see visions through (sometimes known as a 'hag stone'), and a stone that has the capacity to heal. The healing element was inspired by a visit to 'Mary Ann's Cottage' in Dunnet, a preserved croft dating back to the 1800s and home to the late Mary Ann Calder. A 'magic stone' found in the cottage after Mary Ann's departure to a local nursing home may have been rubbed on animals to help relieve them of their ailments – although Mary Ann reportedly professed to know nothing about it when she was interviewed on the matter herself. Whatever the truth, I was mesmerised by this stone and its sense of mystery when I visited the cottage several years ago. According to information at the cottage at the time, the stone may have originally come from the wall of a now-demolished chapel not far away. Mary Ann's Cottage can be visited during the summer months (more details on their Facebook page). On their route to Dunnet Head in *Pieces of Sky and Stone*, Lavellan and Sysa would have walked past the site of Mary Ann's cottage – and possibly the chapel, which may have been the original location of the stone.

Lavellan – Lavellan was inspired by the real-life Lavellan, a giant shrew-like creature once believed to inhabit Caithness pools and rivers. In his book, *Legends and Folklore of Scotland*, R.S. Holland writes that the eighteenth century Welsh naturalist Thomas Pennant once visited Ousdale in search of the Lavellan. He didn't find it, but was told that the preserved skin of the creature abided at a nearby farm. Apparently, the water the skin was soaked in was used to cure various ailments affecting livestock. Holland suggests that the Lavellan may have been a genuine animal, which had long since gone extinct.

Neven, Brigid and the Cailleach – The name Neven (or NicNeven) is often used to denote the Queen of Faeries in wider folklore. Similarly, in Celtic tradition the goddess Brigit is associated with fertility and Imbolc, while the Cailleach is also linked to seasonality and is said to control how long the winter months will last.

Rogart, Fyrish and Never Night – *Castle of Steel and Thunder*'s giant is named after a place in Sutherland – the result of many trips along the A9 since childhood. **Fyrish**, the name of *Castle of Steel and Thunder*'s fae land, is named after an Easter Ross landmark – a monument that sits atop hillside near Alness, and is said to represent the Gate of Negapatam in Madras. Finally, **Never Night**, the fae folk's name for Caithness, was inspired by a trip to the Highland Folk Museum in Newtonmore several years ago, where I saw an old poster announcing trips to John O'Groats – 'the land of the Never Night'. The name stuck with me, conjuring thoughts of magic and drama.

That's the thing about inspiration.

Just like magic, you never know when it's going to strike.

Some of this information was first published on my blog Wellies on the School Run.

ACKNOWLEDGEMENTS

Writing book two is much easier than writing book one, mostly because by book two, you know you can do it.

Thank you to everyone who helped me realise I could write a book, and to everyone who supported the release of *Castles of Steel and Thunder* in 2020 – which turned out to be a very strange year for all of us. To Gary, Christopher, Fraser, Mum, Dad, Jill and Stuart – thank you. To the rest of my family on both sides – you all helped with your encouragement and words. To my friends, who are small in number but take up a large portion of my heart – so glad to know you. To Brody, thank you for lending me a version of your name, and for leaving your paw prints on my books. To Jen Parker at Fuzzy Flamingo – thanks for your patience and your professionalism. To the Ravenskald Writing Group – thank you for helping me to grow. Special thanks to Andrea and June, my first readers, for their constructive feedback and insight. Enduring gratitude to the late Donald Omand and to everyone who has supported my blog *Wellies on the School Run*.

And to Nana and Iain Innes, and Granny and Grandad Gunn – thank you to each of you, for giving me Grey.

ACKNOWLEDGEMENTS